# THE MISSING ONES

ANITA WALLER

Boldwood

First published in Great Britain in 2025 by Boldwood Books Ltd.

Copyright © Anita Waller, 2025

Cover Design by Head Design Ltd.

Cover Images: iStock

The moral right of Anita Waller to be identified as the author of this work has been asserted in accordance with the Copyright, Designs and Patents Act 1988.

All rights reserved. No part of this book may be reproduced in any form or by any electronic or mechanical means, including information storage and retrieval systems, without written permission from the author, except for the use of brief quotations in a book review. This book is a work of fiction and, except in the case of historical fact, any resemblance to actual persons, living or dead, is purely coincidental.

Every effort has been made to obtain the necessary permissions with reference to copyright material, both illustrative and quoted. We apologise for any omissions in this respect and will be pleased to make the appropriate acknowledgements in any future edition.

A CIP catalogue record for this book is available from the British Library.

Paperback ISBN 978-1-83533-924-4

Large Print ISBN 978-1-83533-926-8

Hardback ISBN 978-1-83533-923-7

Ebook ISBN 978-1-83533-925-1

Kindle ISBN 978-1-83533-927-5

Audio CD ISBN 978-1-83533-918-3

MP3 CD ISBN 978-1-83533-919-0

Digital audio download ISBN 978-1-83533-922-0

This book is printed on certified sustainable paper. Boldwood Books is dedicated to putting sustainability at the heart of our business. For more information please visit https://www.boldwoodbooks.com/about-us/sustainability/

Boldwood Books Ltd, 23 Bowerdean Street, London, SW6 3TN

www.boldwoodbooks.com

*In loving memory of Maxine Spittlehouse*
*3.3.76–22.7.24*

But if the while I think on thee, dear friend,
 All losses are restored and sorrows end.

— SONNET 30, WILLIAM SHAKESPEARE

## PROLOGUE
JUNE 2021

'Mr Eke, your 2 p.m. client is in reception. Shall I send him up?'

Ray stared at the girl who was standing in his doorway, and muttered, 'No.'

'I'm sorry?' Hannah Wrightson was already feeling pretty irritated by him as he hadn't answered his phone all morning, and now it seemed he thought it was okay to just say no. What the hell was she supposed to tell his client? 'What shall I tell him? You need a few more minutes?'

'No,' he repeated.

It was very obvious Hannah didn't know what to do; her mantra had always been that clients were prioritised, not the staff, and now she had Mr Eke, the senior partner in the business, playing silly devils.

She stepped inside the room, saying tentatively, 'Mr Eke...'

Ray's head had dropped, and he mumbled as he spoke. 'What do you want?'

She stared and began to feel afraid. Ray Eke had never said a wrong word to her until a couple of minutes ago, although she couldn't count that morning because he hadn't spoken at all each time she'd tried to ring on his internal line. It suddenly occurred to her he had completely ignored her 'Good morning' when he had arrived that day too, and that was definitely out of character.

She backed out of the room and headed downstairs to reception where she spoke to the man sitting on the green velvet armchair, waiting patiently. 'Mr Eke won't be long, he's on a client call at the moment but he'll ring down to me when it's finished. Can I get you a tea?'

The man smiled up at her. 'My appointment is two o'clock, but I'm in a rush today. I'll wait until ten past two but then I'll have to get going. So I'll pass on the tea, thank you.'

Hannah felt even more flustered. She gave the man a brief smile, but in her heart she knew he would be walking out of the door at ten past two, because Ray Eke hadn't looked... right. No, not right at all.

\* \* \*

Ray couldn't control his head. It seemed to be going round and round on his neck, and he kept reaching up with his hands to stop it. He couldn't see much either. Everything was blurred. Had he grown cataracts overnight? He wouldn't have thought that was possible, but something wasn't right. He looked at the accounts sheet in front of him, and poured a glass of water over it, then he switched on his computer for the first time that day.

He couldn't seem to focus on what to do next, and then he saw numbers. Numbers everywhere. Blurred numbers, incomprehensible numbers and he had no idea what they meant. He wiped sweat from his forehead with the accounts sheet he had just covered in water, then pushed back his chair and walked over to the freestanding antique coat rack in the corner. He removed his coat that he'd hung on it some five hours earlier, and picked up the heavy piece of furniture. He carried it clumsily across to his desk, lifted it as high as he could and brought it down with considerable force onto the computer.

Pieces went everywhere and the noise reverberated around the corridors. He repeated the action, although there was nothing much left to destroy, and suddenly his door burst open. Mark Griffiths, his best friend and co-partner in the accountancy firm of Eke, Griffiths and Co, stood in the doorway and looked around. He watched as Ray crumpled to the floor, and he was already pulling out his phone to ring for an ambulance before he reached his friend.

\* \* \*

Three months later, the psychiatrist deemed Ray was fit to return home from the Priory, but not fit to return to work.

Ray had managed a half-smile when he heard that. He had already spoken with Mark, and the working partnership was in the process of being dissolved. No more figures. Ever. The brotherhood would never fade, but the firm would evolve into Mark Griffiths and Co, Accountants.

Following difficult discussions with his mum, she had closed down her home, and moved into Ray's rambling house in the south of Sheffield. Ziggy Duly had always put her son first above all else, and he needed her now.

Divorced for many years from Sam Duly, Ray's stepfather, life had reverted to how things had been when Ray was little – just the two of them, after his genetic father, Martin Eke, had decided fatherhood wasn't for him. And they were back to 'just the two of them' all over again. No Martin, no Sam, just Ziggy and Ray.

Christmas 2021 was a strange time, quiet, no exchange of gifts, but Ziggy insisted they have a proper Christmas dinner, albeit with a ridiculously small turkey.

Ray's breakdown was massive; at odd times he felt he would never recover, at other times he knew he was on the right road. Ziggy watched him for either negative or positive signs, and it was only when 2022 reached March that she knew he had finally started on the road to recovery.

He had cornflakes for breakfast on that Sunday morning, and ate it all instead of leaving some. Ziggy didn't comment on it, she didn't want him to know of her worries surrounding his weight loss. She had a feeling it would make matters worse if she brought it to his attention.

The sun was out, and Ray walked towards the lounge window and looked out at his garden. Spring bulbs were performing well, and he felt a smile appearing on his face. He touched his lips, and continued to watch the petals and leaves with their gentle movements.

Then he walked over to his piano, sat on his stool and opened the lid. He placed his hands on the keys and sat for a few seconds.

Then he began to play Beethoven's Piano Concerto No. 3 as if he had never been away from his instrument.

Ziggy felt the tears roll down her cheeks, and knew he was on the mend at last. He hadn't touched his beloved piano for nine months, and she was beginning to think he would never touch it again.

His breakdown was broken.

**1**

Three years later and a changed Ray Eke loved his job. He walked at least four miles a day with his litter-picking tool, gathering the stuff thrown casually away, by the people he classed in his mind as 'Dirty Sheffielders', and sometimes he found little items that he would put into his pocket instead of into the bin bag he carried everywhere with him.

Today was his day to walk by the side of the tram tracks on Donetsk Way, before continuing on towards Crystal Peaks, the small shopping mall. A lot of the rubbish he collected bore the branding of McDonald's; with two outlets within a quarter of a mile of each other, it was always going to be a high-volume litter area.

Sometimes he even found McDonald's toys discarded, and these he always saved, because he'd once read that these small items were fetching quite a lot of money at auctions. And they looked good on the windowsill in his bedroom.

The May sunshine was warm, and he stopped and ran his sleeve across his forehead. He should have brought his hat, the peaked one that said his name on the front. If the weather people could get things right occasionally, he would have known to shove the hat into his back pocket ready for when it turned really warm, but the forecast had been for overcast with a possibility of rain, so he'd worn a jacket. And no hat.

The collection point for leaving his full rubbish bags was where the tram tracks crossed over Moss Way. He left them leaning against the road sign, notified his boss by text how many bags required moving, and the next day they would be gone, ready for him to start again. His bag was almost full, so he eased it out from the frame that held it permanently open, and tied the top. He left it round the back of the road sign, so the name of Moss Way wasn't obliterated, then straightened his back.

Ray looked around to decide which bit to clean up next, spotted a police car that had just driven from the Moss Way police station exit, and waited until it drove past so that he could wave at it. The two officers inside the car waved back, used to seeing him around the area all the time.

'Good bloke, that,' the driver remarked, and his partner agreed.

'Been litter-picking round here for a couple of years now. Once had a word with him, and he said he used to be an accountant, but had a massive breakdown. Wanted a job away from people and out in the fresh air, and now the council pays him to litter-pick.'

\* \* \*

Ray watched as the car disappeared into the distance, then fastened a new, empty bag onto his frame. Now it was decision time. Should he cross the road and continue down towards Crystal Peaks, or should he go over the tram tracks and head back down Donetsk Way until he arrived opposite the point where he had started earlier in the day? Both sides would then be nicely cleaned, and tram travellers wouldn't have litter to look at, just trees and grass.

He thought for a moment, then realised if he did the other side of Donetsk Way today, with the sun getting hotter, it would make the most sense because the trees and bushes would offer him some shade. He wouldn't get that if he headed towards Crystal Peaks. He wiped his forehead once again, checked the full bag was upright and stable, then headed towards the traffic roundabout.

He had to move quickly. This was an area with a high volume of traffic and the roundabout had a constant flow of vehicles going round it. He ran, reached the middle and stopped, then completed his journey to the other side. He had no idea what the white blossom on the trees was, but every year it made a reappearance, and it was now in full bloom. He touched it gently as he reached the first tree bearing it, and stood for a moment looking at it. Almost every day it occurred to him that he had been so right to leave the rat race of high-level accountancy and opt for the open air. These trees confirmed that feeling.

He picked up his first couple of papers, and took a few steps back towards the beginning of the long curving road. He would complete this side of the road, leave this bag for collection outside the church, and notify his boss it was there. Then he could catch the tram home and hope his mum had been well enough to cook them a meal. She had complained of feeling nauseous that morning, saying she'd perhaps just have some dry toast for breakfast.

They would watch whatever programme took their fancy, and maybe play Scrabble – she always said it kept their brains alert. She had never understood his breakdown hadn't actually affected his brainpower, and he just let her believe what she was happiest believing. Life was much easier if he said little and agreed with what everybody said.

And tomorrow he could concentrate on the stretch of road down into Crystal Peaks, maybe treat himself to a roast pork sandwich from Beres in Peaks for his lunch if he timed it right.

He spotted another police car travelling up Donetsk Way towards him, and he stopped to wave at it. The driver, alone in the car, waved back and smiled. Ray stopped for a moment to watch as it navigated the roundabout and headed back towards Moss Way police station, back to its base.

Ray sighed. At one time in his life, he had considered a career in the police, but he'd almost accidentally fallen into accountancy. He was good at litter-picking now though, and he somehow knew he wouldn't be good at chasing shoplifters through Crystal Peaks, or indeed spending his days adding up numbers.

He added a screwed-up betting slip to his bag, glanced around to make sure he hadn't missed anything and walked around the huge display of white blossoms. There was a lady, seemingly lying down and possibly asleep. Mostly hidden by the tree and bushes he had just circumvented, but she would have been invisible to any passing vehicles such as trams and buses. He walked tentatively towards her.

'Hello?'

He tried again. 'Hello? Do you need some help?'

He stepped closer, automatically picking up a couple of bits of litter as he did so.

The woman's hair was long and blonde, partially covering her face. He'd never seen a dead body on his litter-picking round before, and he knew he would have to report this unusual occurrence to his boss, and quickly.

She was wearing white trousers that had grass stains on the

knees, and bits of twigs and leaves attached to them, and her top had short sleeves. She looked like a professional – maybe a nurse, because it was obvious her clothing was actually a uniform of some sort.

He tentatively touched her arm and she didn't move. Despite the warmth of the sun, she was icy cold. He touched the purply-coloured top she was wearing, pressing it down on to her chest.

There were some flies on her face, and he brushed them off while he debated his next action. He had three things to do – ring his mother, ring his boss and ring the police. With the police station across the road from him, he took that option first, figuring he would have more to tell his mother and his boss once the police had been. He reached for his phone and rang 999, hoping it would be officers from across the road who arrived. He wouldn't want to speak to strangers. He felt uneasy, and this was one of the times when he wished his medication didn't make him feel so spaced out. So slow.

\* \* \*

PC Frank Carter enjoyed being on reception. He was a year off retirement, and policing had changed too much over the years for him to want to be in the thick of it still. No, dealing with the public and their sometimes-crazy queries suited him down to the ground, and he was rather good at directing phone callers to someone who could help them.

When Ray Eke rang, Frank was a little puzzled.

'It's Ray,' the caller explained.

'Ray who?' he asked, thinking it was a member of staff ringing in to explain his absence.

'Ray Eke. I'm across the road. I pick up rubbish.'

The light bulb turned on. 'Oh, hi, Ray. You okay? Saw you a couple of minutes ago when I drove past you.'

'You should have stopped.'

'Sorry! Did you flag me down? I thought it was just a wave, like you always do to the lads.'

'It was. But now I need somebody to stop. I've found a lady and I can't wake her, I think she might be dead. I've rung 999. They've told me to wait here until somebody comes, but I wanted to tell you as well, cover all bases so to speak. Thought somebody from the station could perhaps get here quicker.'

Frank took a deep breath. 'Are you still where I saw you, Ray?'

'I've moved round the big white tree at the corner of the road, but I don't want to leave this lady to come and get you, I have to keep moving flies off her face.'

Again, Frank breathed deeply. 'Okay, Ray. Here's what I need you to do. I want you to step away from her, so that we don't contaminate the scene, because if this is a crime and not a natural death there could be other footprints around. Move to the roadside and wait there for us. We'll be about a minute. I'll ring you in a bit to make sure everything's okay, I've got your number.'

'But what about the flies?'

'We'll deal with them. Don't leave the scene until somebody reaches you, will you, Ray?'

'No.'

'Ray, do you know the lady?'

'No. I don't think so. At least...' He hesitated, then continued. 'She seems to be quite young, pretty, blonde hair, but I don't think I've ever seen her before. But...' Ray wanted to add something, but then changed his mind. His confidence in believing in himself still hadn't fully returned, and he closed his mouth before he could say anything further.

'Okay. Don't do anything with your litter bag, we'll probably need it. And I think the first thing that will happen is the road will be closed off. But we'll make sure you get home, because buses and trams will be stopped. I've sent all instructions through to the right people, so things will start to happen now.'

'Thank you. Can I ring my mother and tell her? She'll be expecting me home in an hour.'

'Can you wait a bit? Just wait till one of the lads sorts you out.'

'Okay. Two cars have just parked wrong on the roundabout.'

'Two police cars?'

'Yes.'

'That's okay, they'll be closing Donetsk Way off, and diverting people up Sheffield Road. Your 999 call will already be activated.'

'I'm standing at the edge of the road. I'm not near the lady now. I think I feel a bit sick. I don't find dead bodies usually.'

'I know, mate.' Frank spoke carefully. He was aware of Ray's social anxieties, but had long admired the man for sticking to doing his job no matter the weather, and for becoming someone that people interacted with all the time, albeit from a distance. It wasn't just police officers who waved, the tram and bus drivers all had time for the gentle man with the slow smile and the fast brain.

'A car is pulling up now,' Ray said. 'I'd better go.' And he disconnected, leaving Frank to stare at his receiver. He knew the lads would treat him properly, and any new officers who didn't know the best-educated, most intelligent litter-picker in South Yorkshire would soon discover who he was. Ray had once confided in him why he litter-picked and didn't do his previous work in accountancy, and Frank hoped he was about to be treated with respect and not as someone who needed help to make them understand the situation. Ray knew exactly what was happening. He was simply a quiet man, a polite man.

Frank quickly logged in the phone call on his call sheet,

noting the time and duration of the call, then sat back. He guessed he would be seeing Ray in the station before much longer, to give a statement. He hoped it would be a pleasant experience for him, and not a scary one. The scary part might come if this were indeed a murder and not a natural causes death – giving evidence in a court of law wouldn't prove to be an easy thing, but he suspected it would certainly be a new experience for Ray.

## 2

The scene changed rapidly, and Ray was sitting in a police car waiting to be officially released to continue with his job, albeit on a different part of his route.

A white tent had been erected over the woman, and the road was utterly quiet apart from various police cars as they moved around. No trams were running, and Donetsk Way was blocked at both ends to everyday traffic.

Ray watched carefully, occasionally taking deep breaths as he felt stress begin to take over in his mind. He couldn't allow that to happen, and he wanted to go home. His fingers began to play the piano across his knees, and he could hear the music in his head, even if it wasn't physically there.

His phone pinged and the text was to tell him to finish for the day. He breathed a sigh of relief. He loved his job, loved the fresh air, loved that he didn't have to think too much, but complications now had to be factored in and he needed to be at home to think things through. He had reported everything to his boss, hence the instructions to head off home.

He returned the text, explaining he had to call in at Moss Way the following day to give a statement, but he would work his way down the A57 if his normal route was still closed off. He pressed send, and the car door opened.

'I'm running you home, Ray. That okay?' The young officer was a stranger to him, and Ray simply nodded his thanks.

'You okay?' The officer sounded concerned as he slid into the driving seat.

'I'm fine,' Ray confirmed. 'It's just been a funny sort of day. Is the lady Lauren Pascoe?'

PC Andy Norman whipped around and stared at his passenger. 'Lauren Pascoe?' The name obviously rang bells in the constable's brain.

'She's been missing for over three years now, and Lauren Pascoe has a small mole on her forehead. The deceased lady did as well, and I know everybody has always assumed she was dead because she's been missing for so long, but I think it could be worth checking if she is Lauren Pascoe.'

Andy took out his phone, sent a swift text to his DI explaining what he was doing, and what Ray had just said, then put the car into gear while checking exactly where he was to take his passenger.

Ray gave him the address, then sat staring out of the car window, saying nothing until they neared his home, where he gave precise instructions to Andy.

He exited the car, thanked Andy, and walked through the front garden gate, at once feeling more at ease. Working in the garden had eased him back into the real world, even if it hadn't led him back to earning the big money he had once earned.

Ziggy had been waiting for him; she hoped what had happened earlier in the day wouldn't cause adverse reactions in Ray, and she pulled him close for a hug.

'I'm okay, Mum, it's over now,' he whispered. 'Need a large mug of tea to calm me down, and help me bury this afternoon.'

'Kettle's already on,' she said. 'Go and get changed, I'll bring it to you.'

\* \* \*

He pulled on jeans and a T-shirt and slipped sliders onto his feet. He immediately felt better, and moved over towards his piano, sitting down and allowing the familiarity of it to wash over him. He rested his fingers lightly on the keys while his brain switched into musical gear, and then he said, 'Gershwin.'

Ziggy smiled at the sound, and poured the tea into the mugs. Gershwin's music was a favourite with both of them, and hearing the old tunes brought back memories of many nights of simply listening to Ray play, before his brain had closed down. She had thought at one time he would never open up the piano again, but he had, and with just as much skill as he had shown before his hospitalisation.

Gershwin had saved them both. She sang quietly along with 'I'll Build a Stairway to Paradise', as she carried their mugs to the coffee table.

'Your drink's here,' she said softly, not wanting to pull him out of his thoughts.

'Thank you,' he said just as softly, then stood and walked over to her. 'Thank you, Mum, and not just for the tea.'

# 3

Donetsk Way remained closed. Fifty per cent of tram travellers grumbled at the inconvenience, the other fifty per cent simply rang work and said they would take a day off and be in the following day.

By lunchtime it was officially confirmed that the victim was indeed the missing person, Lauren Pascoe, who had disappeared in 2021, and despite prolonged searches and hundreds of interviews, hadn't been seen since that time.

It was also confirmed that the body, although quite emaciated, had only been deceased a matter of hours, definitely not three years, and she had clearly been imprisoned somewhere because there were raw marks around her ankles and wrists showing she had been held captive until recently.

DI Chris Chandler had only been at the station for two days, and was desperately trying to remember the names of his team, but he put such thoughts to one side when he read the report from the pathologist, recognising just how big this case was likely to be. He would need all the paperwork from when the female first went missing, but he kind of guessed that might not be so helpful. It was the pathologist's feeling that she had been held captive, mainly on her back, for all the time she had been gone; the healed and unhealed bed sores on her back and buttocks were evidence of it.

He printed off the report and walked through to the briefing room.

'Thank you for your patience,' he said to the five people waiting for him to speak, 'I realised how little we had to go on until this report came through.' He waved the printout at them. 'Even now we have it, we know very little, but I'll itemise what it does say, then I'll forward it to all your inboxes. Thank you to the person who's put a team group email together – you've obviously heard about my IT skills.' Maria smiled but said nothing. 'I'm trying desperately to remember your names, but don't laugh if you have a new name by the end of the week. I get confused by my own kids, so you lot don't stand a chance.'

A red-haired young woman held up her hand. 'PC Sally Duroe, boss. I've sent down a request for all the files we have from the time Lauren Pascoe went missing. It seems there's a lot, and they'll send somebody up with the boxes as soon as they've collated them all.'

'Thanks, Sally. That sounds ominous. Were any of you actually here when our victim first disappeared?' He glanced around at the team.

They all shook their head except Sally. 'I was here, but in uniform. I helped with the door-to-door enquiries. I did know Lauren though, she lived on the same road as me. I remember her disappearing, and I remember all the searches but in the middle of it I moved to Central for a while, and by the time I returned, it had died down for lack of any evidence as to what had happened.'

'So, we start from the beginning. This young lady has clearly been held somewhere for the best part of three years. The report from the pathologist suggests she was very malnourished, and there are bruises and evidence of sexual activity, which I'll leave you to read through. It's not good, I must warn you.'

He glanced down at the compact list in his hand, then lifted his head as he tried to match a name to a face.

'Okay, redhead PC Sally, blonde DS Tia, PC Andy looks too young to be a copper, PC Bryn could be Welsh if his name's anything to go by, brunette PC Maria. Did I identify everybody correctly?'

DS Tia Monroe laughed. 'Smart cookie. You did. And Andy is quite old enough to be a copper, transferred to our team last week. But hang on a minute – Andy's light-haired as well. Don't get us mixed up, will you? The rest of us have been together a while now. Happy to welcome you on board, boss. None of us had chance to say much yesterday with everything that happened, but we're looking forward to cracking on with this. Most of us remember when Lauren went missing, although only Sally worked the case. I was stationed in Rotherham at the time, so knew of it from the periphery. It seems she's had it rough for the best part of three years. I reckon even her mum assumed she was dead. She used the newspapers a lot when her daughter first disappeared, pushing for more action from the police, but the truth of the matter is that there was nothing to find.'

'Thanks, Tia. Let's hope test results from the post-mortem show us a bit more of where she's been for all this time. This report is first results only, but she was identified by her fingerprints. Okay, which of you is our IT guru?'

Maria blushed, then held up a finger. 'That will be me,' she said.

'Well, it's definitely not me,' Bryn said, his Welsh accent very obvious. 'I do have some skills – I can switch on a computer, and I can draft a report and save it, but that's about my lot. If I need anything, I ask Maria.' He winked at the pretty woman who was still blushing at the spotlight being shone on her.

'Well, thank goodness one of us has some knowledge.' Chris smiled at her. He could sense her discomfort. 'Okay, Maria, first thing to do is read the post-mortem, then I need you to open up your mind to whatever it says that hits you the most and go on the internet to research it. If nothing stands out, research Lauren Pascoe, Lauren Pascoe's relatives, friends, anybody she may have had contact with up to the point of her disappearance. It's important that we start afresh with this – the original investigation was for a missing person. This is a murder.'

He glanced around at the others. 'Bryn, can you chase up the old files? I know Sally's requested them, but I'd like them sooner rather than later. We need them in this room today. This isn't a cold case any more. Somebody bloody evil has done this to this lady, and we don't want him hunting down another one because he's lost this one.'

He turned to Sally. 'Sally, I need you to accompany me. We have to go see Lauren Pascoe's mother now we have confirmation of identity. Frank from the front desk – think that's his name anyway – told me as I arrived this morning that she had rung, hysterically asking if the woman was her Lauren. That's our priority now, to put this lady's mind finally at rest.'

Sally nodded. 'Janey Pascoe knows me anyway. As I said, we've been pretty close. Living nearby gave her some comfort, I always thought. Every time I saw her, she asked if anything had shown up, did we have any clues. It was heartbreaking to have to say no every time, but now, although it's not the result she would have wanted, she'll be able to lay Lauren to rest.'

Chris gave a brief nod. 'Okay, Tia, I need you and Andy to go talk to the chap who found her. I didn't see much of him yesterday, he was sat in Andy's car, but we actually need a statement from him, so if you can do that at the same time he won't have to come into the station unless we have some reason further down the line to bring him in.'

'You know who he is?' Bryn asked.

'No, should I?'

'Not really. Thought Frank might have told you. His name is Ray Eke, and he was a pretty smart guy back in the day. Partner with his best mate in an accountancy business, but then some time ago he smashed up his office, and ended up in the Priory for quite some time. He said "no more numbers", and for a while walked the streets picking up litter. Then he was mentioned in the paper as being a good Samaritan doing the work that the council should be doing, and they offered him a job. He's a good guy, quiet, a clever man. He rang 999 when he found our victim, but because he was just across the road from us, he then rang here directly. Within two minutes we had the road closed off, all the litter he had picked up that day safely stashed in the back of Andy's car. Then we had a quick word with him, before taking him home. Andy took him, said we'd let him know when to come in to give a statement.'

Chris listened intently. 'I concentrated more on the body yesterday. It felt a bit like a swimming pool deep end, I'd only been in here for ten minutes when the building emptied as everybody shot off to do what they had to do. I was in with the big boss, itching to get across to the white tent I could see through his window. But never mind, I'm sure we'll all be au fait with the entire thing very shortly, and it seems we're all at the same point with the case files from when Lauren Pascoe disappeared.'

'Our job for tomorrow?' Sally asked.

'I expect so, unless anything crops up from what we're all

doing this afternoon. Tia and Andy, forget going to see Mr Eke, let's concentrate on all this paperwork, keeping eyes peeled for any tiny details. I'll go see our litter-picker tomorrow myself, get his statement, find out his story.'

\* \* \*

Chris and Sally chatted quietly as she directed him to the house where their victim had once lived. She pointed out her own house where she still lived with her mother, explaining her mum was disabled due to MS, and she shared the caring with her sister.

Sally changed the subject. 'You're moving to Sheffield, boss?'

'Already moved. I put in for this transfer about six months ago. My wife and I split up, she stayed in Durham, but I knew where I wanted to be. I spent most of my free time climbing rocks in the Peak District, so I had to be in Sheffield. I bought a house here, at Norton, three months ago, and just waited for the right posting. Everything comes to he who waits,' he flashed a smile at her, 'and this position arrived in my inbox. I did think I might have a week or so to settle in before anything major happened, but I guess stuff like this happens a lot more regularly in a big city like Sheffield.'

Sally leaned forward. 'It's the grey door, the one after the red one.'

'Got it,' he said, and put on his indicators before pulling up to the kerb and stopping the car. He glanced through the rear window. 'You really do live quite close, don't you?'

Sally nodded. 'I do. It can have its drawbacks, but, like I said, I actually think it gave Janey some comfort. And Janey sometimes sits in with Mum, or takes her to a bingo game, so all in all, I have no complaints. How do you want to do this?'

'I'll talk, you make a pot of tea?'

'I'm fine with that. I suspect she's half expecting this, but she's still going to be devastated. She's never got over Lauren just disappearing. She was simply coming home from work. Then nothing, until today.'

They climbed out of the car, and walked together towards the grey door. Curtains twitched in the bay window of the house with the red door. Sally knocked.

Janey opened the door only seconds later, saw Sally and her face crumpled. 'I knew,' she said. 'I knew.'

Chris held up his warrant card. 'DI Chris Chandler, Mrs Pascoe. And you know PC Duroe, I believe.'

Janey couldn't speak. She stepped aside and the two police officers entered a tiny hallway. The older woman waved a hand, still without speaking, and they walked into the lounge, a small welcoming room decorated in two shades of green. Peaceful.

Janey's bottom lip trembled. 'It's my Lauren, isn't it?'

Chris looked at Sally, and she left the room to head for the kitchen. Only tea would do it, she knew, only tea would offer that small degree of comfort that would be so needed.

# 4

They stayed with Janey until her sister arrived then left to head back to the station, travelling along Donetsk Way, unusually devoid of traffic until they were sure all evidence had been collected.

'I just want to check out the site now everybody has gone,' Chris said. 'It was chaotic with most of Moss Way here, so I'd just like to take it all in now it's quiet.'

Sally nodded. 'I know what you mean.' She led the way along the flattened area to where the tent was still standing. After greeting the uniformed officer who was standing outside the tent, she introduced her new boss.

'DI Christopher Chandler, started this week.' She waved a hand somewhat vaguely in the general direction of Chris. 'Everything okay?'

'It is. They're coming to take down the tent in the next hour, then I can stand down.'

'You had to chase anybody off?'

'Two youngsters came and stood by the tape, asking if they

could look at the body because they'd never seen a dead one. They seemed a bit disappointed that I was the only body here.'

Chris walked inside the tent, and Sally left him on his own. Already she was starting to realise he was a quiet man, a thoughtful one, and he would be absorbing the area, especially the part where Lauren had been lying.

\* \* \*

Chris stared around him. The sun was making life easier, giving the white tent an almost unearthly glow on the inside. He relaxed the tension from his shoulders and stood immobile for a minute. Then he bent towards where the body had been and touched the grass. So many questions flooded into his mind. How long had she been here? How had she got here? Where had she been held for the last three years, and did she die in captivity before having to be dumped in this almost hidden spot?

So many questions, so few answers. He needed to speak to the forensics team – he suspected other things would be revealed, as the email had said preliminary findings. The pathologist had obviously appreciated they would be keen to make an immediate and productive start on the investigation once the fingerprints had revealed the identity of the young woman.

Lauren Pascoe. Although he knew little of the case, it was clear to Chris that she didn't disappear of her own free will. According to the early findings, her body was in a dreadful state, and the last three years must have been hell for her. More questions rose up. Had she known her kidnapper? Or had it been just a random grab and run?

He sighed. Time to head back to the office, to visit the morgue, to do all the things that began an investigation before much was known about where it would take them.

\* \* \*

Chris left the autopsy suite feeling slightly sick. The damage to Lauren Pascoe's body had been a graphic description of horrific torture, and he couldn't believe that the woman had been forced to endure such treatment for the last three years.

The official cause of death was cardiac arrest, brought about by exsanguination, but the pathologist had explained how that massive blood loss had happened. A broken bottle had been inserted into the victim's vagina and twisted, causing internal and external bleeding to the extent that blood stopped going to her heart and she died within minutes.

Chris hoped she had died immediately the bottle was inserted; the pain must have been unbearable from the second the jagged glass touched her.

There were so many questions to be answered with this case, and he drove back to the office deep in thought. Where had she been held captive for three years? When she disappeared, it had been a major case, yet nobody had come forward with any suspicions of changes in anyone's behaviour; there hadn't even been any hints of Lauren having been spotted anywhere, either real or imagined. She had simply disappeared, until a litter-picker had found her discarded like the rubbish he was collecting.

And it seemed the litter-picker – what was his name? Was it Ray Eke? – had recognised her, possibly from earlier pictures of her. He nodded his head in agreement with himself. This Ray Eke needed to be interviewed; he may have noticed something, although Chris doubted it. But he had identified the victim, seemingly. He had suggested it was probably Lauren Pascoe. Had he known her before she had disappeared?

His mind was spinning in circles, and he reached the briefing room knowing he would have to tell his team exactly what he had been told in the autopsy suite. He could imagine the silence in the room when he had finished his talk, and then the sudden clamour as his words really sank in.

He opened the door; everyone stopped what they were doing and turned towards him. He walked slowly to where the murder board had been set up, and he tapped just below the face of Lauren. They had used the picture that had been on the poster distributed all around Sheffield when they had first started looking for her, a picture of a beautiful face with a happy smile. The face he had seen on the autopsy table was gaunt, haggard with suggestions of a healing black eye. Several teeth were missing due to having been knocked out and her hair had clearly been pulled out in clumps. As he had left the autopsy suite, he had heard Kevin Hanson, the pathologist, whisper something about *man's inhumanity to woman* and he had known exactly what the phrase was conveying. And now he had to tell his team.

\* \* \*

The team of five listened in silence as he explained everything he had been told and seen. The silence he had imagined would happen definitely did.

Then he heard Bryn Williams say in his Welsh accent, 'For fuck's sake.' He watched as Bryn dropped his head, but Bryn said no more.

Maria stood. 'I'll be back in a minute,' she said, and left the room. Tia waited a moment then followed her; she knew she had headed for the ladies' toilets. She quietly opened the door and heard Maria vomiting.

She waited, then when Maria came out of the cubicle, she put her arms around her. 'I know,' she said quietly. 'It was horrific, and your reaction is exactly what I would have expected. Let's get you a drink of water, and then let's get on with our jobs and find the bastard who did that to her.'

They walked to the water fountain, took a cupful each and headed back to the briefing room. Chris lifted his head as they came through the door, and looked questioningly at Tia. She gave a slight nod, and he understood everything was under control.

'Okay, we need to read every tiny scrap of paper in these boxes, we need to know everything about Lauren Pascoe, what she did, what hobbies she had, anybody she'd ever dated, what size shoes she wore – I mean everything. Something in her past life prior to her disappearance could be the clue as to why she was abducted, and who did it. Maria, you're in charge of that. Tia, we should go have a chat with Ray Eke, preferably in his home. I don't want to drag him in here, he's not a suspect, just the unfortunate bloke who found the body. Can we contact him? Make sure he's not back at work? We can't really chat to him in the middle of the A57, or on Moss Way.'

'I'll give him a ring, see what he's doing.' Tia smiled and picked up the briefing room phone. She spoke briefly to Frank Carter, who obliged with Eke's number, but then added that Ray Eke had rung earlier to say his boss had insisted he didn't return to work until the following Monday, so if he was needed for a statement he would be at home.

Tia passed on the message to Chris, who stood from the desk on which he was perching. 'Let's go and get this ticked off our list. For everybody else we need to go through this lot.' He indicated the piles of boxes. 'But we mustn't skip through them. Every interview needs to be logged, every little point digested. Once we've finished the immediate work on this poor woman, we'll all be doing the slogging work. I'll let you all have copies of Mr Eke's statement when we have it, just in case you don't have enough to look at with this lot.'

'Thanks, boss, you're all heart,' Bryn said, and groaned. He walked across to the stack of bankers boxes, checked the contents and picked up the earliest dated one. 'This is the earliest dated one,' he announced, and everyone held up a thumb. What that meant was unclear, but he guessed they would then take the next earliest and slowly work through them all. It had obviously been a long and detailed search for the missing woman, judging by the sheer volume of reports and interviews.

\* \* \*

They pulled up outside Ray's home and sat for a minute just looking at it. It was a large house; Tia guessed four bedrooms. The path leading to the front door was long, and divided a beautifully laid out front garden. The centrepiece on the left-hand side was a granite sundial; the right-hand side displayed a stunning rock garden with a gnome as its centrepiece. A gnome playing a piano.

They approached the front door and pressed the Ring doorbell. The music they could hear stopped abruptly, and Chris knew he hadn't recognised the piece, even though he had recognised the quality of the pianist.

Ziggy opened the door and cast an eye over her visitors. 'Police?' she asked.

Both officers held out their warrant cards, and Chris asked if they could speak with Ray, just to get his statement and check he was okay.

Ziggy nodded. 'I'm his mum. He's fine, just sorry he couldn't do anything to help the lady. I'll take you through to him.'

She led them through to the lounge, and Ray paused with his

hands on the piano keys. 'Sorry,' he said, 'I was lost in this.' He indicated the sheet of music in front of him on the music rest. 'Taking a bit of composing time. I didn't hear the doorbell.' He stood and walked across to Chris and Tia. 'You're from Moss Way?'

Chris nodded and held out his hand. 'We are.' Ray shook it, and Ziggy left the room, saying she would make some tea and coffee.

Ray led them to the sofas and they sat around the circular coffee table. Tea and coffee appeared quickly, and Ziggy left, adding that if they needed her, to give her a shout.

Tia poured the drinks, then pulled her notebook towards her. She waited patiently for Chris to speak.

'That was beautiful music, and seeing the paper on your piano explains why I didn't recognise it. It's your composition?'

Ray nodded. 'It is. I'm taking advantage of these couple of enforced holiday days to get it finished. It's only for me, but the tune is constantly in my head, and needs to be down on paper. And I'm lying,' he confessed with a grin, 'it's called "For Sigrid", and it's for my mum.'

Chris nodded. 'It certainly does need to be on paper. When it's finished, I'd like to hear it all.'

Ray smiled for the first time. 'My first audience,' he said, 'I'll make sure to invite you.'

# 5

'You told PC Norman you thought you recognised the victim.'

Ray nodded. 'I did. Funnily enough it was the mole on her forehead. Her face didn't really look like the face on the posters we handed out, it looked much older, but then I saw the mole and wondered if it could possibly be her. Now you're saying it definitely is, and I think I kind of knew that, but something awful must have happened to her over the last three years. That lady I found hadn't been dead for three years, that's a certainty.'

'No, we believe she had been dead about five or six hours. I can't give you any further details, but now we have the problem of finding out just where she's been since June 2021. You formed part of the original search teams?'

'I did. One of the girls at work was a friend of Lauren's, and asked if she could take a day off to help look for her. We closed down the office and everybody went. At that time, it would have been nine or ten of us. It started to become too dark to see much around half past nine, but we'd given out hundreds of those posters with her details on. Such a pretty woman.'

Chris's mind went immediately to the body he had seen

earlier, and little of that prettiness had been obvious. She had aged dramatically; her skin was sallow as if it needed a wash and some sunlight, and her body in general was emaciated. It seemed obvious that food had been withheld.

'I did a couple of extra searches after that, the case kind of got under my skin, I suppose. But eventually it dropped out of sight, apart from the occasional reminder by her mother – on her birthday, the anniversary of her disappearance, that sort of thing. But that mole couldn't be disguised, could it?'

'It's now been confirmed because the original team managed to get her fingerprints from her diary in her bedroom, and they match with the victim. It is definitely Lauren Pascoe. DNA will follow and will be matched to her mum's DNA, but there's no doubt of the identity.'

'Oh, God, her mum. She'll be devastated. But at least now she knows she can lay her to rest. I remember her as being very vocal, pleading with the police not to drop the case, but I suppose if there's no evidence to push anything along, there's not a lot you can do.'

Chris finished his coffee and replaced the cup on the saucer. 'So that's it, Mr Eke, Unless there's anything else to add, you need to sign the statement Tia has been putting together, and we can get out of your hair, let you go back to your piano.'

'Thank you. I'd prefer to be working, but my boss wouldn't hear of it. The council has certain rules, it seems.' He pulled the pen and the statement form towards him and signed his name with a flourish.

'Do you play other instruments?' Tia asked.

'The piano's my favourite, but I also play saxophone and violin. When I'm in a jazz mood, it's the saxophone, but if I'm a bit down, or just feeling quiet, it's the piano or the violin.'

'Such a gift. I'm envious,' and Chris leaned across the coffee table, shaking hands with Ray as he stood.

Ray smiled. 'It wasn't enough to save me when I needed an anchor, but it's saving me now.'

He accompanied them to the car, and they spoke of his garden, which he clearly loved. He pointed to the gnome. 'I wouldn't ever have considered having gnomes in my garden, but Mum bought me that to welcome me home after my illness. It's lived proudly in my rock garden ever since. He's called Mozart.'

Ray and Ziggy waved as Chris and Tia drove away, and Ray continued to watch until they were out of sight. He had been slightly dreading having to go into the station to make his statement, and he now felt a sense of relief that it was over and done with.

Ziggy joined him by the garden gate, and he slipped his arm around her. 'Thank you,' he said.

'You're welcome, but what for?'

'Just for being there for me. You've seen me through the most awful time in my life, given up your home to care for me, done everything to keep me safe and you've never complained.'

She smiled. 'When you're ready for me to go home, you know my house is empty waiting for me, so just say the word. I'm sure you're well enough to be alone now, but I don't want to pre-empt anything and leave you when you don't want to be left. Does that make sense?'

'I think so. Mum, you can stay here forever, as far as I'm concerned. I'll never ask you to leave, that will always be your decision. I owe you so much.'

'Well, that's all right then. I'm staying. Unless I find someone who looks like Paul Newman and has oodles of money. Then I'm going.'

And they returned to the lounge where Ray headed straight

to the piano. He could get some more of his tune down, take advantage of this free day off work. And tomorrow maybe the two of them would go out to the garden centre, grab some lunch there, and look at arbours. He quite fancied an arbour at the top of the back garden... his fingers lightly touched the keys and he played and hummed softly to himself, lost in his world of music.

Ziggy shook her head as she left him to his composing – the kitchen was calling. The ingredients for a cake had been added to a bowl, and then baking had been suspended when she realised it was the police at the front door. Time to get back to the lemon drizzle cake they both enjoyed.

\* \* \*

Chris and Tia sat in the car at the police station. A sudden heavy burst of rain was holding them prisoner, and they decided to give it a few minutes in the hope that the downpour would lessen.

'Did you like him?'

Tia nodded. 'I did. Seemed genuine. He hasn't let it faze him, finding the body, and he must realise he'll never lose that image for the rest of his life. Neither will we, come to think of it.'

Chris peered through the windscreen. 'Does it always rain this heavy in Sheffield?'

'Only when it wants to give hard-working coppers a five-minute break.'

'Thought I might head out into the hills this weekend, but maybe this rain will keep me in the back bedroom to get it decorated. The kids are coming to stay in a couple of weeks, and I've done my daughter's room, easy because she wanted everything on the walls to be cream so she can add her own posters and stuff to it, but my son wants a Sheffield Wednesday room, so that's going to involve a trip to the Sheffield

Wednesday shop for bedding, and hopefully they sell wallpaper.'

'You just have two kids?'

'I do. Twins. Simon and Ava. When we found out were having a baby, my mum had just died, and we said immediately that if it was a girl it would be called after her, Ava. When we discovered it was a boy and a girl, we used my wife's late dad's name for him. They're very much alike, Simon and Ava, in character and attitude to life, but not in looks. Simon is like me, you'd know instantly he was my son, but Ava is blonde, very pretty, and she'll go far. Simon's into football, but Ava is creative. She'll cover those cream walls in her artwork.'

'How often will you be able to see them? They don't exactly live around the corner, do they?'

'We have a flexible arrangement. It was an amicable divorce, and it's stayed that way. Luckily, my ex-wife understands my job, but deep down I think that's why we drifted apart and when she met someone who had a nine-to-five job, it was the end for us really. But the kids are our priority, and they don't suffer as a result of incompetent parents.'

'Good. I'd like to meet them someday. The rain's not as bad, shall we make a run for it?'

Chris peered through his side window. 'If we have to.'

They raced across the car park, and burst through the doors of reception.

Frank Carter grinned. 'Raining then, is it?'

'Just a bit,' Chris said. 'Anything happened while we've been battling through the monsoon?'

'Not a thing. All the bad lads stay indoors when it's raining. They might have come out to play when it was sunnier earlier, but they'll not come out and risk getting their stolen designer gear wet, will they?'

They both grinned and lifted a hand in agreement before headed upstairs to the briefing room.

It was an afternoon of quiet. Heads were down, buried in the paperwork from everything that had been issued during the period of the initial searches for Lauren, and Chris felt satisfied that fresh eyes would uncover something.

He moved into his own office and logged into the case. He added the statement taken from Ray Eke, then sat back and let his thoughts roam. He had liked Ray, and had completely understood his reluctance to return to the life of stress that had caused such a major breakdown.

Money clearly hadn't been an issue; he lived in a beautiful home and that wouldn't be possible without a solid financial background. He had an air of what could almost be described as pleasantness, if indeed pleasantness was a word. He talked with a touch of gentle capability, as if nothing was too much trouble. He had spoken of how much he enjoyed his job and couldn't wait to get back on track on Monday morning, wanting reassurance that Donetsk Way would have reopened by then.

Chris had been able to confirm it, and the smile on Ray's face had been genuine. 'I need to finish off that second side,' he explained. 'Then I can tick it off as complete, and move onto the road down into Crystal Peaks. I have to be methodical with it, or bits get missed.'

Chris smiled as he recalled the conversation, and thought how alike they were. He too was 'methodical with it', and as a result he pulled a notepad towards him as his telephone rang. Not much point answering a phone that inevitably would issue some information for him, and not have pen and paper to hand to record the content for posterity.

'Chris Chandler.'

'Boss, it's Frank in reception. I've somebody on the phone wanting to report a missing person.'

'How long missing?'

'Today. But could be since last night. It's the girl's mother on the phone.'

'Can you take details?'

There was a moment of hesitation. 'You know that inkling us coppers get? I've got it. I'm not saying it's linked, but...'

'Put the lady through.' Chris knew better than to ignore an experienced copper's inkling, whatever the inkling might throw up. He didn't think they had inklings up in the north-east, but it seemed they did in South Yorkshire.

'Her name is Paula Wrightson, and the missing person is Hannah Wrightson, her daughter. I've taken a few more details, in case she doesn't tell you it all, she sounds a bit upset.'

'Thanks, Frank. Put her through.'

# 6

It transpired that Hannah Wrightson was twenty-seven years old, lived at Birley in her own home, but never missed speaking to her mum every night, even if it was just to ask if everything was okay at home. Before his recent death, her father had had several health issues, and Hannah was always available to help, or cover for her mum if she had to go out. They were a truly closeknit family.

And now it seemed that Hannah couldn't be reached. Chris had a sudden overwhelming feeling of the 'inkling' as described by Frank, and began to coax information out of the clearly worried lady at the other end of the line.

'I texted her at work yesterday morning, Wednesday, about ten o'clock. She replied and said everything was good, and then I've heard nothing since. I actually rang her at work earlier, which I wouldn't normally do, but it was a different receptionist who answered, and she said Hannah hadn't been in work since around eleven yesterday. I nipped round to her place thinking she must be poorly, and she's not there.'

Chris could hear the sob in Paula Wrightson's voice. 'Mrs Wrightson, tell me where she works and we'll begin there. It may be they know more than their receptionist does. Has she worked there long?'

'Yes, a few years now. It's Mark Griffiths Accountancy. I don't know the full address but it's quite a large place on White Lane, at Gleadless.'

The inkling tingled a little bit more.

'Mrs Wrightson, we'll be popping round to see you later, but your daughter is an adult and could be doing something a little out of character, but perfectly normal. If you hear from her, please contact me directly, and we can close everything down. I wouldn't normally open a file for at least another twenty-four hours, but you're obviously worried, so I'm going to make initial contacts now, in the hope we can put your mind at rest.'

He disconnected, and sat back in his chair, deep in thought. Accountancy. Too much accountancy hovering in the air. He'd always thought figures and financials to be somewhat dull, but suddenly they seemed to be centre stage.

He stared at the notes he had taken. Hadn't his litter-picker acquaintance been senior partner in an accountancy business?

'Good morning, Ray. Chris Chandler. Just a quick question.'

'DI Chandler. How can I help? Did you forget something this morning?'

'No, it's a different matter. I know you have nothing to do with numbers and suchlike now, but when you did, did you come across a company called Mark Griffiths Accountancy?'

He heard a slight laugh in Ray's voice. 'Mark Griffiths is my best friend, and was the man I brought into the business when I first started. It was called Eke, Griffiths and Co Accountancy until I walked away. Mark bought me out of the business and now we're the closest of friends instead of business partners. He saved my life. I was at a terrible point when he found me smashing up my office, and got me the help I needed. Please don't tell me he's in any sort of trouble, because I wouldn't believe it.'

'No, he isn't. The firm's name just cropped up in connection with something else, and when I heard "accountancy" I immediately thought you might know them. You okay?'

'I'm fine, thanks. I'll be glad when Monday gets here and I can go back to work, I'm not used to time off during the week. I've just got Friday, Saturday and Sunday to get through.'

They said goodbye, and once again Chris leaned back in his chair, deep in thought.

According to the files, Lauren Pascoe had been a trainee veterinary nurse. It was something she had longed to do since being a child, and had targeted her exams towards doing that job. She had been with the vet's practice, Paws and Claws, for two years when she had disappeared.

Could there be a connection with an accountant's business? He needed to know who did the annual accounts for the vet's business to check a link, but he didn't feel particularly hopeful. He looked up his name in the files. Stewart Phillips.

And was he simply clutching at proverbial straws? Was he assuming that because one woman had turned up dead, a replacement for her killer was now required? He hoped with all his heart that Hannah Wrightson would suddenly arrive back home, confessing she had met the most gorgeous man on the planet and had spent time having ecstatic sex with him before the most gorgeous man on the planet confessed his wife was due home any time.

A telephone call to the vets told him that there was no accountancy connection. It seemed Stewart Phillips had a brother who was an accountant, and had seen to his tax affairs for many years.

Chris thanked the man, and then listened to Phillips's grateful words for finding his absentee animal nurse. He spoke of how much she had been sorely missed, but they had never lost hope she would be found.

Chris almost felt as if he had cheated – he hadn't found her, and definitely nobody had found her in time to save her from some brutal treatment that had caused her death.

\* \* \*

'DI Chandler,' Chris said, holding up his warrant card. 'I'd like to speak with Mr Griffiths for a few moments, please.'

The receptionist smiled at him. 'I'll check if he's free.'

Chris nodded, but didn't move. He really didn't care if Griffiths was free or not, he intended speaking with him in the next five minutes.

The receptionist disconnected and switched on her smile once more. 'He'll be down in one minute.'

Chris nodded. 'Thank you.' He moved away from the desk and walked around the small reception area. The pictures on the walls were of old Gleadless, and he wondered just what the area had looked like a hundred years earlier. These pictures showed a very rural Gleadless, nothing like the thriving township it had become over the years.

He turned as a man came through the door to his left. Smartly dressed in a dark navy suit and sporting a yellow tie with navy stripes, he looked every inch the boss.

'Mark Griffiths, how can I help?'

'DI Chris Chandler.' He briefly flashed his warrant card once again. 'Is there somewhere we can speak?'

Mark nodded. 'Let's go to my office.'

Chris followed Griffiths down a corridor until they reached a door marked with his name.

'Coffee?' Mark asked.

'No, I'm good, thanks.' They both sat.

'How can I help?'

'Apparently you have a missing receptionist. Hannah Wrightson. We've been asked to look into her disappearance.'

For a slight moment, Mark appeared shocked. 'Missing? I thought she was ill. I assumed it's why we have one of our junior staff on reception. Oh my God, I'm not sure what to say now. I wasn't in work myself yesterday, had a proper migraine, but when I saw it wasn't Hannah on duty this morning, I assumed she was off for some reason and the girls had done their usual job of making sure reception was covered. I feel awful now for not checking. My only defence is that the headache is still there and I'm not thinking straight.'

Chris leaned forward. 'Her mother has been trying to contact her. She has no idea where she is. Apparently she came into work yesterday morning and hasn't been seen since. The information we have is that she went missing around eleven yesterday morning. After I've finished our chat, I'd like to speak with any members of your staff who are here.'

'Of course. I'm quite stunned. Don't really know what to say. And because I was out of it for the biggest part of yesterday, I know absolutely nothing. This place could have burnt down for all I was aware.'

'Do you have a full list of employees?'

'I do. There aren't many of us. I made the decision to remain as a one-man business when my senior partner was taken ill and I had to buy him out. I've never been particularly ambitious, so decided to remain small.' He turned to his computer and clicked on a couple of items before sending them to his printer. He passed the printed copies to Chris.

'This is a list of names, plus a sheet with their home addresses. We go out to clients, as well as work here on accounts. The bigger clients obviously need us to go to them, but I specialise in the smaller businesses that bring cartons of paperwork to us and say sort this out. Ray Eke, my ex-partner, left the business as a thriving concern, and I hope I've continued it as he would have done.'

'You miss him?' Chris detected a note of despondency in the other man's words.

'Very much so. But he wanted out of figures. Those were his words. He's such a genuine bloke, been my best friend for years, but it's a different relationship now.'

'Now I'd also like to ask you about Lauren Pascoe...'

'The girl who went missing? Who's now been found? I heard that much, but it's all I know. Yesterday wiped me out – started Tuesday evening, and I feel as if I've just re-surfaced. Migraine can be a bugger, excuse the language. It's plagued me for years, and the staff know I occasionally have to give in to it.'

'You joined Ray Eke in the searches?'

'We all did. She was a friend of one of the girls who worked here at that time, and we kind of supported her so joined the hundreds of people in the area who were out looking in the woods and fields around Gleadless. I personally went out several times, just looking, totally disorganised but you just never know, do you? I know Ray did the same. We printed off a lot of copies of the leaflet with her face on it, and delivered loads of them through doors in the area. But it fades, you know. I can't even remember the name of the girl who was her friend, she didn't work here for very long. I can look it up if ever you want it. I haven't thought of Lauren in a long time. It's been a busy period with the re-structure of the business, missing Ray, and coming to terms with being the main man. I was happy being second in command, but seeing Ray that day when he was smashing everything up...'

Chris stood. 'Thank you for your help, Mr Griffiths. If you can point me in the right direction, I'll have a quick chat with the members of your staff who are here, just see if they know what happened yesterday with Hannah – they may have seen something that made them stop and think.'

'Of course.' Both men went out into the corridor. Mark pointed. 'Two are in that room, they do general secretarial work, and the two offices down at the end have names on the doors indicating who is in which space. They are Marsha Jackson and Caroline Bent. Caroline is currently on sick leave.'

Chris shook his hand, thanked him and entered the first room containing two women. They both looked up as he entered, and he introduced himself. They weren't able to tell him anything, other than Hannah had been on reception when they arrived, and then she wasn't. Their office junior had stepped into the breach, and was there again at the moment.

He thanked them and left for the other two small offices. Again he found nothing useful, and ended up back at reception. It seemed that Hannah had called the office junior, seventeen-year-old Lyra Grayson, to sit on reception for a few minutes while she nipped across to Sainsbury's to get fresh milk for the drinks some clients had said yes to. That had been around ten o'clock, Lyra thought, and Hannah never came back with the milk.

Chris thanked her, left his card with her just in case anything else came to mind, and walked outside. He climbed into his car and looked across at the Sainsbury's shop. Had she really gone there? He would send someone up to check their CCTV for between ten and eleven the previous day.

He mulled over his thoughts as he drove back to the station, reflecting that Mark Griffiths hadn't appeared to know that it was Ray Eke who had found the body of Lauren Pascoe.

And then he smiled. They had asked Ray not to talk about it. He clearly had taken their instructions to heart...

# 7

Maria flashed her warrant card at the manager of the shop. 'PC Maria Fletcher,' she said. 'I need to take a look at your CCTV covering the entrance doors for Wednesday morning, 9.30 to 11 a.m. If I see what I'm expecting to see, then I'll download it. That okay?'

The manager smiled at the pretty police officer. This was brightening up his day and making his Friday more bearable, was his initial thought. He followed up that first notion with a hope that he wasn't in some sort of trouble for sticking out a foot as the teenage shoplifter went charging past him. The resulting crash to the floor had been a bit brutal. 'Follow me, I'll take you to my office. That's where the screens are.'

\* \* \*

Maria cradled the obligatory cup of coffee while she sat with her eyes glued to the slow-motion visuals scrolling across the screen. Her phone, with its picture of Hannah Wrightson showing on it, was propped in front of her.

Although not a huge shop, its steady stream of visitors made Maria slow down the action a little more. And then she saw her. She screenshot the paused moment, took a note of the time, then continued to watch. Four minutes later she saw Hannah walk back out of the doors, carrying a two-litre bottle of milk. She took a second screenshot, then downloaded the relevant section to a data stick.

After thanking the manager, she left the shop. She texted Chris with the results, saying she would be back in the office in ten minutes. He responded with a smiley face and a thumbs up.

She was slowly starting to like her new boss. She hadn't been too sure at first. He was a quiet man, and she always felt that you only saw the surface when anyone was quiet, but gradually he was starting to open up.

\* \* \*

She put the stick into her computer and everyone gathered around her desk to see the results of Maria's unusual foray from the office. Being the IT expert left her tied to her desk so much, and today had been a real treat.

'That's her,' she said, lightly touching her screen with the tip of a pencil. 'I am right, aren't I?'

'You definitely are. She's an attractive girl, isn't she?'

'She is. You think somebody took her because of that?' Maria asked Chris.

'We still don't have any proof at all that somebody has abducted her. For all we know, she has a boyfriend she's trying to hide from her mum. She could be having a couple of days with him.'

'But the milk she's carrying was for the office.'

Chris frowned. 'I know, and what's more, I know it never

reached the office. I checked with the young girl currently manning the front desk at Griffiths Accountancy. One of the others ended up nipping across the road to get some. She was only twenty-five, maybe thirty-five yards away from her office when she left Sainsbury's. It's that close, and yet she didn't make it back there. Nobody has reported an abduction of any sort – you think she got in a car with someone she knew? I'm quite sure she wouldn't have done so with a stranger.'

Maria nodded. 'We need to see other CCTVs from the area, but to be quite frank, I had a bit of a look after I came out of Sainsbury's. She turned slightly right as if to head back across the road towards her office, so any cameras to the left of her wouldn't have caught anything. The Sainsbury's shop is the last one on that small row, so nothing there. There's a pub car park, but she walked towards the road, as if to cross it. We need to know if the frontage of her own office has any cameras. Other than that, I'm with you on the possibility that she knew whoever has taken her. And I'm sorry, boss, but I don't go with the theory she might be with a boyfriend she doesn't want anybody to know about. She had a bottle of milk in her hand, and it was the middle of the morning. You don't just suddenly decide to walk out of work and go off for a bit of sex. We shouldn't waste time even considering that as an option.'

The others turned to look at her. Maria was their quiet one, their clever and smart one. Suddenly she had spoken, and all of them knew that her words were ringing uncomfortably accurately.

'And,' she continued, keen to get her thoughts out before her courage went back to its usual place, her big toes, 'are we, in our minds, linking this disappearance to the death of Lauren Pascoe? Because we have no link, do we? Hannah Wrightson worked at an accountancy firm, and wasn't Lauren a vet nurse? Or are we simply scared that whoever has killed Lauren now wants a replacement?'

Chris kept his eyes trained on her. 'You think that's a possibility?'

'Of course it's a possibility, but it also could be mere coincidence that Hannah has gone missing within a few days of Lauren dying. I think we have to be careful not to close our minds to other circumstances.'

Chris allowed a smile to break through. 'And the rest of the team are in full agreement. But thank you for putting it so succinctly. They are two separate cases, and must be treated as such unless facts link them together. However, we are working both of them, and we can call on uniforms for help whenever we need them, for the foot work and suchlike. As a result of that I'm sending a team of half a dozen or so up to Gleadless, simply to mingle, to post flyers through doors in the close locality, say half a mile radius, of Mark Griffiths and Co Accountancy, and to talk to people who visit Sainsbury's. It's a small shop in comparison to the superstores, and used almost as a corner shop by the locals. They may have known Hannah, may have seen if she got into a car, or even carried on walking instead of going back to her desk. I can't think of a reason for her taking that last action, but that doesn't mean it didn't happen in that way. She may have simply thrown a wobbly, thought sod them all, and walked.' He paused for a moment. 'I expect we've all had days like that.'

There was an automatic nodding of heads. 'Okay, I'm going downstairs to organise a few bobbies to infiltrate the Gleadless community, get the leaflets sorted and have them start up there on Monday morning. That gives us the weekend to see if Hannah returns home under her own volition.'

\* \* \*

It didn't take long to organise who would be doing what on the Monday morning, and to get someone to photocopy images of Hannah. Chris found himself cursing the weekend – but the people who would be out and about around the Sainsbury's area would probably be totally different to the residents who frequented the area during the week.

He headed back up to his office and sat going over the facts. It seemed that Lauren had disappeared in June 2021, reappearing nearly three years later, sadly deceased. The search for her had been huge, with large numbers of people heading into woods, playing areas – anywhere that a body could possibly be hidden. Because it seemed they had believed a body would be the end result, as there had been no mobile phone activity, no bank card usage, nothing to indicate Lauren was still alive.

He sighed. But she had been, and according to the pathologist had been kept under appalling conditions. The torture had been excessive, and he couldn't imagine the pain she must have experienced, but that broken bottle inserted into her vagina and twisted had been the final straw to her poor battered body and her heart had given up.

Chris recognised his fear – that Hannah had been taken as a replacement and could be suffering the same sort of treatment. Gut instinct was telling him the two women were somehow connected, and yet he had nothing to confirm the theory.

When his phone rang, he knew it would be Paula Wrightson. He took a deep breath.

'DI Chandler.'

'It's Paula Wrightson. I still haven't heard from her, and she hasn't been home. Please...'

'Mrs Wrightson, we've been out making enquiries, have confirmed she went across to the local shop at Gleadless for milk for the office, and then she never made it back across the road.

Monday morning, if we still haven't heard from Hannah, we have a large team of uniformed officers ready to blanket Gleadless, interviewing everybody who is out and about. This hasn't been put onto a back burner, we've already been checking CCTV which is how we know she actually went to the shop, but since then there have been no sightings that we know about. We're going to post on Facebook at six o'clock tonight with a missing person's post, so hopefully something will come from that. I promise you that if we hear anything, the tiniest whisper, that will lead us to Hannah, I will contact you immediately. I'm a parent myself, and I can't imagine how you're coping.'

Paula Wrightson burst into tears. 'I just feel...'

'I know,' Chris said gently. 'Hannah's never gone so long before without contacting you. It's why we're taking it so seriously at this early stage, but I promise you a lot of work has already been done as we search for your daughter.'

He could hear Paula's struggles as she tried to control her tears. 'She's all I have, DI Chandler. We're so close, and that's why I know something is wrong. We chat at least twice a day, and suddenly that isn't there. She's not asked to use the car – we share one just for shopping trips and suchlike because she uses the tram to get to work – and everything feels so wrong. Have you checked with her bank...?'

'We have, and there has been nothing, no activity at all apart from a direct debit. We won't give up,' Chris said gently. 'Something will break, and I'm hoping with everything I have that somebody will be interviewed on Monday who actually saw something, that will lead us to where she is.'

'So you think she has been taken?' Paula's voice had dropped to a whisper as she digested what Chris was saying. Chris heard the hope die in the woman's voice.

'I'm saying nothing because we know nothing from the point

when she left Sainsbury's. You're absolutely sure she doesn't have a boyfriend?'

'I'm positive. We're very open with our conversations. There hasn't been a mention of anyone recently.'

'What is recently?'

She paused for a minute to think. 'Oh, I would say nobody to speak of for at least six months. She was talking about booking a holiday in Spain, but that was with one of her old school friends.'

'Do me a favour, Mrs Wrightson. Make me a list of any love interests or even casual acquaintances that have been in your daughter's life for the last four years or so.'

There was a sharp intake of breath. 'Of course I will. I'll ring you tomorrow.'

They said goodbye and Chris sat back, rubbing his hands up and down his cheeks as if to revive himself. Paula Wrightson was clearly at the very edge of her self-control, and while he didn't think a list of ex-boyfriends would help, it gave Hannah's mother something to focus on apart from a silent mobile phone.

# 8

Pain. It filled Hannah's mind, body and even deep into her soul. She tried desperately to recall how she had arrived at this moment, and thought she could remember walking past a white van with open side doors, and someone with a white coat on. The driver had asked her something in a very quiet voice and she had leaned forwards to ask for it to be repeated.

And that was it. She had no idea where she was; she could neither move nor see. A blindfold was across her eyes very tightly, and a scarf had been tied across her mouth to stop her talking. It had been removed twice to give her a drink of water but then immediately tied again. She was hungry; she was uncomfortable because she had needed to wee and could hold it no longer, but the pain that had ensued from that normally natural action had been unbearable. She was chillingly, frighteningly cold. And she had pains in her stomach which meant weeing was going to be the least of her problems with regard to bodily functions.

She was aware she was naked, but she had no coverings of

any description to ease the coldness. And being cold seemed to aggravate everything else.

Her pain seemed to be everywhere. Her entire body was suffused with it and she suspected she had been raped, so severe was the throbbing between her legs. But her biggest problem at the moment was that she felt sick. She wouldn't be able to expel the vomit if she couldn't stop this awful sensation, and she could easily choke on it.

She forced herself to remain still, to move her thoughts to better things such as the cinema outing she had planned with her mother, and slowly the nausea faded, although not altogether. She didn't want to think about food in case it started again.

The cramp in her stomach hit her in waves and she knew her bowels were about to explode. She tried to scream out for help but the gag was effective at quietening her, and she moaned inwardly.

\* \* \*

The door opened quietly and someone stood in the entrance.

'You stink.'

She heard the door close and she didn't know whether to feel relief or terror. Her thoughts drifted to the joys of a red-hot shower. Hearing the door open again brought her mind out of the pretty white tiled bathroom at home and back to her current domicile. She felt footsteps approaching her, and then stop. There was a clang and then she felt a splash followed by a bucket full of ice-cold water as it splashed over the bottom half of her body.

She felt the roughness of fabric rubbing into her skin and she prayed for it to stop. It was aggravating the agony already present in her genital area, and she couldn't even scream. She heard the fabric being thrown into the bucket, knocking it over.

The second bucket followed the first and Hannah actually thought she was dying, so cold was the water.

She was rolled onto her side and her captor took hold of her right hand. She briefly wondered if she was going to be allowed some freedom from her bonds, as the pain in her shoulders from lying permanently on her hands tied around her back was almost unbearable.

A new pain completely engulfed her. Seconds later she was returned to her usual position on her back, then something was stroked across her forehead.

'Your little finger. Next time we have another mess like this it will be another finger. And, by the way, your first pee cost you your left nipple.'

She felt consciousness slipping away from her, and a hand touched her neck to check her pulse. Losing this one wasn't an option yet. The fun had only just begun.

The idea was for one more day and it would be smart to introduce a toilet system, maybe give her a biscuit or something. There were no intentions of killing her; the three years with Lauren had been amazing and if God was good, he'd give this one her life for even longer than that.

She just needed to be trained.

\* \* \*

When Hannah surfaced after fighting back to semi-awareness, she realised she had no control over her body. She was shaking, enough to be making a noise, and she tried to stop it. She didn't want Whitecoat coming back. Her memory was slowly surfacing, and she remembered the back view of a white coat, like doctors wore in hospital. Her captor, in her mind, was now Whitecoat.

Her hand was throbbing, and painful waves were washing over her. It seemed she now had an explanation for the rawness across her chest – her nipple had been cut off. A huge shudder engulfed her, and she wondered just how long it would take her to die if body parts kept being removed. She hoped it wouldn't be long, because the utter agony coursing through her entire body was reaching unbearable levels. What she was struggling to understand was why she hadn't felt the loss of her nipple. Had she been drugged first? All she had been aware of was pain, but it had blended in with all the other pains. Had the sips of water really been just water? Had she been injected with something?

In some ways she was dreading having the freedom to open her eyes once the blindfold was removed. She felt she must have closed them automatically when the tight fabric had been put on her face in the back of the van, but at least she couldn't physically see the mess she must now be in. There must be lots of blood. Nothing had been done to clean whatever she was lying on, so her finger stump was probably bleeding, her nipple would have bled, and whatever had been done between her legs had probably caused a loss of blood, if the pain was anything to go by.

Hours drifted by and Hannah slipped off into a dreamworld. She was only wakened by cramps in her stomach, but different cramps to when she had been forced to give in to the demands of her bowels. These were cramps of food withdrawal. She had no idea how long she had been held captive, no idea what her prison looked like, but she knew that right at that moment she would absolutely kill for a bag of crisps. Cheese and onion.

* * *

Although Hannah had no idea of time passing, her abductor did. Knowing she would soon be at the stage where she would be desperately craving food and water, two slices of toast and a cup of tea were prepared and then carried down the stairs and into her room.

She was immobile during the approach to the side of the camping mattress. Then she involuntarily moved; it was an obvious reaction to the fear she must be feeling.

'Food,' was all that was said. She was helped to sit up; rough hands removed her gag and snipped the plastic ties binding her hands together. She groaned as her shoulders screamed with the pain of moving for the first time in many days. The plate was placed on her lap and her hand was guided towards it.

'Toast.'

She nodded and felt in front of her. The relief was evident as she said a whispered 'Thank you.'

'Tea,' was said with a snarl, and the mug was placed on the floor.

She held out her hand. 'Please. I'm so thirsty.' It was passed to her and she carefully sipped at the scalding liquid. Her tongue felt huge, but she swilled the hot liquid around her mouth, trying to reach every dried-up corner.

The toast was almost cold, but she didn't care. Her stomach needed it. She ate it quickly, afraid it would be removed before she could eat it all. She heard footsteps moving away from her, and suddenly she recognised the click of a switch being turned on. She guessed it was a light.

'I'm going to remove your blindfold, but not the straps on your legs. You're going to have to learn to move around in a different way. If you're still behaving yourself in another week, I'll untie your legs.'

She swallowed the final bit of toast as she sensed the footsteps walking towards her. A bit of tugging and pulling at the blindfold caused it to suddenly fall from her face. She slowly opened eyes that hadn't been opened since the blindfold had been tied on her, and stared at the figure in front of her.

Dressed completely in a white forensic suit, there was also a black balaclava that completely covered the face and head. A gloved finger pointed into the corner.

'That door isn't an escape route. There isn't one. That is your toilet. Use it, don't use it, I don't care. But if you don't use it, I'll cut off bits of you.'

The black and white figure turned and walked away carrying the plate that had held the toast. 'I'll leave the cup, there's a small water tap in the toilet where you can get drinks of water. Don't break the cup, you won't get another.'

She didn't dare speak. Afraid of the removal of some or all of the privileges she had just been allowed, Hannah kept quiet. There had been no mention of clothes, or even a blanket to cover her. Maybe they would be rewards later on, if she behaved herself. And who the hell was her captor?

If it was a man, he was only of medium height; average build, and with a generic accent. Not Yorkshire, not Derbyshire, accents she would have recognised. But she wasn't sure it was a man. The height could have belonged to either sex, as could the voice, because every word spoken so far had been almost in a whisper. Whitecoat disappeared through the door and she heard the click of the lock.

She slowly drank the tea and massaged a little of the warm liquid into the corners of her mouth and her cheeks. The gag had been so tight, so painful, and she hoped a little liquid might make them feel a bit more normal.

Then she knew she had to make it across the tiny space to the door she had been told led to a toilet, with her legs still securely tied together with plastic garden ties. She swung her legs around then eased her bottom onto the floor. She began to use her arms to navigate the few feet to the toilet and tried to ignore the tears of pain running down her face. Her arms had been behind her back for some time – she had no idea just how long – and the agony as she tried to bring them to their normal position was almost too much to bear.

Plus she had the raw stump that was making her feel sick – Whitecoat had taken the finger then left her hand without any sort of dressing. She had to sort out the toilet facilities no matter how much she was hurting. She didn't want to lose any other parts of her body because she had wet herself, or even worse, soiled herself. This toilet business had to be mastered.

She reached the door, lifted up her arm to open it, and the light went off. She was plunged into instant blackness, disoriented, and she heard her voice croak, 'No, not yet…'

She managed to pull open the door and did a quick shuffle into the tiny room. She felt around with the hand that wasn't throbbing as though it was going to explode, and touched the toilet. She heaved herself upwards and launched herself at the porcelain toilet. It cast a tiny bit of brightness because it was white, so she sat on it and immediately her bladder opened and she breathed a huge sigh of relief.

She felt around the miniscule space and touched a tiny sink, then found the tap that would give her water. She turned it on, and tried to wash herself then let herself slide down onto the floor to exit, and make her way back to the bed.

She knew she should have placed her finger stump under the tap, but had been too afraid. What if it caused even greater pain and she passed out? That might cause the loss of another finger for that sort of transgression.

With a sigh of utter relief she made it back to the bed, and waited for what was to happen next.

# 9

Sunday was a quiet day, beautiful sunshine and a gentle breeze to bring a little comfort in the heat.

Ziggy was up early and wandered down to the kitchen, looking forward to her first coffee of the day. Not having heard Ray, she was a little surprised to see the coffee already made in the pot. She glanced outside the back door to see her son comfortably ensconced on a garden chair, cradling a large mug of coffee.

'Morning, sweetheart,' she said.

He casually waved a hand. 'Morning, Mum. The coffee's only been made about five minutes.'

'Thank you, I'll go get some. You want anything?'

'No, I'm good, thanks. Just enjoying the day before it gets too hot. I'll mow this back lawn later, when I manage to find some energy.'

Ziggy felt happy. It seemed normality had returned to her life; she didn't look for hidden meanings behind Ray's words any more, and at one point she had been constantly on the lookout for what he said and what he meant. It now felt as though if he said he was going to mow the lawn, it wouldn't be him wanting to clean the windows.

She grabbed a mug and poured a coffee, debating with herself whether to join Ray, or whether to leave him on his own. He had obviously been enjoying the peace without her, so she decided to head into the lounge and wallow in her own little bit of stillness. She picked up her Kindle, asked Alexa to play piano music, and settled on the sofa.

\* \* \*

The knock on the door made her jump, and she put down the Kindle and peeped around the curtain. She smiled.

'Mark,' she said, as she opened the door. 'Lovely to see you. You here for breakfast? We haven't eaten yet.'

'Well, I promise I didn't time the visit to coincide with breakfast, but what are you having?'

'Could be bacon sandwiches.'

'Could be here for breakfast then,' he laughed. 'Is the lad up?'

'The lad is on the patio. Go through to him, I'll go and sort breakfast.'

\* \* \*

With a fresh pot of coffee made and three bacon sandwiches on thick crusty bread all covered with tinfoil, she carried everything out to where the two men were chattering, clearly putting their worlds to rights. Ziggy loved it when Mark called round. It sometimes seemed as if he was the only person who could really get Ray to talk naturally, and to get her son to laugh out loud.

They both stood as she approached the table, and Ray lifted

the tray from her arms. 'You should have shouted, I would have sent Mark to get this,' Ray said with a grin.

'Shut up, and pour the coffee,' she retaliated.

It was only when the bacon sandwiches had been all but totally consumed that the conversation returned.

'We're going to the gym,' Ray said.

'Good grief, are you ill?'

'Don't be clever, Mother dear,' Ray laughed. 'I'm going a little reluctantly, Mark's going because he goes most days. We're going to mow the lawn first, then I'm going to get fit.'

Ziggy snorted. 'In one visit? Mark? Are you sure you want him to go with you?'

'Course I am. He's my best mate, and if we can't talk numbers any more, we've got to find some other common ground. I thought he'd enjoy the gym. I'll make sure he starts off slow...'

'Very slow, I hope.' She waggled a finger at Ray. 'And don't damage those hands!'

\* \* \*

The stripes in the lawn were immaculate. Ray had dealt with the edges, and Mark had tackled the lawn itself. They left her an hour later and Ziggy breathed a sigh of relief.

Ray hadn't seen Mark for some considerable time when he was first hospitalised, but slowly the doctors had said he could start to introduce his previous life back into his present one. Mark had been the first one he had messaged, and the two had met within an hour of that first tentative contact.

She would always be grateful for that visit. It had revealed the first flickering of a return to normality in her son and apart from the finalising of their split within the partnership, Mark had never spoken of work again with Ray.

Now their conversations were of gardening, enjoying a pint on the patio, driving out into Derbyshire; gentle activities that eased the two of them into a totally different type of relationship which seemed to have strengthened their friendship.

Ziggy loaded the dishwasher before heading upstairs to change the bedding on both their beds – such a lovely day she deemed it might be a good idea to wash bigger items and get them on the washing line outside to dry.

\* \* \*

It was very clear that Ray had been awake most of the night, just snoozing in his armchair. The bed hadn't been disturbed; the laundry she had placed on his bed to be put in his drawers was still there, and the covers were unruffled in any way. There was a light quilt on the arm of the chair, his iPad on the other arm.

She backed out of his room, closing the door behind her. If he needed to talk about what was keeping him awake at night, she had to hope he would talk to her, or Mark. He knew he would eventually have to talk, to get back to peace of mind.

He had talked at some length about the discovery of the body of Lauren Pascoe, and she hoped he had talked it out of his system and settled it inside his head, but maybe he still needed to talk more. She had read behind his words, and knew he was deeply troubled by the death, but he was an adult. She couldn't make him talk to her, but she would try for a quiet word with Mark when they returned from the gym.

\* \* \*

After a hard gym session and a hot, then cold shower, the two men found themselves accidentally in the coffee shop, and equally accidentally with a plate with a huge piece of chocolate cake in front of each of them.

'Cake's nice,' Mark said.

'Probably got more calories in it than we burnt off in that hour or so in the gym.' Ray smiled as he took a second mouth full.

'I know, but it's Sunday.'

'That makes a difference?' Ray looked puzzled.

'It does. Calories don't count on Sundays.'

Ray thought about the statement for a moment, before digging his fork back into his portion of cake. 'I'll be able to walk them off anyway tomorrow.'

Mark lifted his head. 'You back at work?'

'I am. I didn't really need to be off, but the council has rules, and they said I needed a few days. Most of my round was cordoned off anyway, but it's clear now. I'm starting on the A57 bright and early tomorrow, it's supposed to be another hot one, so I can get my six hours in and finish.'

'And you're okay?'

Ray nodded, digging out another forkful of cake from his plate. 'I'm fine. I told them I thought it was her, you know. She didn't look exactly the same, but I saw the mole...'

'My God, Ray. I'm not sure I would have handled it like you did. Calmly ringing the police, waiting there until somebody turned up, giving a statement. It seems unreal. You actually said it's Lauren?'

'I did. As I say, she does look different now, her hair was quite long, not like it was on those posters we took out when she went missing, but the mole stuck in my mind, so I mentioned that to them. There was something else that I told them seemed strange. The top she had on was the same one as she was wearing on the posters. Nobody in the police had noticed that, or at least they hadn't said they had.' Ray glanced around the room as if checking who was close enough to hear their conversation.

'Let's hope one day they give out some details. I'm just glad it's out in the open now, it must have given some closure to her mum.'

'And Hannah?' Ray asked.

'Her mum doesn't know where she is, and the girls at work don't know either.' He looked up as if he'd suddenly had a light bulb moment. 'You think the police have decided it's connected?'

Ray shrugged, wiping the chocolate from around his lips with a napkin. 'I don't know. I always liked Hannah. I know I upset her on that last day...'

'Hey, don't worry about that. She understood you'd had a breakdown, kept asking me how you were doing, and she was over the moon when you sent her that huge bunch of flowers after you came home. No, Hannah was cool about it all, which is why the police think it's a little strange that she went out for a bottle of milk for the office, and nobody has seen her since. The police have spoken to me, of course, but I told them I wasn't really aware of anything because I was in bed all day with another blessed migraine, and then we were into the weekend, but Monday I'm going to bring everybody into my office and talk to them. Maybe one of them knows something without realising they do, or perhaps she's confided in one of the others about a boyfriend, or something. See if I can get something to pass on to the police. I may find something I can tell them that will help, or at least get them off our backs.'

Ray nodded, and cleared off the final remnants of the cake from his plate. 'Delicious. Will you keep me informed if you hear anything from anybody? As I say, I like Hannah, and I do feel guilty for the way I was with her, and then for smashing up my office virtually in front of her. She must have been scared. Wonder if she's feeling scared now...'

'Your office is still there, you know. You only have to say the word...'

'I've walked away from numbers. I'm in the fortunate position of not having any money issues, and that's the way I like it. My music and my garden – and my job – are enough for me now. I know Mum watches me like a hawk, but I'll be honest – I'm dreading the day she tells me she's moving back home to her own place. She doesn't place anything on me. We talk when we need to talk, she never says anything about me playing the piano at any time, and actually sings along with the ones she knows. Loves a bit of Frank Sinatra, does Mum. My job demands nothing of me, and I've actually told them I can take on extra if they want to extend my patch, but I'm still done with accountancy. There's no fresh air in an office, you know. And just think about this... maybe it's the numbers that give you your migraines?'

Mark grinned at him. 'That's the longest speech I've heard you give since you came home from the Priory. I'll not mention it again, just pop in every now and again, will you? Let the girls see you're alive and well. I've actually been interviewing for a new trainee, and I've kind of made the decision to take a twenty-one-year-old lad called Gareth Thompson on. He lives in the area which is a bonus for him, and he's already well on with the qualifications. I liked him, so if I definitely can't tempt you back then he'll probably take over my office, as I think I'm going to move into yours. I never wanted to make that move before, I think I always felt you might come back even after I'd bought you out, but after listening to you just now, I know I'm being stupid. You're so much happier, so why the hell would you want to come back to a life of figures? You seem to have found your niche in life, strikes me.'

'You ready to go?' Ray smiled at his friend.

'I am. Can I keep the coat rack you used to smash up your laptop? It didn't break, obviously stronger than the laptop.'

'You're very welcome. The trick to getting a baseball cap to hook onto it while sitting at the desk is to stand slightly, thumb on top of the peak and flick it in the direction of the stand. Definitely thumb on top of the peak.'

'I'll remember that. Thing is, I don't think I've ever worn a baseball cap.'

Ray glanced once more around the café as they left the building. It had suddenly become busier but he didn't recognise any of the new arrivals. He breathed a sigh of relief. He was quite happy with his anti-social life.

They were laughing, easily and in close friendship, as they climbed into Mark's car, heading back to Ray's home, where the newly washed sheets fluttered in the softness of the warm breeze.

## 10

Ray got off the tram at the Donetsk Way stop and walked across the road. It was a deliberate move on his part – he needed to face the spot where the body had lain and move on. He needed to change the image of that tiny piece of land in his brain, because it was his tiny piece of land, part of his working route, and he wanted a different image to the one now imprinted in his brain of a once very pretty girl.

He paused at the exact spot, and waited for all images to settle. The grass was starting to recover and he knew within a week it would return to how it was before it was flattened by a white tent erected over Lauren's body. Ray wasn't a churchgoer, wasn't sure what he felt in regard to any religion, but in that moment he softly whispered a small prayer, asking that someone, anyone, take care of the soul of Lauren.

'Amen,' said a quiet voice, and he spun round. DI Chris Chandler was standing a few feet away. 'We obviously had the same idea,' Chris continued.

Ray nodded. 'This little bit of land is always going to be part of my round, and I came here in the hopes it would become what it was before, and not somewhere I found a dead body.'

'Speaking from experience of many crime scenes, it will fade, but it won't happen overnight. It's not a good thing to happen to anybody, finding a deceased person, and if you need counselling...'

Ray shook his head. 'I had a breakdown. A bad one. I have counsellors coming out of my ears, but they can't control or adjust anything you've seen. This will be dealt with in my own way, and this today, me being here at this ungodly hour, is my way of getting through it. I don't know where the little prayer came from, I've never prayed in my life, but at that moment it felt like the right thing to do.'

'If it felt right, it was right.' Chris turned to walk away. 'Have a good day, and try not to be too hard on yourself. Everything you did, the way you handled it, was spot on, so now I'm off to find out who did it to her and then we can all rest easy.'

As Chris stepped away, he heard Ray speak again. 'She was wearing the same top.'

He stopped and turned back. 'What?'

'If you look at the posters that we handed out, when the whole of Gleadless was out and about looking for her, she's wearing the top that I found her in. It just seemed strange...'

Chris looked at him for what seemed like forever to Ray. 'You're sure?'

'I'm sure. I printed enough of those pictures to be absolutely certain.'

Chris gave a quick nod of acknowledgement. 'Thanks, Ray. Try to enjoy your day. At least it's not raining.' He walked quickly down to the edge of the road, heading back towards Moss Way.

Ray waited a couple of minutes before sighing, and following in Chris's footsteps. His journey started at the roundabout, and he remotely clocked in with his supervisor before heading down the A57. He loved this section – dense woodland, paths made by many years of feet walking along them, and the Pennine Way stretching across the top of the road via a man-made bridge. Although the bridge wasn't, strictly speaking, part of his route, he always included it, kept it litter-free before returning back to the opposite side of the road and heading back up towards Moss Way. It was a secluded area, virtually guaranteeing the body would be found quickly, because if her body had been taken into woodland, or even up towards Beighton Tip, she could have lain undiscovered for some time. It flashed through his mind that he could set up an evening class and teach people where the best places to bury or simply hide bodies would be around Hackenthorpe and Beighton. They'd soon get A levels in that subject – the whole area was a tree-filled haven, and ideal for murderers to take their pick of grave sites.

He shook his head, not believing where his idiotic thoughts were taking him. After checking the bag was fastened securely to the frame that held it open, he picked up his first piece of litter for that day, and wasn't at all surprised it had originated in McDonald's.

\* \* \*

Chris sat in his office for a while, pondering on his strange meeting with Ray Eke. Then he realised it wasn't such a strange meeting, it was more an odd one. Different word, different meaning. It had been early. Just after six, and while it wasn't unusual for a policeman to start work at that ridiculous hour, he guessed it was pretty unusual for a litter-picker to begin work so early.

Frank Carter had been another early starter, and had been reading the *Star* as Chris had entered through the front doors opening into the reception area. He had confirmed that all the lads required up at Gleadless that morning were having hot drinks before heading out around seven-thirty, and they would be reporting back in around three-thirty before going home for four.

Chris thanked him and headed up to his office, his thoughts all over the place. Door knocking, street interviews, private CCTV cameras, Ray Eke, Sainsbury's, same clothing...

Same clothing. When he had attended at the crime scene he hadn't yet seen the poster with Lauren's picture; later, at the morgue there had been no sign of any clothing. Lauren Pascoe had been covered by a sheet so the clothing must, at this point, have arrived with forensics to be checked. It was probably a fact that nobody in the forensics team had seen the flyer handed out when Lauren had first disappeared three years earlier, and therefore wouldn't have made the connection that the top she was wearing was the same top she was sporting as she was abducted. It may have become obvious at some point, but that moment certainly hadn't arrived with him until Eke mentioned it.

What the hell did it mean? Where had those clothes been during those three years? Had she really had to wear them for all that time? He needed to speak with the pathologist, find out if they appeared to be old, if they were worn out in places. He regretted more than ever that he hadn't seen her photograph when she was first discovered, but nobody had connected any dots; Lauren Pascoe's disappearance was a cold case, and it was only after Ray Eke mentioned Lauren's name to Andy Norman that bells began to ring loudly with everybody. Except himself, he thought grimly.

He heard the briefing room door open and close, then the sound of voices began to filter towards him. A glance at his watch told him it wasn't yet seven o'clock, but it appeared his team were all arriving early. They obviously felt like him; they needed to get on with this case, needed to be in touch with the lads out on the streets of Gleadless, just on the off chance that a snippet of information came through to them.

Chris took a deep breath and left the security of his own tiny office for the open space, multi-desked briefing room. 'Morning, everybody.'

There was a chorus of 'Morning, boss,' and everybody stopped their chatter and turned to face him. Expectantly.

'Okay, Maria and Andy, I want you both inside today. Handle any calls coming in from any of the uniforms out taking statements, and Maria, do what you do best on that computer. If you catch anything, no matter how insignificant it might be, ring me. Remember, we have a missing girl as well as a dead one. We're treating them as separate cases, until something happens to give us a link. Work together. Two calls may come in at the same time, so we need two people on phones. Okay?'

Both officers nodded their understanding, and Chris walked over to the whiteboard. He pointed to the picture of Lauren.

'This top that Lauren is wearing is the same one she was found in. Think about that. I'm going to the morgue to have a look at it, get some idea if it's been worn constantly for three years, then I'm going to speak to Lauren's mother to ask if she knows when that photograph was taken. Something's not sitting right with this. Sally, you saw her in the tent, didn't you?'

Sally nodded. 'I did. And if her top had looked tatty, or torn, or anything other than how it did look, I would have noticed. But to be honest, it looked as though it was fairly new. That needs some thinking about. Could whoever took her have made her wear his choice of clothes for the entire three years?'

'Possibly. I can't think beyond seeing that top and getting a feel for how much it's been worn. You're with me, Sally, as we're going to see Janey Pascoe again, she responds well to you. We'll be walking on eggshells, I fear, because I don't want her knowing just how brutal her daughter's death was, but she may have some answers for us, and I'd rather see her face to face than just chatting on the phone.'

'Anything in particular for Bryn? I'm happy to do whatever,' Tia said.

'Bryn, I'd like you up at Gleadless. The lads know you're with Major Crimes, so just keep them going because it can be a thankless job trying to get people to talk, and it's usually people who don't like being stopped by the police. Find me some CCTV in the area. We're really struggling to know how Hannah Wrightson managed to completely disappear. And I'm definitely struggling not to link these two cases. I want proof they're not linked, rather than proof that they are, believe me. I don't want to consider Hannah may be going through what Lauren went through.'

Tia stared at Chris. 'Great minds think alike, boss. Can I make a suggestion? I know you spoke to the employees at Griffiths Accountancy, but maybe I can get more out of them. Woman to woman sort of thing. I'll use the old excuse of needing official statements, try and commandeer a boxroom or something, and interview them a little more formally. They may let something slip that they hadn't considered when you spoke to them last week. They've also had time to think about it now, as well.'

Chris nodded. 'Interview them singly. I was shown into an office where most of them were, there was really only the receptionist who was on her own. Go for it, and ring me if anything comes up that's the slightest bit helpful. I want something a little more concrete on either of these two women before the end of the day, but I am aware we've already made a start that needs building on.'

Everybody began to move. Within five minutes, only Andy

and Maria remained in the office. Maria shook her head. 'Bit of a whirlwind when he wants to be, our boss. Right, I'm going to do some deep diving on Lauren first, then move onto Hannah. I actually feel Hannah is more urgent, but if the two are linked within one case, I need to start with Lauren.'

Andy nodded. 'No problem. And I'll keep us topped up with coffee. This could be a busy day.'

## 11

Janey looked old. She had spent three years worrying about her daughter, and her whereabouts, but she had always had hope that she would one day walk back through the door. That hope was now gone, and Janey had allowed the grief and despair to envelop her entire body.

She had on Mickey Mouse pyjamas, with an old grey dressing gown casually wrapped around her. She stared for a moment at her visitors, then stepped back to allow them to enter.

'Can't offer you a drink,' she said. 'I'm out of milk.'

'That's fine, Janey,' Sally said gently. 'But if you would like me to make you one, I can nip to mine and get you some milk?'

Janey shook her head. 'I'm okay with water,' she said. 'Have you found him? Have you found the bastard who's had my daughter for three years, doing God knows what to her? And when can I see her? You said you needed me to identify her, but I've heard nothing.'

Sally helped her neighbour to sit in an armchair. 'We do need that, but we also need the go-ahead from the pathology department to say that we are cleared for you to confirm it is Lauren. I suspect that may happen tomorrow, and we will come and get you and escort you to the room where you can spend a bit of time with Lauren. We can't really tell you much more at the moment, it's an ongoing case, but we wanted to ask you a couple more questions. You okay with that?'

Sally and Chris sat on the sofa facing Lauren's mother, both of them wanting to make everything go away for her. The grief was palpable, coming off her in waves.

Chris reached across and took her hand. 'Janey, I need to ask you something. I want you to think back to when Lauren first disappeared. Tell me about the photograph that was used to make the posters everyone was handing out. Where did that picture come from?'

'One of the girls at the vets had been asked to take photos of all the staff in their new workwear. They wore white trousers and that coloured top, and the owner of the practice wanted to make a board for the reception area with pictures of each individual staff member on it, along with their names. He'd bought all of them two pairs of trousers and two tops. These days they wear all white tops and trousers, but at that time it was that purplish-blue top. I think the girl who took the photos was called Katie, but don't quote me on that. The picture was taken on the day she disappeared, so the police were pleased they had an up-to-date photo of her to get that image out there. I have an unopened blouse thing upstairs that's never even been tried on, she was wearing the other one for the first time the day she was taken.'

'Thank you,' Sally said. 'That's really helpful. Would you mind if we took it?'

'Not a bit. If it will help find who did this, take whatever you need. I'll go and get it for you.'

Sally stood with a smile. 'You stay there. You're out on your feet, Janey. Not sleeping?'

Janey shook her head. 'Not since she was found. It's in Lauren's room, top drawer in the chest of drawers.' She looked down at her hands, her intertwined fingers that never seemed to stop moving.

Sally quickly returned with the top, and placed it into an evidence bag. 'Thank you for your help, Janey,' she said. 'And it will be me collecting you for the identification at the morgue, not a stranger. I won't leave you to carry this alone.' She glanced across to Chris to confirm she wasn't out of order saying it, and he gave a brief nod of his head.

The two officers stayed for a while, talking about Lauren, allowing Janey to talk about her daughter and bringing out memories of good times they had enjoyed as Lauren grew from babyhood to adulthood. When they left, it seemed as if Janey was feeling a little brighter and speaking about going to have a shower, maybe even getting dressed. They drove away, neither of them wanting to talk, both shocked by how rapidly Janey had changed over the last couple of days. Sally vowed to herself that she would keep a close eye on the woman who seemed to have been on the periphery of her life for such a long time.

\* \* \*

Bryn had spoken with each of the six shirt-sleeved officers; all had been respectful of the job they had been tasked with doing, and said they would stay as long as it took. Bryn told them no later than five o'clock, and they all nodded their agreement, but he wasn't convinced. The shock ending to the Lauren Pascoe mystery had rattled them, and now they were out asking questions about a second missing woman who had disappeared, virtually concurrent with the finding of the body of Lauren. Bryn soon realised they were linking the two cases, and he explained they weren't officially being tied together, but they did need to keep open minds.

The day grew hotter and he provided bottles of water for them, but still they worked through, determined to speak to everyone they could in the local area. And then there was a tiny breakthrough.

\* \* \*

An elderly lady by the name of Marjorie Bird got off the tram at Gleadless Townend and walked back towards her home. She was spotted by one of the uniforms, who had been keeping detailed records of properties that he hadn't managed to check because nobody was in.

He gave her a few minutes to get herself organised before knocking on her door. Her home faced Sainsbury's, and overlooked the tramlines.

She heard the doorbell and hurried to answer; she had seen several police officers in the area, and hoped it would be one of them, and not Old Man Peters from next door, who could be a bit of a pain.

As a result, her smile was a genuine smile of pleasure as she met PC Danny Moore. 'Come in,' she said. 'Would you like a cold drink?'

He liked this lady. 'Mind if I make room for it and use your toilet first, please?'

'Not at all. First right, top of the stairs. Iced tea or lemonade?'

'Wow. Iced tea if you have some.' He disappeared at some

speed, and five minutes later was sitting at her kitchen table, explaining why he was there.

'I'd not heard anything about this,' Marjorie exclaimed, her eyes wide. 'This is so exciting. I had to go stay at my sister's about ten days ago, because she was taken into hospital and she has cats.'

Danny felt a little bewildered. 'She took the cats into hospital?'

'No, I went to stay in her home until she was discharged, because there are three cats and they needed looking after. I'm back for a few hours, then I'm going back over there to look after her as well as the cats. I had to come home to get some tablets and stick a wash load in, because I've run out of the ones I took with me.'

'I see.' He didn't really, but he thought it best to just go with the flow. He wasn't sure whether she'd run out of tablets, or clothes.

'It seems I came home on the right day. This is quite exciting. Nothing ever happens in my life.'

'Ms Bird...'

'Marjorie, call me Marjorie.'

'Thank you, Marjorie. That camera on your bedroom windowsill, is it live?'

'It most certainly is. I watch what's going on through an app on my phone. My grandson set it up for me. I can show you how to work it, if you like?'

'Thank you,' he said, sipping at the peach iced tea. Truly delicious.

Marjorie stood and walked towards the window. Her bag was sitting on the kitchen side, and she reached into it to find her phone.

It was the latest model iPhone.

'Nice,' Danny said.

'My grandson bought it me for my birthday. It does all sorts of things.' She clicked on the security camera icon, waited for a moment, clicked again and passed it to Danny. 'It covers all the front of my property, the car park across that belongs to the Red Lion, and the layby and tram tracks in front of Sainsbury's. It's a very clear picture,' she said with a laugh. 'You'll have to track down the time you want to look at it, and take it from there. Can I leave you to do that while I get a wash load put in?'

'Of course,' Danny responded, totally in awe of this tech-savvy pensioner. And he'd kill to have this phone.

He worked carefully through the listed recordings and checked to see if there was anything at all that looked in any way suspect at the relevant time. He watched a white van pull up, parking carefully in the designated parking area that was really just a small layby for Sainsbury's, and well clear of tram tracks. The driver didn't get out. Hannah Wrightson walked into view, swinging the bottle of milk. Within a minute, the van pulled away and Hannah was nowhere to be seen. The angle of the van in relation to the camera on Marjorie's house meant that the number plate couldn't be read, but he doubted it really belonged to that vehicle anyway.

Danny took out his own phone and rang the control room number they had all been given before starting work.

\* \* \*

Maria leaned back in her chair, shook her head to clear her brain and answered it. 'Please God,' she whispered, 'make this something we can get our teeth into, and not just one of the lads reporting in that they had nothing to report.'

Her prayer was answered.

'I have something. CCTV. Can I have somebody to download, please?' Danny gave Marjorie's address, and Maria said she would be there within ten minutes.

\* \* \*

Marjorie couldn't help but smile. She now had a young lady police officer, albeit not in uniform, and life had suddenly become exciting. She'd had the most boring few days in the universe, having to share her time between hospital visits and feeding cats, and now she was the star of the show.

She thought Maria was a lovely girl, and pretty smart too, just like her grandson was smart when he'd installed the camera. He wanted her to be safe, he had said, wanted her to know how to use it, to read the information it held, but most of all he wanted her to use that very expensive iPhone to its full capabilities. And she could and did.

And when these two very nice police officers had returned to Moss Way, she would have a close look at what they had seen, just for the sheer hell of it!

\* \* \*

Maria and Danny finished their cups of Earl Grey that Marjorie had persuaded them was the finest tea this side of Ceylon, and Maria had thoroughly enjoyed it. She'd make sure there was Earl Grey in the kitchen at work from now on, but she would pay attention to Marjorie's words when she had said Marks and Spencer's was the best brand.

They thanked her for her time and waved from the end of the path as they left her to continue with her postponed afternoon of things to do before returning to the cats.

Marjorie gently closed her front door, checked how much longer was left on the washing machine and sat once again at the kitchen table, picking up her phone as she did so. She clicked on the icon for the camera and Maria had left it exactly where they had been downloading the footage that had caused all the afternoon's excitement.

'Thank you, Maria,' she said to herself. 'You knew I would want to look at whatever you had looked at, didn't you?'

## 12

Chris arrived at the morgue on his own. He'd dropped Sally back at Moss Way to write up their morning's work, and he'd turned around to take the top recovered from Lauren's bedroom, just in case the forensic team could use it for comparison issues.

He hated the initial smell of chemical overload, but was learning it was a fact of life in a lab technician's world, so he had to put up and shut up.

Kevin Hanson pushed his sandwich to one side and held out his hand. 'We didn't really meet properly the other day, I was a bit busy with your young lady, and I needed to get her back here and out of the sunshine. Kevin Hanson, supposedly in charge here.'

'DI Chris Chandler, but call me Chris, please. And I'm supposedly in charge of Major Crimes. It was a bit chaotic the other day. I'd only just started at Moss Way, and I'm still trying to find my way around. I'm not very good at remembering names, so don't expect me to know yours next time we meet,' he said with a grin. 'You have anything new to tell me?'

The smile disappeared from the pathologist's face. 'Bloody

horrific, wasn't it? I know I shouldn't say this, but thank God her death was quick. What he did with that broken bottle…'

'Was there semen? Anything at all that could give a DNA result?'

He hesitated. 'No semen. So in truth we don't know if it was a man or a woman who killed her.'

For a moment, Chris was shocked. It took a lot to make him feel that way, and he knew deep down he had stereotyped this killer. Of course it could just as easily be a woman. He knew statistics would say it was more likely to be a man, but that didn't mean it was a man, did it?

'So we have nothing?'

'Very little, but I think Ms Pascoe hasn't worn clothes for a long time. Her skin is… strange. It feels almost rubbery, as though it's had no air to it. It actually makes me believe whoever took her kept her locked away for the entire three years in a closed, almost airless room, possibly a cellar, and naked. She has been tied with plastic ties, and she has many marks that indicate this. They would have worked pretty much like razors on her skin every time she tried to free herself. I've done a much more comprehensive report on this lady now her body has had time to settle, and I believe the killer dressed her to dispose of her.'

'I have something to add to that. The top she was wearing on the day she disappeared was brand new. It was staff uniform at the vets where she worked. I've just dropped a spare one that has never been worn in with your forensics team, just in case it could help. We've no idea at what point she disappeared but her mum was sensing things were wrong almost immediately. They were very close, kept in touch constantly, and she hadn't heard from her.'

'It bothers me that I can give you so little.' Kevin frowned as he spoke. 'We're waiting on blood results, but I suspect this killer hasn't been drugging her to make her compliant, I think he wanted her to feel everything. Both nipples had been removed but I believe that was early on in her captivity, they were fully healed. Most of her fingers had gone, her suffering must have been immense. I know life is precious, but I can't help but feel that death was the ultimate wish for her.'

Chris nodded. 'Truly horrific three years for Lauren. The biggest fear now is he or she has already replaced her.'

'I've been following the news. You think this latest disappearance is definitely connected?'

'We have no proof,' Chris admitted, 'but she has definitely disappeared. There doesn't appear to be a connection between the two women, but there wouldn't need to be. The only thing, at the moment, that links them is that they both have a mother who is close to them, and both women knew from the outset that their daughters were in danger. Sometimes a missing person can be off the radar for weeks before somebody reports it, but not so with Lauren Pascoe and Hannah Wrightson. Janey Pascoe and Paula Wrightson knew immediately. They had phone conversations or visits every day, and when that didn't happen alarms rang immediately. I've tried not to link this second disappearance with Lauren, but I feel sick when I think about it. If she is with him, if he has taken her...'

Chris stood. He reached across and shook Kevin's hand. 'Thank you for letting me talk. If anything else shows up from test results, you'll let me know? Janey Pascoe is keen to see her daughter, and I said possibly tomorrow. Will that be okay with you?'

'Of course. I'll make sure Lauren is clean and tidy – the parts that her mother will see, anyway. Find this bastard, Chris, find him quickly. Or her.'

\*\*\*

Maria had issued pictures of the van to ANPR, the automatic number plate recognition department; she didn't hold out much hope of them tracking it. There simply weren't enough active cameras, but anything was worth a try. And if the number plates were false, it could only be tracked up to the point when the number plates were changed to fresh ones...

Following Chris's return to the office, she showed everyone the footage taken from Marjorie's camera. Chris asked for a second viewing with it slowed down, but still nothing was obvious. Hannah had walked towards the van as she was preparing to cross the road to return to her office, and then she had simply disappeared.

'Okay,' Chris said, deep in thought. 'We need to know the exact make of this van, and if it has side-opening doors. If those doors were open, he could very easily have tipped her into the van. It was driven away immediately, and Hannah wasn't left standing by the roadside waiting to cross. She was in that bloody vehicle, probably scared half out of her mind.'

'It's a Ford Transit, will either have one or two sliding doors on that side next to the pavement, and two locked back doors. He would just need to tip her in, slam the doors shut and get into his driving seat. I'll bet anything there's a partition between the load area and the driving area so that she couldn't get to him.' Maria put a picture on the screen of a white Ford Transit. 'It's definitely this model.'

'And nothing from ANPR?'

She shook her head. 'Not yet, but it's early doors.'

'The old lady, she didn't actually see it?'

'Don't call her an old lady.' Maria laughed. 'Marjorie Bird is one smart cookie. And no, she didn't see it because she was looking after her sister's cats at the other side of the city. She's going back there tonight, but we have her mobile number now. Brand-new top-of-the-range iPhone,' she said wistfully. 'She promised to keep checking her camera just in case the van came back – let's face it, it could be perfectly innocent, and he could be a delivery driver to either the pub or Sainsbury's, or even one of the shops round the other side of the road.'

'The thing that's really bothering me is that this is real time, and Hannah Wrightson was there by the side of the road, walking to go past that van before crossing the road, and then she wasn't anywhere, twenty seconds later. I'm absolutely sure she was taken in that van, all we need to do is find it.' Chris gave a deep sigh as the enormity of doing just that enveloped him. 'But of course it had to be a Ford Transit. There's millions of them.'

'I've made sure everybody has notification of this Transit, but indicated that the number plates may be different by now. So basically, every beat bobby up to the Chief Constable has a picture of it, and I've stressed how urgent it is that we find it. I've also added a picture of Hannah Wrightson, so fingers crossed we don't get inundated with white Transits from Leeds to Nottingham and all points in between.' Tia looked at Chris. 'Did I do right?'

'You certainly did.' He looked around at the rest of his team. 'Don't feel you have to get permission to do stuff – you're all experienced detectives, you know the score. We use whatever we can to get the right results, and what Tia has done is smart. Yes, it can mean an extra workload, but it can also mean it leads us directly to where Hannah Wrightson is being held.'

Tia sighed. 'Thanks, Chris. It's always difficult getting used to a new boss's way of working. It was only after I'd set up the info going out to all and sundry that I suddenly realised maybe I should have run it by you first. Can I assume we've now accepted that this could be another Lauren Pascoe situation?'

Chris looked across towards the whiteboard. Both women were on it, but on separate halves. 'I'm coming round to thinking they should definitely be together, not seen as two cases. I think he accidentally killed Lauren, and Hannah is his replacement. Or her replacement.'

Five heads swivelled towards him. 'Her replacement?' Bryn asked.

'I popped in for a chat with...' Chris hesitated for a moment, while he searched through his brain, 'Kevin Hanson. You know, the new pathologist.'

They all nodded, and Tia laughed. 'Don't worry, boss, we'll try and make it that you're never on your own, and then you won't have to remember any names. It is Kevin Hanson. He had something new to say?'

'Kind of. For a start he believes Lauren was naked for the three years she was missing. He also believes she was kept inside, possibly in a cellar of some sort, for all that time because her skin was wrong. I think he meant sort of leathery, but he didn't go into details about that because I think he wants to run more tests. However, when I asked about DNA and the possibility of semen on the body, he said there was no evidence of it, and then asked me if I was sure it was a man. It could just as easily have been a woman.'

There was silence for a moment and then everyone began speaking at once.

'Surely not,' Maria said. 'Surely a woman wouldn't have pushed a broken glass bottle inside another woman's vagina.' She shivered at her own words, and repeated, 'Surely not.'

'Myra Hindley killed five children,' Chris said. 'We would all have said surely not before that happened, wouldn't we?'

Tia lifted her head. 'I know what Maria means though. There's a huge amount of women who don't go for smear tests when they should because it bloody hurts, at least in my experience. And let's not talk about childbirth...'

'Point taken,' Chris said. 'Don't tell me anything more. I'm just glad I was born a man. Let's slightly change the subject, because I need to organise Sally for tomorrow. Can you make arrangements with Janey to take her to the morgue, please? Kenneth is going to tidy Lauren for viewing, so if you can arrange to collect Janey around ten?'

The five members of his team spoke as one. 'Kevin!'

## 13

Janey was awake by six, showered and dressed in black trousers, a white top and a black cardigan. She wanted no colour. Colour had been in her life when she still had hope. This morning she would be seeing the body of her daughter, her beautiful Lauren, and now she wanted no colour.

She needed no breakfast, but the coffee was welcome. She limited herself to the one cup, so that she didn't have to ask to use the toilet while out with Sally. Today was all about Lauren, not her mother's erratic bladder.

But Janey was nervous. She knew she was going to Watery Street, but she had no idea where it was. She guessed Sally, now she was with Major Crimes, would know exactly its location, but if Janey was being completely honest, she hadn't even heard of Watery Street.

She walked down the garden, trying to find some peace in her soul, but the sun was really bright and she headed back indoors. She switched on the kettle, then immediately switched it off again. No second cup till she was back home.

Maybe she should go and have a wee, just in case. She

climbed the stairs, used the bathroom, then went into her daughter's bedroom. She sat on the bed, and let everything wash over her. She hadn't changed a thing in this room, had always believed that one day Lauren would walk through her front door, give her usual shout of, ''S me,' and they would fall into each other's arms. The tears came thick and fast, almost taking Janey by surprise; she thought she would be all cried out after three years of tears, but apparently there were still some hiding away inside her.

She laid her head gently on the pillow, and realised she could no longer smell Nina Ricci's L'Air du Temps on the pillowcase. She hadn't washed it in all the time Lauren had been away because the fragrance of her daughter's favourite perfume had lingered and lingered, but now it had gone. Along with Janey's hope.

She hugged Eeyore tightly to her and realised he still carried a faint aroma of the perfume. Eeyore had been Lauren's constant; he never let her down, and he was the recipient of all her secrets, problems and joyful moments.

Janey stayed in the room, lost in remembrance and experiencing an almost painful longing to hold Lauren for one last time. Eventually she sat up, placed Eeyore back on the pillow and headed downstairs.

Five minutes later, Sally arrived.

* * *

Sally pulled into the car park of the Medico Legal Centre and they got out of the car. Janey was trembling.

'Can I do this?' she whispered, half to herself and half to Sally.

Sally took hold of her hand. 'We're doing it together. I won't leave you, I promise. You've been an absolute rock, so strong, for the last three years. We're reaching the end now, so do Lauren proud and hold your head up when we go through those doors to the autopsy suite. Don't be afraid, just be you. You ready?'

Janey nodded, and Sally pressed for admittance, giving their names through an intercom. The door catch was released and they walked through.

Five minutes later, a calm and composed Janey confirmed it was her daughter lying on the table, and Sally left her alone for a few minutes, watching her carefully through the small window in the door, ready to go in if Janey showed any signs of needing help.

But Janey was numb. She didn't need help; she needed to say her goodbyes and to go home and make arrangements to bury her most precious only child.

They left the building, Sally supporting Janey with an arm linked through hers. 'Shall we go get a Costa?'

Janey nodded. 'I think we should. Do you know I was up at six, and I've only had one drink because I was worried I might want to wee? How stupid is that? Everybody here has been so nice, so kind, and all I had to worry about was possibly wanting to wee.'

Sally smiled. 'It'll be a large latte, then?'

'The biggest one they do,' Janey said. 'And I need to talk about Lauren, I just need to quite desperately, because I've buried all thoughts of this day for three years and I've now got to stop.'

'No problem, we can talk for as long as you want. Nobody is expecting me back in any sort of rush, they know we are friends.'

\* \* \*

Sally returned Janey to her home, went inside with her and made her yet another cup of coffee to get her through the afternoon, then headed down the street to pop in to check her own mum was okay. Fortunately it was a fairly good day for her, so Sally gave her a kiss and headed back to the station.

She parked her car but didn't get out immediately. She needed a couple of minutes away from everything to deal with the day that had mentally wiped her out. In the end, the heat inside the car drove her out, and she crossed the car park and climbed the steps up to the reception. She waved at Frank Carter, who leaned forward and asked if she was okay.

'I'm fine. Lauren Pascoe's mum is an absolute star.'

'I know,' he acknowledged. 'She's been in here a lot asking what we're doing to find her daughter, many, many times over the years. I really hope she has some peace now. I know it's the wrong outcome for her, but she's no longer in limbo wondering what's happened to Lauren.'

'Is everybody in upstairs?'

'I think so. Maria hasn't been out, but everybody else has. They've returned in dribs and drabs, but I think you're the last one.'

'Good. I need them to be here. See you later, Frank.'

She climbed the stairs to the Major Crimes Unit, glancing around as she went in. She dumped her bag on her desk and headed for Chris's office.

'We have a link,' she said.

'Between?' Chris wasn't following at all.

'Between Lauren Pascoe and Hannah Wrightson. Not a massive link, but a link nevertheless.'

'Hang on, let's go into the briefing room or you'll be telling everybody individually.'

She nodded, and they walked to the whiteboard together.

'Need some concentration, folks. Sally has some additional info that could be handy for us. Sally? Over to you.'

She immediately felt stupid. The intention had been she would tell Chris, and he would then run a briefing, passing it on to the others. And she hated it when she blushed.

She took a deep breath. 'I've been out with Janey Pascoe today, as you know, and I took her for a Costa after she'd confirmed it was Lauren. She said she wanted a large latte and to talk about Lauren. So we did. As you know, Lauren worked for a vet, a chap called Stewart Phillips.' Sally cast a quick glance over her notes. 'The shop is called Paws and Claws. She had worked there for quite some time when she disappeared, and it had always been what she wanted to do, to work with animals. She couldn't get taken on by any local vets, so to get a wage coming in she took a job with an accountants. Her second love, after dogs and cats, was figures. She applied to Eke, Griffiths and was offered a job as a trainee receptionist, starting with doing general secretarial duties. She only lasted half a day, because during that first day she got an offer from Paws and Claws. She spoke to one of the partners at Eke, Griffiths, told them she was leaving with immediate effect and she didn't want any wages for the half day she had been there. Hannah Wrightson then got the receptionist/general dogsbody position, and has been there ever since.'

She paused for another quick glance at the copious amount of notes she had made. 'Apologies for this,' she said, 'but I didn't want to run the risk of forgetting anything. This hasn't cropped up before, it's only the Hannah Wrightson abduction that has made it mega important. So, we have Lauren happily settled in at Paws and Claws, doing exactly what she wanted to do, and she seemingly never gave a backward glance to Eke, Griffiths and Co. Janey explained she had a long talk with Lauren when the vet's offer came up, because deep down, she thought the accountancy job might be better financially for her daughter, but Lauren was adamant that come Monday morning she would be heading for her new job at the vets.'

Chris glanced around at their faces as they listened to their colleague delivering the new information.

'So we definitely have a connection between the two women,' Andy Norman said slowly, his mind obviously churning through everything he had just heard. 'This is excellent news, but it doesn't seem they knew each other, if Hannah only took the job vacated by Lauren. We need to talk to Eke, Griffiths again now, in view of this information.'

'And we also have to consider the fact that they haven't withheld this information from us, it was a long time ago, she just wanted to leave and take the job she had always wanted.'

It was Chris's turn to join in. 'Think about this, and factor it into what we now know. Everybody at that accountancy firm went out searching for Lauren. Ray Eke told me that, but he didn't say it was because they knew her. He said she was friends with one of their other girls in the office. We need to know stuff before we start locking people up in a cell just on the off chance they took Lauren. We need to know if Ray Eke and Mark Griffiths actually remember Lauren worked for them for half a day because it's quite possible they didn't. We need to know who gave her the job, if it was suggested she went to work there by the friend who also worked for them – we need to know it all before we start breathing heavily on them.'

'You want to bring them in, boss?' Bryn spoke slowly, as if deep in thought.

'You don't think I should?'

Bryn shook his head. 'Not till we have a plan. This is a link, yes, but it's a very tenuous one. It could simply be coincidence, because both these women actually lived locally, and it's always good to work near to where you live. Doesn't cost anything to get to work, for a start. And it's always good if you finish at five, and you're home for five past five.'

'My thoughts exactly,' Chris said. 'In view of what the killer did to Lauren, we have to be mindful that he could be doing the same to Hannah, but just because there is that little link doesn't mean it's a dead cert he's taken Hannah.' He held up a hand to stop the arguments. 'I know it's a big possibility, but it's not a fact. I might just pop over to Ray Eke's home tonight, just to check he's doing okay after his first couple of days back at work. And I might just let it slip that we are aware that Lauren worked for his company. Let's see his reaction to that bit of news, and we'll take it from there.'

## 14

Chris felt as if he was doing something wrong. This wasn't normal for him; he played everything by the book, and yet here he was walking down a front garden path for an informal sort of chat with a man who was a potential suspect.

Although he didn't really think Ray was.

And he hoped he was right in those thoughts.

He raised a finger to press the doorbell and the door opened. 'He's in the back garden,' Ziggy said. 'You want a beer? Or a cuppa?'

'A cup of tea would be very welcome,' he replied, smiling at her. 'A beer would also be welcome, but I'm driving.'

'Then tea it is. Go through to him, he's at the garden table. Ignore all the papers, he's working on a new tune and it's kind of taking over, I think.'

Chris stepped down into the garden and he saw Ray lift his head. A wave of the hand followed, then Ray stood up. 'Welcome, DI Chandler. Is Mum getting you a drink?'

'She is. I thought I'd pop round and have a little chat. A piece of information has come to light, and I'm hoping you can fill me in a little more on it.'

'Happy to, if I can. Let me clear some of this stuff away before it starts blowing around the garden.' Ray began to tidy up the sheets of manuscript paper, and Chris remained quiet.

Ziggy brought them a tea each, and disappeared back into the house, leaving the two men to enjoy the late-evening sun, and the peace of utter quiet.

'Next-door neighbours are on holiday,' Ray said. 'That's why it's quiet. They've got twins, eleven-year-olds, both mad footballers, so you can imagine what it's like most evenings in the garden.'

Chris grinned. 'And I'm here disturbing you. Sorry.'

Ray popped the sheets into a plastic folder, and picked up his cup. 'You're not disturbing me. I lead quite a strange life, every day is basically the same. Don't get me wrong, it's through choice. I don't ever want to get back to the state I was in when everything imploded, but sometimes I need a bit of change in that life. Currently, you're it. So what can I do to help?'

'It's something that we've only just been made aware of, but it seems Lauren Pascoe worked for you for a very short time.'

'What? I think you may be wrong there. My connection, if that's what you want to call it, to Lauren is through one of our ex-employees. They were close friends, and when Lauren went missing her friend, and I honestly can't remember her name but I'm sure it will be in the files, asked if she could produce some flyers on our photocopier. She was really upset, and so we said no problem, and it grew from there. The entire company went out several times searching for her. It was a massive search, coordinated by the police. But I'm pretty sure she never worked for us. When was this?'

'September 2021. She was only there for half a day and never on your books because she started with you then was almost immediately offered the job she really wanted, at the vets where she was working when she disappeared.'

Ray frowned. He was clearly deep in thought. 'Hang on,' he said. 'I'll get my 2021 journal. I started keeping a journal when we went into lockdown, and I quite enjoyed it, so apart from a period of about three months when I was so out of it, I've continued that. I'll be back in a minute.'

Chris sipped at his tea, totally enjoying the evening sun, and the fragrance wafting over from the rose garden to his right. Perfectly positioned, he thought.

Ray returned carrying a blue book. 'I'll see what it says in here. I'm sure I would have mentioned something so out of the ordinary as a one-day employee. I know my memory is a bit suspect, which is one reason I now write every day without fail in my journal, but this one was my first. So, September.'

He opened the book and flicked through until he found the ninth month. 'Aaah, that might explain why I knew nothing about it. I went to Crete on 28 August, and returned 19 September. I deliberately had no contact with work during this period, so there's absolutely nothing about anything other than sunshine and walking and eating and the odd glass or two of wine in my occasionally wobbly handwriting. Quite apart from that, Mark had taken on the role of hiring and firing, although I don't think we ever fired anybody. He was exceptionally good at recognising skills in people. Much better than me. So he would have set Lauren on, and if she left within a day, probably I wouldn't have ever known about it. I'd made it very clear to him I wanted to know nothing about the business unless it burnt down while I was on holiday. We were in the process of buying me out of the business and I actually rarely went to the office. I should imagine a day-long employment history didn't merit me hearing about it, ever. I bet he barely remembers it, but I would suggest you try asking him.'

Chris nodded. 'I will. That explains why you didn't mention it when you clearly recognised Lauren on the day you found her, but if you didn't actually know you'd given her very brief employment...'

'I promise you, this is the first time I've heard about it. I actually feel even more sad about the whole situation now, knowing this. I was with Mark this weekend, but we have a sort of pact that he doesn't talk about the business, because he would love me to return, and the pressure would be too much for me. The thought of that puts me into a... I want to say a depression, but it's not really. It's almost as if I want to keep a firm line between what I had before and simply walking the streets keeping them clean and tidy.'

Chris smiled. 'You do what suits you best. Thank you for this information. I'll pop in to the office tomorrow and have a chat with Mark. Put the issue to bed, so to speak. Thank your mum for the tea, I won't disturb her evening any longer.'

'She's probably gone across the road. She's teaching one of our neighbours to crochet. Patience of a saint, she has. Apparently Janet, the neighbour, has been trying to follow instructions on YouTube, and Mum said she could teach her, so they spend a couple of hours a night crocheting bedspreads.' He shook his head in amazement at what two elderly women got up to in their spare time.

It caused Chris to erupt in a guffaw of laughter. 'Whereas you, Ray, play the piano, compose wonderful tunes, play the violin...'

'Okay, okay,' Ray answered with a grin. 'I get you. You want me to prewarn Mark you're popping in to see him tomorrow?'

Chris thought about it for a few seconds then shook his head. 'No, don't say anything. If I miss him, I'll pop back when I know he will be in. I like to see initial reactions, and if he knows I'm coming, I won't get that. I'll see myself out, Ray. Thanks for your time.'

He let himself out of the front door, closing it carefully behind him. Damn it, he liked the man. He didn't like the fact that Lauren, working at his company, put him into a different place to the one where he had been the man who had found her body. It now put him firmly into the suspect category, but Mark Griffiths was much more firmly entrenched. It seemed he had been the one to have offered Lauren a job at Eke, Griffiths three years earlier. And it had never been mentioned...

\* \* \*

Chris called to pick up fish and chips before heading home. He too, just like the man he had so recently visited, moved into the garden to eat, this time enjoying the added attraction of a bottle of beer.

His mind was less on Lauren, more on Hannah. Two females both employed by Eke, Griffiths, both taken. There had to be a connection. He speared a chip and popped it into his mouth.

Hannah Wrightson. Had she ever known Lauren Pascoe? Was that the link they were looking for? Okay, they had no proof at all that the same person had taken Hannah, but sometimes you had to follow a gut feeling. And his gut feeling was screaming at him that when they caught him or her, they would be charging the perpetrator with two counts of kidnap. He hoped with all his heart it wouldn't be two counts of murder as well.

He finished his meal, tidied everything away and moved back inside. A wave of stress washed over him; they basically still had nothing. The white Transit hadn't been traced, there had been no reported sightings of Hannah despite considerable social media posts on Facebook and X, and they seemed to be waiting for something to break, even accidentally.

He thought back to the time he had just spent with Ray Eke, and the way he had produced a journal in which he had annotated everything, starting his first one as the whole country had gone into lockdown. He had been able to confirm a trip to Crete in his 2021 journal, proving he was out of the country when Lauren disappeared.

Although it hadn't been mentioned at any point, he briefly wondered if the stress and problems unique to Coronavirus times had contributed to Ray Eke's mental breakdown. Had he been unable to cope with being confined to home, unable to access his business, with clients he could only communicate with by telephone and Zoom? The personal touch was gone.

Did Chris believe that the litter-picker hadn't known that Lauren Pascoe had worked for them, albeit for only a half a day? Yes, he did. She had told the company that she was leaving and didn't want remuneration, so she wouldn't have been added to any payroll; and it had all happened while he was on his great Covid escape to Crete.

It seemed that he didn't hear her name for a further year. She moved to the job of her dreams, a trainee veterinary nurse at Paws and Claws, where she disappeared from in June 2021. And then came his breakdown, his slow recovery, his litter-picking job, then his first sight of the woman he had only ever seen on a flyer.

Chris let his thoughts simply wander around his brain, trying at times to put himself in Ray's shoes, wondering how he would have coped if he was actually locked into Ray's life.

He couldn't, of course, wipe Ray from the suspect list, not without absolute confirmation, but Chris was back to gut instinct on that late Tuesday evening. If a man had been the sole cause of the amount of damage done to Lauren Pascoe's body, then that man wasn't the gentle Ray Eke. He had seen the tenderness in the way he touched piano keys, the fluidity of the handwriting in his journal – this was a man who didn't give house room to violence, and was the reason Mark Griffiths didn't hesitate to send for an ambulance when Ray had smashed up his computer and his office. Because his best friend had known that sort of violence wasn't a part of Ray Eke's make-up.

No, he and his team should put Ray on some back burner and focus on tracking down the real killer of Lauren. And deep down he knew, without proof, that they would find Hannah Wrightson there. The question would be, would she be dead or alive, or so severely damaged she could wish she was dead.

Chris switched off the television, completely unaware of the programme that was broadcasting, threw the remote control onto the sofa and stomped angrily to bed. They needed to find Hannah and find her quickly.

## 15

And still the sun continued to shine. Ray started work early, keen to finish before the sun's heat became unbearable, but after reflecting on the previous evening's visit by Chris Chandler, he found himself starting his day's work at the spot where he found Lauren. It felt as if the image was burnt into his retinas, and he sighed deeply. This wasn't good and it had to stop.

The grass was now almost as it had been before the body had unceremoniously been dumped, not caring about her any longer. You couldn't do anything to hurt a dead body and enjoy their pain.

Once DI Chandler had left, he had spent the rest of his evening thinking about Lauren Pascoe. He was thankful he had been able to refer back to his journal to prove he hadn't known her at all, neither socially nor at work.

And now he knew, without hearing the words said out loud, that they were linking Hannah's disappearance with Lauren's abduction.

He stood silently for a few moments, then turned and crossed over Donetsk Way. His route today would take him down Ochre

Dike Lane, up through the bus terminus at Crystal Peaks, and back onto Drakehouse Crescent. Then he would decide which way to turn next depending on how hot he was. He could, of course, call into Crystal Peaks, pick up a roast pork sandwich and a bottle of ice-cold water for his lunch, and sit on a bench in Peaks enjoying the air conditioning for half an hour…

\* \* \*

Chris Chandler's Wednesday started with an early-morning chat with his children, who were about to leave for the airport to fly to Spain. It seemed their mum had suddenly decided they needed a holiday, picked up a last-minute booking for the three of them, and so his visit with them would have to be postponed. He had tried desperately to sound upbeat in front of the kids, but secretly he wanted to verbally rip his ex-wife to shreds.

They were obviously excited to be going, and that cheered him up a little, so he left them with a definite date to visit him before they had to return to school. It was a bad start to his day, and he hoped it could only get better.

He made a coffee before tackling anything once he reached his office. His plan was admin work, then head off up to Gleadless to see what Mark Griffiths had to say about their brief employment of Lauren Pascoe. He hoped it was going to be a mere tying up of loose ends, but it was a *definite* loose end.

He checked his emails, saw the final post-mortem report from Kevin Hanson had arrived, and forwarded it to his team for their input to add to his own thoughts. He then typed up a report of his visit to Ray Eke the previous evening. As he was typing, he realised with surprise that he had actually enjoyed the visit. It was clear that Ray lived for his music, and it was also clear that Ziggy, his mother, simply left him alone to get on with it. She had given up her own home to move in with him, to take care of her broken son, and there seemed to be no evidence she was planning to return home in the near future. Maybe Ray wasn't as far into his recovery as he tried to project, and she knew he still needed her?

Chris shook his head. This case wasn't about Ray, or his crochet-loving parent. Ray was simply the person who had found the victim. Some other evil bastard was the killer, and he had absolutely no idea where to look next. He felt the entire team needed a brainstorming session, because he knew they would be carrying this case home with them at night, and he also knew that the best ideas usually arrived around three in the morning, so after he had ruled out Mark Griffiths from the equation he would have a briefing meeting with everybody.

He finished his coffee, contemplated having a second one but decided against it, and headed out of the office after telling Sally where he was going.

'I'll be back by about half ten, so can we have a briefing meeting at eleven? Is everybody here?'

Sally nodded. 'They're all going through old files from when Lauren first disappeared, and I'm going through every report collected by the lads on Monday and Tuesday when they were out interviewing everybody. I'll pass on the message. You need anybody with you this morning?'

'No, it's a straightforward chat, should be a ten-minute thing and I'll be on my way back here.' He handed her a twenty-pound note. 'Can you nip across to Asda while I'm gone and get us some nice buns for the briefing? It always works more efficiently with buns.'

'Certainly can. You read the PM report?'

'I have. We have to find Hannah Wrightson, and quickly. I dread to think what he's doing to her now.'

'So we've decided there's a connection?'

'My feeling is he didn't expect to kill Lauren. I think that poor woman was set for many more years of torture, but the glass bottle was a step too far for her battered body. But once Lauren was gone, he needed a replacement.'

'Why are we saying he? In the PM report, it definitely says no evidence anywhere of semen. No semen, boss. That scares me even more, because if this does carry the possibility that the killer is a woman, that really doesn't bear thinking about.'

'And this is exactly what I want to hear at the briefing. We're going to be brainstorming with buns. I'll head off now and see this chap at Gleadless while you're out shopping, but warn the others it's eleven sharp for tea, coffee and buns. And talk.'

\* \* \*

Chris drove to Gleadless with his driver and passenger windows down. The forecast for Thursday was for ten degrees cooler and he couldn't wait. There was a slight breeze, but it was minimal and did nothing to help. He navigated the confusion of traffic lights at Birley crossroads and headed over Birley Lane. A tram snaked its way across the field by the side of the road and he marvelled at the wonder of the transport system in Sheffield. He'd never lived anywhere with trams prior to moving to South Yorkshire, and he still hadn't been on one. He intended taking the kids to Hillsborough for a match using it, but that would have to wait for the new season.

By the time he reached the Griffiths Accountancy office he was thoroughly fed up with the heat and traffic lights. He slipped on his jacket which he'd retrieved from the floor behind the driver's seat, and gave it a tug in an effort at looking more like a senior police officer and less like a homeless person.

The receptionist – someone he hadn't seen before – smiled at him. 'Can I help you?'

'Yes, I hope so. DI Chris Chandler.' He showed his warrant card, and she waited. 'I'd like to speak with Mr Griffiths, please.'

'I'll see if he's free.'

Chris smiled kindly at her. 'He's free. Tell him I'm on my way through.' And he moved round the back of her desk and through the door leading to the offices.

Mark reached his door quick enough to open it as Chris arrived.

'DI Chandler. How can I help? I hope this is good news about Hannah.' He waved Chris through. 'Coffee?'

'I'd settle for a water if you have one.'

'Certainly do.' Mark walked across to the fridge in the corner of the room and reached inside to produce a bottle with a sports top.

'Perfect,' Chris said, and flipped the lid smoothly, taking a long and satisfying drink. 'I needed that.'

Mark grinned. 'Is that what you came for, a drink of water?'

They both sat at opposite sides of the desk, and Mark waited.

'No, I came to talk to you about Lauren Pascoe.'

Mark frowned. 'Lauren Pascoe? I thought... Hannah...'

'We believe the two disappearances could be linked, although we have no proof of that. Yet. We understand that Lauren was employed by you and Mr Eke for a short time.'

Mark frowned. 'When?' He was clearly baffled.

'I'll explain, maybe it will come back to you then. She started work here in June 2021, when people were starting to drift back to the office to go to work after lockdown. She started on the Monday then told you she was leaving at the end of the day because the job she really wanted, at a vet's, had been offered to her. She didn't want any pay because she was messing you about. Does that ring any bells?'

His face cleared. 'God! Was that Lauren Pascoe? I do remember now. She was a friend of one of our other girls, can't remember which one, and she had asked if we had an opening for her. I think she was suitably embarrassed when her mate walked away after only a day. I didn't connect the Lauren Pascoe we were out searching everywhere for with the girl who had worked here. She was never on our payroll or anywhere in our system. I'm so sorry, I would have said if I'd remembered. And of course, I set her on, not Ray, so he wouldn't have known about it probably. He left me to do the hiring and firing.' He paused for a moment. 'He was in the process of winding up here so rarely in the office. He actually had no idea at all that she had even been through the doors.'

Chris emptied the bottle of water and stood it on the desk. 'I'll leave you to dispose of that. Thank you for your help, I just needed to complete my report.'

He stood, and Mark did the same. They shook hands, and Chris left, removing his jacket as he got back into the car.

He sat for a while, windows closed and aircon trying very hard to work efficiently, before he gave in, switched it off and opened the windows. He stared across at the layby where the white van had been parked, feeling slightly angry that the only camera to have caught the shot wasn't positioned to capture the number plate, although he did suspect that the number plate wouldn't have helped anyway. You don't go out to kidnap a woman with genuine number plates on the vehicle.

He looked at Marjorie Bird's house and wondered if she was still cat-sitting, or if she was now back at home. He had no intentions of troubling her, but he had really enjoyed hearing what a feisty lady she was, and would have genuinely liked to have met her. When this was all over and the killer was safely ensconced in a cell somewhere, he would take her some flowers and have a little chat with her about cats and suchlike. And top-of-the-range iPhones causing much jealousy amongst his team members.

He drove back to Moss Way, having to wait at red traffic lights for yet another tram to thunder down the field and onto White Lane where it mingled with everyday traffic. Wonderful, clean form of travel, he mused.

The lights eventually changed and he took his time by driving a different way home, going over Thornbridge. It was one way of learning his way around this newly adopted city of his, and he had a lot to learn.

He parked up at Moss Way and entered the reception where he caught Frank with a mouthful of doughnut.

'Sorry, boss,' he spluttered. 'Thanks for the doughnut. Sally said you'd bought them.'

'That's fine, Frank. You'll be at the briefing then?'

Frank spluttered even more. 'Not likely. That poor lass, I can't sit and listen to all the details about it. No, I'll be on guard for you down here.'

# 16

Once again Chris settled for a bottle of water. He added two paracetamol tablets to his throat in an effort to conquer the imminent headache, and sat down at the head of the large round table. Everybody was present, there were several boxes of buns, and he tapped on the table to call everybody to order.

There was instant silence and he burst out laughing. 'I'm not that scary a boss, am I?'

'We don't know yet,' Bryn said. 'But I'm guessing not.'

'Thanks for the vote of confidence, Bryn. Now let's get down to some work. The aim of this briefing is a little odd. I'm not here to pass information on that you don't yet have, I think we need to have a brainstorming session where hopefully somebody will come up with a bright idea. Personally, I'm feeling more and more convinced that Hannah Wrightson has been taken to replace Lauren Pascoe, which means we need to find her fast.'

'Has anything come in on the white van?' Maria was the first to speak.

'No. We need to get the picture of the van out to every beat bobby and on every television screen before the end of today.

Maria, can you book us a two-minute slot on this evening's local news programmes, *Calendar* and *Look North*, please?'

'Certainly can. A picture of Hannah and a picture of the van?'

'Yes, and add where the picture was taken. Locals hearing it was parked outside Sainsbury's at Gleadless may just give an extra bit of consideration to what we're asking. We need to stress we believe the number plate was false, so it's just the van everyone needs to be looking out for.'

'Unfortunately, when the killer sees this on *Calendar*, that van is going to be locked in a garage somewhere until it can get a respray.' Andy Norman frowned as he spoke, then reached across for a Cherry Bakewell. 'Love these,' he said.

'You're probably right, Andy,' Chris concurred, 'but we need to get everybody looking for it. We may even need to say we're linking the two abductions, put every woman on their guard. He may have got a taste for killing them now, rather than just torturing them.'

'There's no semen,' Sally declared, loudly. 'There's no fucking semen!'

Chris stood, slowly. 'My apologies to you all. I keep saying he, because torture is typically a man's thing. But Sally is absolutely right, there is no semen, fucking or otherwise. This killer could, of course, very easily be a woman. Can we take it that if I say he I actually mean he or she, because life will get difficult if I have to be politically correct all the time.'

'Sorry, boss,' Sally said.

'No problem, Sally. You are quite right to bring it up, that's exactly what I mean by brainstorming.'

'And can I just say I've known Sally for a number of years,' Bryn said, 'and I've never heard her swear with anything stronger than bloody before. I'm impressed.'

Sally tried not to laugh, but couldn't hold it. It spread around the table, easing the tension and eventually opening up the next point of discussion, getting a list of owners of white Transits within a ten-mile radius of Moss Way police station.

'Leave that one with me, boss,' Maria said, adding that note to the ones she had already scribbled in her book. 'I've got a good contact at DVLA. He'll get it to us as fast as he can.'

'There's something that's occurred to me only this morning, and forgive me if I'm wrong because I really know nothing about them, but do your trams have CCTV on board?' Chris glanced around the table, inviting anybody to respond.

'They do,' Tia said. 'It's not our usual first thought for CCTV because the trams run partially on roads and partially through fields and off roads. But in this case, of course, we have the exact time the van was parked in that layby, the trams go within a couple of feet of anybody parked in that spot, and it would be on CCTV if a tram went past while it was there.'

'It didn't,' Maria said. 'There's never a tram when you need one, is there? It would have shown on the CCTV we got from Marjorie, because the van was only there for about ninety seconds, long enough to get Hannah into it and drive away immediately. No tram went past.'

'How the hell did the driver know she was inside Sainsbury's? Could they have been parked in that car park where the church is? Or at the top of Seagrave Crescent? It would have been simple to watch her walk into the shop, wait a couple of minutes and then pull across to the layby. She would have walked to the kerb of the entrance to the pub car park before crossing the main road, and that's exactly where our killer parked. Surely Hannah going for a bottle of milk was a random timing. I shouldn't imagine for one minute that she went for milk at exactly the same time, on exactly the same day, all the time. It doesn't make sense. He or she had to have been parked up on the off chance she would come out. Or would any of the staff at Griffiths have done? Was Hannah the unlucky one?' Chris looked around the table. 'Talk to me, somebody. Tell me I'm seeing problems when there aren't any.'

Nobody spoke. They had followed his mini speech in silence, each of them understanding as little as their boss was understanding the situation. None of it made sense, because it all boiled down to a random trip to a shop to a get a bottle of milk.

Tia opened her mouth as if to speak, then closed it, then opened it again.

'Tia?' Chris waited for his DS to sort out her words, her thoughts.

'What if...' She hesitated, still not sure if she was making a complete fool of herself. 'What if she had arranged to see someone? Strictly speaking, she could have come out of Sainsbury's and crossed the road at that point. There's no zebra crossing or anything to help get across the road, but she didn't. She walked a few yards further down to cross once she'd moved by the van, or was she actually walking to the van? Did she know him or her? Was it a pre-arranged meeting? Did she text somebody to say she would be going out to get some milk, and she could stretch it to quarter of an hour if they fancied a brief interlude in the van? It bothers me that if she had been forced into that van, she would have fought back. It's quite a populous area, somebody would probably have gone to help, but nobody has come forward to say they noticed anything.'

Chris smiled. 'I knew some genius would come up with something logical. I stupidly assumed Hannah was taken against her will, and I think it's quite possible she was, but I don't think she saw that at the time. Now Tia has shown me the way, I'm leaning towards thinking it was a pre-arranged meeting. Has she been groomed? Was the killer getting bored with Lauren and looking for a replacement? This abduction of Hannah happened very soon after the body of Lauren was ditched on Donetsk Way. Further thoughts anybody?'

'Yes,' Bryn said. 'Now we need to know if Hannah liked men, or if she liked women. Do we know? This could actually solve the he/she conundrum.'

There was a general consensus around the table that nobody knew, but questions could be asked.

'I'll find out,' Maria said. 'I'll try and glean information from Facebook, but if that's not forthcoming, I'll simply ask her mum. They seem really close, and I'm sure she would know her daughter's sexual leanings. I'll start to look as soon as we're done here.'

'Thanks, Maria,' Chris said. 'Can I have a doughnut now?'

'I'll make fresh coffee and tea while we're all thinking everything through,' Sally said. 'For what it's worth, I think this briefing has been brilliant. It's opened up our minds, and that's partly because we've all accepted the two cases are definitely linked. Let's hope this killer isn't getting bored with Hannah yet.'

Sally moved to the kitchenette and switched on the kettle. She was getting to like the boss more and more; he was open to discussion, and definitely open to new and controversial ideas. She refilled the coffee pot, and rinsed all the cups out before reloading the tray and carrying it through to the briefing room.

'I hope you lot haven't eaten all the coconut macaroons,' she said, carefully placing the heavy tray on the table.

'We've saved you the last one,' Tia said. 'But don't expect any doughnuts to be left.'

Sally poured out the fresh drinks, then grabbed the macaroon before it disappeared. Not as good as the ones her mum made, but passable. More than passable, quite delicious.

There was some small talk for a few minutes, and Chris told them a little more about Ray Eke.

'I really like him,' he said. 'There's something special about somebody who can expertly play the piano, write his own music and also play other instruments. It makes him sort of... gentle. That's the right word. If you get the chance, I advise you to talk to him. Very interesting man. His mum lives with him. He was telling me she locked up her own home and moved into his place in order to look after him after his breakdown. They get on really well together, she gives him space from what I'm seeing. She made us a drink when I turned up unannounced last night, then left us together. He explained she was teaching a neighbour across the road how to crochet, and they spent many a night making blankets. Two very nice people, Ziggy Duly and Ray Eke, who I don't suppose I would ever have met apart from the waves that Ray gives to all our squad cars. I'm pleased I have met him, it's such a shame it was because of a murder.'

'I don't know how Lauren lived as long as she did,' Maria said quietly. 'I've had a really close look at the post-mortem report and it's horrendous. I know the pathologist has to state cause of death, but as far as I can see she died slowly over many months. He kept cutting bits of her off, like fingers and toes. And both her nipples had gone.' Maria shivered. 'If it does turn out to be a man, I'd like to volunteer to cut off his dick.'

There was a moment of silence.

'Well,' Bryn said, trying desperately to keep a straight face, 'it's been an education, this meeting. First of all, I heard Sally swear, and now we've got quiet little Maria talking about cutting off a dick. I tell you, boss, this has to be your influence. It's a slippery slope...'

His laughter boomed around the room, and everyone followed suit.

Chris held up a hand. 'If it is my influence, I apologise. Okay, who's been taking notes and who's writing up the report of this meeting?'

Sally held up a hand. 'I'll do it,' she said, holding back on any further laughter. 'I'll email it to all inboxes when it's done because I think we really need to look at what's been discussed today – the facts, the suppositions, everything. If we can all read it by tomorrow, we could maybe meet up without cakes and thrash the more proven theories out, and discuss the unproven but possible ones.'

'Then let's close for today. My report on the meeting with Ray Eke last night and Mark Griffiths this morning will both be on by the time I go home, so I'd like you to read through those as well. And that's it, we're done for now, but thank you. A most productive brainstorm.'

# 17

Hannah dragged herself painfully to the toilet. With her ankles bound tightly with plastic ties, it was a struggle to move, but the consequences of not reaching the toilet in time just didn't bear thinking about.

She was concerned about her left breast. It hurt constantly, and where the nipple had been removed it was leaking pus. She had nothing to clean it with other than cold water, and, just like when she wanted a drink of water, it all had to happen in the small toilet room because if she tried to carry the cup with water in it back to her bed area, the water was non-existent in the cup after the hazardous journey on her bum across the room.

Her finger stump was raw but looked reasonably clean. She had braved the risk of passing out and allowed water to run on it directly from the tap; she hoped she had done enough to save Whitecoat from having to amputate the entire hand.

There had been no more food and she had no idea when her tormentor would return. Time seemed irrelevant, night and day blended into one with the absence of any sort of window. She slept when she could, and slowly the pain in her shoulders was fading.

The last time she had woken she felt a presence, and she chose to keep her eyes closed, pretending to be still asleep, Eventually the footsteps crossed the room, and she heard the key turn, locking her in on her own once more. Still she waited for some time before opening her eyes.

She longed to feel her mother close by. They never went more than a few hours without either chatting or texting, and this prolonged absence was almost unbelievable. She thought things might feel better if she could understand why she had been taken. She'd only nipped out for a bottle of milk, and now look where she was.

She sat up and carefully massaged her shoulders. They felt so much better, but the stiffness hadn't disappeared altogether. She was careful not to catch the bloodied stump where her pinkie finger used to be. Her legs were rapidly becoming another problem to worry her. The plastic ties had cut into her, and the flesh was swelling around the ties. She could see blood seeping from around the wounds, and hoped Whitecoat had meant it when promising to remove them soon.

She glanced across at the door, unsure if she had heard something on the other side of it. Fear enveloped her, and she waited.

The door was plain, no window, but a tiny spyhole had been fitted into it. Her captor could be watching her right now, and she shivered. She could also do with something, anything, to give her a bit of warmth. She had been completely naked since her arrival, and while that had been embarrassing at first, it no longer affected her in that way, but she was permanently cold. She suspected she was somewhere in a cellar, certainly underground, because it had a dampness in the air.

The tiny toilet built into one corner of the equally tiny room had no window, just one very small sink and the toilet itself. It did have a door, but no lock on it. She could see no way of escaping her captor, and from the pains in her stomach she was getting concerned that her period was about to start. She needed to see Whitecoat at some point to request tampons. She rubbed at her stomach, hoping it would make the aches and pains disappear. She had enough pain to deal with without one of nature's usual pains making everything worse.

She gently slid back down onto the mattress and curled herself into a foetal position, hugging her stomach.

Damn Whitecoat, where the bloody hell was he/she when you needed them?

\* \* \*

Hannah slept for two hours, and woke to the sound of the slight squeak she had come to recognise as the door opening. She felt scared, inexplicably scared. She hadn't done anything wrong as far as she was aware...

Whitecoat didn't speak, simply left a wrapped sandwich, a bottle of water, a pack of Tampax and two painkillers.

'Thank you,' Hannah called out as the door closed and she heard the key turn in the lock.

She dragged herself to the toilet with a feeling of dread. The pain in her genital area had lessened but she was still very sore and the thought of trying to insert a tampon with her legs tightly bound together was horrifying.

She checked and discovered she hadn't actually started bleeding so left the packet balanced on the back of the sink, took the painkillers to help with the stomach pain, then crawled back to her bed.

She was just dropping off to sleep once more when she heard

the creak of the door. She was instantly awake and she stared at the white-clothed figure, hoping the fear didn't show on her face. Then she saw the knife in the gloved hand.

Her first inclination was to scream and she knew she would fight back now she had free hands, but the consequences of that would be dire. Whitecoat had the upper hand, both physically and mentally. She remained immobile, her eyes never leaving the knife.

The gloved hand touched her leg and she couldn't hold in the sob. No words were spoken, but she could feel the blade of the knife pressing against her skin. The pain of the leg sores increased and then suddenly she could move her legs independently. Whitecoat left the room and Hannah heard the key turn in the lock.

The pain that came with moving her legs was almost welcome. She couldn't help the cry that left her lips and she struggled into a sitting position while she attempted to assess what damage had been done.

It was bad. Blood was leaking from open wounds and her legs looked hugely swollen. She had no idea what to do, but she didn't reckon she could walk. Her legs were too badly damaged at the moment to support her, and trying to clean the wounds was unthinkable.

She slowly and carefully stretched herself out on the bed, and closed her eyes. It was easier to move, but pain engulfed her when she did. Sleep was out of the question, so she simply kept her eyes open and stared at the ceiling. She was getting used to the dim light being on all the time, and allowed her body clock to dictate when she should sleep and when it was time to wake up. Now she doubted she could have naps, because her legs would move and that wouldn't be good at all.

She couldn't believe how awful her life currently was proving to be. She had to assume people would be looking for her, just not very successfully because she was still imprisoned, and her captor was still tormenting her.

How much longer could she accept these limitations without attempting to tackle Whitecoat? And she knew that when she reached the point of making the decision that life was unbearable and she would be better off dead, that was when she would begin to fight back. And she would probably die. If she didn't die, further bits of her would be removed, and Hannah simply couldn't get her head around what to do next.

She certainly needed legs that worked properly, just in case the opportunity presented itself to run, to at least attempt an escape from wherever she was being held.

She forced herself to sit upright, then she ate the sandwich. The bottle of water meant she didn't have to struggle over to the toilet room to get a drink, and she realised she now had a second item that would hold water, which was a huge plus as far as she was concerned.

Exhaustion eventually took over and she closed her eyes. Sleep still didn't come easily, but she knew it would eventually. She heard the click of the door and she knew Whitecoat had entered the room. She kept her eyes closed.

Hands ran down her body, and she tried not to flinch. Her legs were pulled apart and it took all her strength to make no sound.

Something was placed by her mattress, but still she didn't show any signs of waking.

Then she heard the whisper.

'Lauren, cream for your legs.'

* * *

She forced her body to remain inactive for some considerable time just in case she was being watched through the spyhole. She actually counted to sixty, thirty times. Her Fitbit might have disappeared from her wrist, but she knew how to calculate half an hour. She couldn't say the same about her brain being inactive. Lauren. Whitecoat had called her Lauren. Lauren Pascoe had been kidnapped and held captive for three years and had only just turned up. Dead.

Had Whitecoat needed an urgent replacement? If her thoughts were accurate, she knew she was in deep trouble. If there had been a way of escaping, Lauren Pascoe would have taken it. Had she also been held in this tiny room? Was this her bed? And had Whitecoat called her Lauren to try to recreate the woman who had died? Was Lauren to be her name from here on in? Or was it just a slip of the tongue?

Hannah knew nothing about any injuries Lauren may have had, but she was starting to realise Whitecoat enjoyed the torture, enjoyed the pain being inflicted. Hannah was annoyed that she couldn't tell if her abductor was a man or woman, but she truly hoped it was a man behind the balaclava. It meant he would have balls that could be kicked, that would drop him to the floor.

If Whitecoat was a woman… she had no idea how to handle that situation. Scratch her eyes out? Rip her hair from her scalp?

It was while Hannah was letting her thoughts run riot that she realised Whitecoat had never actually called her by her name. If the name Lauren was used again, should she just pretend she hadn't heard it? That she was in so much pain her brain wasn't working properly? She didn't want to admit to knowing of Lauren and risk any further amputations.

There had been a few steps forward; she had worked out her situation by Whitecoat using Lauren's name, and there had been a glimmer of kindness with the packet of tampons and the two painkiller tablets. The sandwich and bottle of water had been a welcome surprise, and despite the absolute terror she had felt when she saw the knife, it had proved to be a tool for cutting off the plastic ties slowly killing her legs.

Now she knew her priority. Her legs had to heal, and heal fast. If Whitecoat proved to be a man, she would need strong, fast-moving legs and feet to target his balls, and a pottery mug to smash it over his head as many times as she could. The broken shards of the cup would be perfect for pushing into his eyes.

She sighed. Good plan, Hannah, she said to herself, but what if Whitecoat is a bloody woman?

**18**

The entire team continued to work that Thursday evening. Yes, they had returned to their individual homes, yes, they had said hello to partners and family, yes, they had eaten a meal, but no, they hadn't settled down for a quiet night watching television or reading, they had logged in to work and read any reports that had been uploaded.

Chris's reports on his visits to Ray Eke and Mark Griffiths were detailed and well written; Sally had written the report on their afternoon brainstorm of a meeting, and Maria had detailed the work she was doing to get photographs of the van out amongst the general public, but also out to beat bobbies over a wide area.

All of them read the reports, making notes on anything new that occurred to them, and nobody switched off. Deep into the night, their thoughts returned constantly to the plight of Hannah Wrightson, what she could be going through, and why.

Had she been taken for sex? For modern day slavery? Just because she was available at the right moment? The same questions rattled around the brains of every member of Chris's team, without any answers becoming apparent to any of them.

As a result, Friday morning saw the team meeting up by seven, looking equally haggard.

Chris had picked up Maria on his way into work, and they had called for seven lattes from Starbucks. He knew exactly what sort of a night they had all had – exactly the same as his own.

They went straight to the large table and sat quietly, drinking the more than welcome coffees.

'Thoughts?' Chris started their morning.

Nobody spoke.

'So we're all in the same place,' he said. 'I've been over and over everything we discussed yesterday and nothing new has occurred to me. We have to widen this. We have to go back to when Lauren was taken. I know she simply disappeared and nobody saw it happen, which is different to the abduction of Hannah, if we're right that she was taken in the Transit. But Lauren was working at the vet's place, and we've done nothing about that, really. We've concentrated more on Hannah's connection to Griffiths Accountancy and Ray Eke, but let's face it, Ray was just the poor sod that was unlucky enough to find Lauren.'

'He was senior partner at the accountants though,' Maria pointed out. 'He may not be there now, but he was there – and he did do a lot of volunteer searching when Lauren went missing. He is connected, even if we don't want him to be.'

'I know, but let's not forget he was out of circulation for a long period of time because of his breakdown, and this was during the period Lauren was missing. He definitely wouldn't have been able to get to her to take food while he was in rehab. I just don't see it, that he's involved. Mark Griffiths may need closer attention – he had a migraine and wasn't in the office on the day Hannah was taken. Find out if he has access to a Ford Transit.'

Maria nodded. 'And we have a list of Ford Transit owners in the area coming through from the DVLA later. My contact has promised it by lunchtime.'

Chris stared up at the ceiling for a moment, deep in thought. 'Has the vet got a Transit?'

It was Tia's turn to offer information. 'I went by their place last night on my way home and they do have a white van. I can't guarantee it's a Transit, but it does have "Paws and Claws emergency pet ambulance" written on it.'

'On both sides?'

'I saw it on one side, the side facing the main road, but it was also on the back doors. The back doors and the left-hand side of the body of our Ford Transit were visible on Marjorie's CCTV and they were plain. You want me to nip up and check?'

He shook his head. 'No, I was clutching at straws. Of course it will say it on both sides. But we haven't investigated Paws and Claws, and from what I can see trawling through the initial work done on Lauren's case, the employees at the vet's were never considered to be suspects. We should look more into them.'

'I'll do it, boss,' Bryn said. 'Can I use force and threats? I had a bad night.'

'It might be better if you simply used questions, Bryn, but if you don't get answers, try the force bit.'

Bryn gave a deep sigh. 'It's like we're no further forward than when we found Lauren's body. And heaven knows where Hannah has been taken to, but I'm betting it's where Lauren was held for three years. This three years bit was playing on my mind all night. It's almost three years since Eke had his breakdown, it's three years since Lauren was taken – was that a connection? Did Eke know something? I certainly don't think he took her because somebody was feeding her as well as cutting bits off her, for all of that three years, but it's a definite link. And his mother's been with him and looking after him for all of that time, so I'm pretty sure he wouldn't be able to just disappear to cut off a finger or a toe.'

'It seems when he came home he did nothing for the first six months, so you're right. Practically speaking he would have made a rubbish kidnapper because Lauren would have been dead a long time before we found her last week. And it would take a clever man to dump a body during the night then fake finding her the next morning on his routine litter-picking round. I imagine he knows lots of good places to dump bodies round here where they wouldn't be found for some time.' Chris shook his head. 'No, I don't see Ray Eke in this at all. I haven't written Mark Griffiths off, but it could be anybody if, as we half suspect, it was just a random snatch of a woman. We're a little bit in danger of losing sight of the main thing here – we have a definite murder to investigate, that of Lauren Pascoe, and if we can solve that we'll also solve the disappearance of Hannah Wrightson, if all our theories are correct. We must focus on Lauren, she has a mother in the deepest of despair and she wants answers. As we do.'

Everybody nodded, drained the last of their coffees, and looked to Chris for guidance.

'Are we done, boss?' Tia asked.

'For the moment, but if you come across even the slightest thing, I need to know about it. As we've shown over the last few days, we all link things in different ways, and that's what I call star quality in a team. It gives an overall bigger picture, and one person's thoughts can trigger a different direction in another, so keep talking, not just to me but in between each other. Now go find me a killer.'

\* \* \*

Bryn parked on a side road and walked round to Paws and Claws. The company van with the name on both sides was parked outside the front doors with its back doors wide open. A large German Shepherd was being carried out, sporting a heavily bandaged front leg. He waited until the patient had been carried around to the back door of the surgery, and then moved towards the pet ambulance.

There was nothing on the front of the vehicle to indicate it was anything other than a Ford Transit, but the side panels both showed Paws and Claws with the registered address of the practice and the telephone number. The back doors held the same information, with half of it on each door. He moved closer and realised the names hadn't been sign-painted, they were magnetic. Removable.

He glanced around to see if anyone was watching, and then peeled one back slightly. There was a distinct line. Underneath the sign it was white, the van itself was ready for a wash. These stickers hadn't been off this van in quite some considerable time, as far as he could see. They needed to look closer on Marjorie's CCTV, to see if there was any evidence that the van used to abduct Hannah Wrightson could have normally had magnetic stickers on it. It was a very clear demarcation line on this vehicle.

Stewart Phillips was in the waiting room when Bryn walked in. He was handing over some medication to a lady carrying a bright orange cat basket, and giving her the instructions as to its use. 'One tablet in the morning and one in the evening for three days, then one every morning until the course is finished. Any problems, you have our number.'

She thanked him, lifted up the carrier a bit higher and Bryn held the door open for her to exit. He turned and Phillips was just leaving to return to his work through the rear door.

'Mr Phillips,' Bryn called.

Phillips stopped. 'Can I help?'

Bryn showed his warrant card. 'Two minutes of your time would be appreciated.'

'Two minutes is about all I have. I am about to spay a cat.'

'It won't take long. I just want to talk about issues around Lauren Pascoe.'

Phillips held up a hand. 'Let me just tell my nurse to hold off on the anaesthesia.'

Bryn nodded, and Phillips disappeared for a moment. He returned and beckoned to Bryn. 'Let's go and talk in my office. The cat isn't going anywhere.'

It was a crowded room. Thank you cards adorned the wall, his desk was covered with paperwork, and a couple of coffee cups showed he rarely got a chance to finish an entire drink. He used a PC for his work, and it was currently showing a black screen.

'Please,' he said, 'sit down.' He lifted some files and indicated the now empty chair. Bryn thanked him and sat.

'So what can I help you with? Lauren was a valued member of our staff, destined for much better things than the level she was at when she disappeared.'

Bryn gave a brief nod to indicate he understood. 'As you know, we found Lauren Pascoe's body recently, and it is now a murder investigation. We're following up on several issues and reworking leads going back three years. I can't disclose anything more about what those leads are, but white vans are a factor. We are aware, of course, that there are thousands of white vans, and your practice has one.'

Phillips smiled. 'I'd be a bit daft to use our van for anything nefarious, it's got Paws and Claws all over it.'

'On magnetic pieces. Once they're removed it becomes any old white Ford Transit.'

'Of course it does. That hadn't occurred to me. I've not seen the van without our name on it for years, I have nothing to do with the vehicle other than driving it to see poorly animals, really. Once a month we pay a lad to clean the van inside and out. It's a thorough job because it all has to be disinfected, and sterilised. Takes him about four hours on a Saturday morning. He does all the inside, and it gleams when he's finished. Then he removes all those stickers, washes the outside and replaces them very carefully, particularly on the back doors so that they line up correctly.'

'When is it due for washing?'

Phillips leaned across and woke up his computer. He glanced down his reminders. 'This coming Saturday.'

'Is the ambulance scheduled to go out again today?'

'No, why? There's always the odd emergency, but I'm hoping our emergencies are over for today. We've just brought in a German Shepherd that needed transport. Its owner ran over it while reversing the car. Badly broken leg. They're stabilising it for surgery as we speak.'

'I'd just like our forensics people to check it out, to cross it off our list. We'll be quick, I promise you, but we do have to do this.'

Stewart Phillips stared at him. 'You have another missing woman, don't you? Is it connected to Lauren?'

'Possibly. We have no concrete proof yet.'

'Get your people here. The keys are kept behind our reception counter. I'll tell my staff the ambulance isn't available until tomorrow.'

# 19

Bryn spoke to Chris, who completely agreed with his actions, and Chris put in the request for an immediate forensics team to head up to the vet's.

Bryn wasn't convinced anything would be found – the van definitely had four weeks of grubbiness on its paintwork, which indicated the magnetic names hadn't been removed. But if this proved to be the elusive van they were seeking, the back had held Hannah Wrightson, and something of her would be in that back compartment. It could be accessed by both the sliding side doors and the back doors, but they knew the van on the CCTV hadn't opened its back doors, so therefore Hannah had entered through the sliding doors.

Phillips hadn't argued at all, recognising that having forensics go through the van would clear him, but there was blood in the back. Animals bled, as did humans. And plenty of animals had been inside the ambulance over the last month. He almost felt as if he should apologise in advance for wasting taxpayers' money. All that blood would have to be tested, and it would come back as cat's blood, dog's blood, rabbit's blood.

Because of the size of the van, only two members of the forensics team arrived. Bryn had a word with them, and explained why their actions were necessary. 'If you find anything suspicious, and by that, I mean stuff connected to humans and not animals, then impound the vehicle. But if it all seems animal-based, because let's not forget it is a pet ambulance, then get whatever samples you need to prove that, and hand the keys back into their reception. The ambulance is a necessary part of their work, and I don't want to keep it away from them any longer than is necessary.'

The first member of the team climbed into the back wearing full PPI gear, and announced, 'It stinks.'

Bryn laughed. 'I saw them carrying a rather large German Shepherd out of it as I arrived less than an hour ago, with a broken leg and lots of blood. Good luck, lads. Let me know when you've finished, will you?'

\* \* \*

Maria received the file of white Transit vans from the DVLA, and took a deep breath. The list was huge. She started by writing down the names of anyone who had already come under their radar for any reason, and checked those names against the record. Neither Ray Eke, nor Mark Griffiths, had white Transits. Stewart Phillips was shown to have one, but she felt disappointed to realise that she didn't recognise any other names on the list. At times it felt as if everywhere they looked proved to be a dead end.

And then she remembered Sally's words, speaking them out loud with a giggle. 'No fucking semen!'

She clicked on the file showing everyone who had been interviewed as part of the investigation, whether it was the Lauren Pascoe or the Hannah Wrightson case, and checked every single name against her list. This included all the women who worked at the accountancy, the women who had been interviewed from the vets as part of the initial steps taken in the Lauren case, and even Marjorie Bird. Maria smiled to herself. Marjorie Bird was more likely to drive a jet-propelled rocket.

But there was nothing. Just who the hell had bought all these white vans? It seemed that, apart from Paws and Claws, nobody attached to this case had one. And Bryn was busy proving the pet ambulance wasn't the van they were looking for.

*** 

Chris stopped by Frank Carter's reception window to tell him he was going out for an hour.

'A lady friend?' Frank asked.

'Ha-bloody-ha,' Chris responded. 'When do we have time for lady friends?'

'I'm married,' Frank said.

'Happily?'

'Just about.'

'I meant your wife.'

'Ah, that's another story. I'll ask her tonight, unless she's going out.'

'Exactly. Even when we're married, we're not really. But no, I'm not going out to see a lady friend, as you so politely put it, I'm going out for some thinking time in the sunshine. There's a problem niggling away at me, so I'm going to do what I'm paid to do, and investigate.'

Frank looked at him. 'You're wondering how they got young Lauren to that spot to dump her without being seen.'

'You a mind reader as well as being Chief Constable then?'

'I am, but only because I've been wondering the same thing. Let me get young Danny down here to cover for me and I'll have a walk across the road with you. Four eyes and two heads, sort of thing.'

Danny Moore arrived within a minute, and grinned at Frank, not realising Chris had sat down to wait for his arrival. 'You off to the pub, Frank?'

'Oh, aye, Danny. Bit thirsty, I am, so thought you could handle the thugs and suchlike for an hour.'

Danny headed into the tiny office, and then he saw Chris stand. His face couldn't have been any redder, and he said nothing further, simply watched as they walked out the door together, mimicking having a pint of beer.

The two men headed across the busy road, Frank's police uniform not being at all helpful in slowing drivers down to the 30 mph speed limit. They reached the other side with a huge sense of relief.

Skirting the corner, they reached Lauren's final resting place within a minute, and simply stood and looked. Remembering it, in Chris's case, as it had been on that day. She had been fully clothed so they had no idea of the horrors that awaited the pathologist when he came to do the post-mortem. Chris had asked if there was anything at that moment in time to suggest cause of death, and Kevin Hanson had merely shrugged. 'Not yet, I would only be guessing,' had been his words.

Frank hadn't been present, he had been busy directing people back at the station. There were guidelines to follow with sudden unexplained deaths, and this one had been definitely unexplained.

Chris took out his phone and opened his photos. He showed it to Frank, who flinched. 'This was with the tent over her, I wanted a record of the scene, so I took this one inside the tent, one from outside the tent, and several from the surrounding vegetation. Last night, or maybe this morning around two o'clock,

I looked at them again. It was easy for Ray to see her because he was actually on that stretch of grass, but anybody just walking by probably wouldn't have seen her. Then there's that huge bank of tall shrubs, trees, bushes, all sorts of greenery to hide the houses over the back and to prevent them seeing and hearing the traffic and the trams. It's a really built-up wooded area, not particularly trees, but plenty of brush. I don't believe for a minute that someone stopped on Donetsk Way, not this close to the police station anyway, and manhandled a dead body out of their boot, or even their front seat! That would not have been a good idea.'

Frank looked around him. 'You think they came through from that little housing estate the other side of the bushes?'

'It's the obvious answer, but I'm not saying it's the right answer. Let's have a walk round the corner and look at possible ways from the other side of this lot,' he said, waving to indicate the bank of shrubs.

They retraced their steps, going back around the corner, then turning left up Sheffield Road. The next left led them onto the fairly new housing estate where houses sold well because of their proximity to a tram stop. They walked down the roads that led them close to the shrubbery separating their back gardens from Donetsk Way, and came away feeling disgruntled by the lack of damage. There was no way a body could have been hauled over and dumped where it had been found, no way at all. Fences were intact, gardens undamaged. A couple of people came out to speak to them after seeing Frank's uniform, but could offer nothing in the way of assistance. They seemed to believe the body had to have been left by a vehicle taking a risk and stopping on Donetsk Way, and both Chris and Frank found themselves in agreement.

They returned to the station but not before revisiting the corner and looking back down Donetsk Way.

'Just suppose,' Chris said thoughtfully, 'if you travelled to here around three in the morning. There's bugger all happens at that time of day. You could pull up here,' he pointed to the spot, 'lift up the bonnet to make it look as though you were having car problems, and this is a long road with a good clear view. You wait till there's nothing in sight, pick up the body and dump it, slam the bonnet down and off you go. She was definitely lightweight, she'd not had much food for the last three years, and she was literally just thrown on the ground. She wasn't posed in any way, just dropped onto her back and left.'

'And our cameras around our building wouldn't pick this up. The bushes and trees on the corner would block it. I reckon you're right.'

'You think a woman could do it? Could carry a dead body?' *No fucking semen*. It was starting to haunt him.

Frank laughed. 'Have you met my wife? She could definitely do it.'

'Do I need to interview her?'

'Wouldn't recommend it, she'll tie you in knots.'

They relieved Danny of his reception duties, with Frank sending him off to get him a sandwich from Asda – all this walking, he explained to the young officer, was making him hungry.

Chris returned to his office, swinging his chair round to face the window. It wasn't much of a view looking down onto the staff car park, but it was a sunny view. He needed to bring pictures of his kids into work, start to make this office his own. He was actually feeling it was okay, this working in Sheffield.

* * *

And so the week came to an end, an unsatisfactory one to most minds. The two linked cases felt as they were progressing, but they were progressing on suppositions. Even the two cases were only supposedly linked, nothing was definite.

Chris Chandler wanted a quiet weekend to mull over everything, to revisit the files, and he would contact both Janey Pascoe and Paula Wrightson, just check they were holding it together. He knew he would feel dreadful having very little to tell them, just like he also knew he would be back in the office at some point during Saturday or Sunday, reworking everything, hoping to spot something he had missed, something that hadn't occurred to him the first time of seeing it.

It was hard when absolutely nothing shed any light on the issues involved in the case. Their only hope was the white van, and even that could just be a delivery driver taking goods to one of the many shops at Gleadless Townend.

Chris walked through to his kitchen, rummaged around in his pockets for his phone, and opened up the app for takeaway deliveries. Burying his concerns and thoughts under a Chinese meal would help solve most of his present angst, he decided.

King prawn chop suey and a portion of chips sounded just about right, and he clicked on his order for delivery as soon as possible.

The bottle of beer he found lurking in his fridge would complete his gourmet meal, and he walked out into his small back garden to set a lonely table for one.

## 20

By Monday the weather had changed. A drizzly fine rain had replaced the glorious sunshine of the previous week, and people were saying they were pleased to see the rain because their lawns needed the moisture.

The entire team were at their desks, computers fired up, by seven. It seemed they had continued working all weekend, reading through reports, waiting for results from the forensic examination of the white van, and generally itching for some tiny new piece of information.

'Okay, let's have a chat. Bryn, the vet's van was not our van. Have I got that right?'

Bryn scowled. 'I don't know why I'm so upset about it, because I knew, we just had to have it formally checked. There was no human blood anywhere in the van, and it's now been thoroughly cleaned by the young lad who does it for them. So it seems we can cross Stewart Phillips off our list. At least as far as the van is concerned, anyway.'

'Maria? Any suspicious white vans?'

'Not that belong to anyone we've had contact with about

these two cases. It's a nightmare. You wouldn't believe how many Ford Transits there are, and most of them are white.'

'Anybody else have anything new to report?' He looked around them all, and Tia spoke up.

'I think I'm speaking for everybody, but we know every word of every report going back the full three years for these two cases. We took the kids out to Chatsworth, and I took the reports with me. They played in the river with their dad, I sat on the grass and read. I was the one with the sore bum caused by sitting on the grass instead of playing rounders on it. And there's nothing. We still have no idea where Hannah can be, or where Lauren was held. It's so damn frustrating.'

Chris nodded. 'I agree. The only thing that occurred to me is why there? Why put Lauren's body there? We all know there is a dedicated litter-picker for this area, we all actually wave at him at least once a day, so why was that body placed there? Was it so that it would be found quickly? Or was it *so* that it would be Ray Eke who found it? Is somebody trying to harm him, to send him back into a bad place? Talk to me, folks, tell me I'm not losing it and going off at a tangent.'

There was silence as his team digested his words. 'That hadn't occurred to me,' said Tia slowly. 'If that is the case, it's an awful thing to do. Do we accept it's a possibility that Mr Eke is being targeted? Do we need to ensure his protection while we're looking for this murderer? Do we actually need to tell him? To bring him in on what we think may be happening. This is a bloody nightmare, isn't it?'

'It is. And I may be looking at it completely from the wrong angle, but I'd be a bit remiss if I didn't consider this angle, and i proved to be an attack on Ray Eke. I intend half suggesting i and then we'll see what his reaction is. Who on earth would want to cause him even more distress than the turmoil he' already been through? Could it be somebody not yet on our radar?'

Chris stood and walked over to the whiteboard. He picked up the black pen and raised his hand as if to begin writing. He hesitated and then turned to face them. 'What do I put?'

Tia stared at the board. 'I have no idea. I don't know where we go next, what we do that's more than what we're doing already, and I think it's a pretty safe bet that we all put in upwards of eighty hours last week on these two cases. We're not slacking, boss, we're baffled.'

Chris grinned at her. 'There's never been a hint of a suggestion that anybody's slacking, Tia. I've reached the point where I'm scared to come out of my office to check something, because you've all got your heads down doing what you do best, or you're out following up leads, as Bryn was on Friday. I couldn't be prouder of you all, and I know that sooner or later we'll recognise the answer, but it mustn't be later. One thing I'm convinced of is that Hannah Wrightson is in mortal danger somewhere. I know linking the two cases is brave, but it's gut feeling that has got to me on this one. She's the replacement for Lauren. We have to get her before too much damage is done to her.'

'I drove around all day on Saturday,' Bryn said. 'I had a chat with Danny Moore – he was asking if the van had been found and when I said no, he said we should go look for it. So we did. I printed off the DVLA list and we checked off fourteen of them, making sure the owners had alibis for the day and time we believe Hannah was taken. It seems Transits are the workhorses of the van world, and without exception all fourteen of them were out being used in connection with the owners' jobs. We couldn't do Sunday because Danny teaches football to eleven-year-olds in the morning, and teenagers in the afternoon, but we're going out again tonight.'

'Then let's bring him into the team for this case. You can go out whenever, you're not having to wait for him to finish his beat bobby job before becoming a part-time detective. Give me five minutes.'

He went into his office, checked with Frank to find out who Danny's sergeant was, and the temporary transfer was swiftly arranged, with the warning that his sergeant did not want Danny to be returned damaged in any way.

Within minutes, Danny was warily knocking on the briefing room door, wondering what he could possibly have done wrong. It was clear his sergeant had only said DI Chandler wanted to see him, leaving the young officer to sweat it out on his way upstairs.

His face lit up when Chris explained what he wanted, and said he had been seconded for the duration of the case.

'Thank you, sir. I'm a bit gobsmacked.'

'You will be, literally, if you persist in calling me sir,' Chris said with a smile on his face. 'Boss will do, unless we're speaking to a member of the public, when it's DI Chandler. Okay?'

'Okay, boss,' was the quick response.

'You're directly answerable to Bryn for the foreseeable future, as between the two of you it seems you did a sterling job on Saturday. Thank you.'

'You're welcome, boss. There was no Sheffield Wednesday match – Saturdays can be a bit boring when it's not the football season.'

'We'd best crack on and get this solved before the season starts then,' Chris said. 'Bryn and Danny, get your heads together and make a proper plan so that you're not chasing your own tails, and see what you can do. I suggest starting with a map of the area, divide it into sections and enlarge the sections on the photocopier. If you don't know how to do that, Maria is our expert in all things that require some tech knowledge. Then use a red pen to mark where you're working. This suspect, whoever it proves to be, is a dangerous person. I need to know your planned whereabouts all the time. I'm serious – apart from Danny we've all seen the pathologist's post-mortem results. You stay together, you don't interview individually. Understood?'

'Yes, boss.' Bryn walked across to the photocopier and pulled out a large A3 map of the area. 'Come on, Danny, let's start off in the canteen, we'll claim a table and get this split how we want it to work. Besides, I need a coffee.'

The two men left the briefing room, and Chris turned to face the others. 'That issue arrived sooner than I anticipated, but I'm serious. This is someone who we have no knowledge of at all, and we know the depravity they obviously enjoy. Nobody, and I include myself in this, must visit anyone in connection with this case on their own. Minimum two persons, maximum the entire team if it's considered necessary.'

'Do we have anything further we want to discuss?' Sally asked. 'I want to go check in on Janey Pascoe. Andy? You'll go with me?'

Andy held up a thumb.

'Any particular reason, Sally? Is there a problem?' Chris sensed she sounded troubled.

'Not really a problem, but she told me she was going to spend the weekend emptying Lauren's room. She hasn't touched it since Lauren disappeared, and she said she wanted to do it, to have one last final immersion in her daughter's life. I think she's hoping for some sort of closure, but it occurred to me last night that she might just come across something that would point to something.'

'Something that would point to something?' Chris gave a small laugh. 'Okay. Text me when you get there. And when you leave.'

Sally gave a brief nod, and it was echoed by Andy.

'Maria?'

'I'm going to try something. I'm not very skilled at it yet, but I'm going to have a go at enhancing the Transit. As you know there are millions of the damn things, fortunately not all in the south-east of Sheffield, but I want to find something that could potentially identify it from all of the others in the area. I can enlarge it, but it loses some clarity when you do that. I know a feller in forensics who might be able to help, might be able to teach me how to do it properly, so I'm going down to see him. That's where I'll be if you need me.'

'Thanks, Maria. So, Tia, we drew the short straws. Fancy a walk?'

'You do know it's raining?'

'That's what I meant by short straws. It's stopping around eleven, though, according to Alexa.'

'Do I need to change into my trainers? And don't believe everything Alexa tells you, she said expect rain around 4 p.m. for yesterday, and so I didn't water the garden. Did it rain? Not till six o'clock this morning.'

Chris laughed. 'I would think trainers might be a good idea. We're going to find our stalwart litter-picker, and I have no idea where he is this morning, so we could be out quite a while, or we could find him in the first five minutes. If we do, I'll treat you to a Starbucks, and we can discuss the conversation I think we have to have with him. I like him, and I'm concerned about him. Definitely uneasy, anyway.'

'Okay, I'll nip down to my locker and swap shoes, meet you in reception? We'd best give our whereabouts to Frank, as we don't have anybody in our team more senior to report our positions to.'

'You being sarcastic, DS Monroe?'

'As if,' she said, and left the room.

\* \* \*

'We're going to find Ray Eke and I need you to know our location,' Chris said to Frank, who grinned at them.

'It's raining.'

'We know.'

'So where is he, our Ray?'

'We don't know.'

'So what do I put down in my book for location?'

'I don't know.'

'So how can I have you rescued if he decides to knock you both out with his litter-picker tool?'

'I don't know that either.'

'This system doesn't seem to be working, boss.'

'Sod off, Frank. I could make you go instead, you know, out in that damp drizzly rain.'

'I was just saying, boss, just saying.'

# 21

Hannah couldn't remember her name. She felt intensely cold from the very core of her to the surface of her skin; everything felt so icy, and she had nothing to cover her to get warm again.

And she couldn't remember where she was, why she was here, or who she was. She tried to speak but it felt as if her tongue was glued to her teeth, so she stopped trying. She rolled over slightly and saw the bottle of water and a packet of crisps by the side of her mattress. She tried to reach for the drink, but her arms and her hands didn't want to obey.

She closed her eyes and tried to concentrate but within a minute she was fast asleep once again. She hadn't seen the rivulets of blood flowing down her legs where Whitecoat had used the Stanley knife to draw patterns on her skin, and to puncture the swollen areas left where the garden ties had eaten into her flesh.

She didn't hear the door close, nor the key turn in the lock. She wasn't to know that she would wake up in a few hours with legs that would be screaming with the agony of all the cuts, and the realisation that she had been drugged once again. The bottle of water was therefore undrinkable, just in case drugs had been added to it, and she could hardly walk to get to the toilet room to get water from the tap.

She thought she could risk eating the crisps – she was so hungry she would eat anything. The bag hadn't been tampered with, so she quickly ate them without moving from her bed, then sat for some time wondering how to get to the toilet without screaming. And what the hell was her name?

\* \* \*

Ray quite enjoyed working in the drizzly rain. The atmosphere was still muggy, and the rain gave that humidity a pleasant feel. He had started his morning shift outside the police station, and had worked his way down, heading towards the bypass running through the Shirebrook Valley. He was lost in his thoughts when he heard a shout from behind him.

There was a wave of a hand from the man, and he paused. This was something new, hardly anyone spoke to him during his working day, and now somebody was actually shouting his name.

As the couple drew nearer, he realised the man was DI Chandler, and Ray began to walk back towards them.

'Morning,' Chris said. 'This is DS Monroe. We were hoping to have a bit of a chat, but the rain seems to be getting heavier. What time do you finish?'

'Around two. You want me to call into Moss Way?'

'That's a much better idea than standing under a tree trying to keep dry. Just ask for me, and I'll come down to reception and collect you.'

'Am I in trouble?' Ray looked puzzled.

'Not at all,' Chris reassured him. 'We just want a chat. Nothing more than that.'

Ray gave a slight nod. 'You could have rung me.'

'I could but I fancied a walk. It was just a slight drizzle when we set off, but it's taken a turn for the worse. We'll leave you to get on with your job, and see you when you've finished.'

'I was going to call in anyway.' Ray hesitated as if deciding whether to speak or not. 'There's something…'

'What?'

'Tell me something first, before I make an absolute fool of myself. Did you find out how Lauren's body came to be at that particular spot?'

'No, we're running on pure guesswork with that one. Why?'

'There's a wheelbarrow. It looks as though it's been dumped, but it's in good condition. I had to go into that copse up by the 30 mph sign because somebody had dumped some rubbish, so I cleared it all up, came out of it by a different route and saw something yellow. It proved to be a wheelbarrow, dark green but with a yellow handle. I honestly think if the handle hadn't been yellow, I wouldn't have spotted it. I didn't touch it. Had a sort of feeling about it, so thought I'd call in after work and let you know where it is. It's not been dumped because it's no good, it looks to be absolutely fine. If anything like that is found that, I can't add to my bag, I have to ring a special number and they send a little truck out to get it, but I felt you should know about it before I did anything. You can transport a body in a wheelbarrow.'

'You certainly can. Can you show us? I'll make it okay with your boss, don't worry.'

Ray smiled. 'I don't worry about anything like that. Even if he sacked me, he couldn't stop me doing this. I don't do it because I get paid, I do it because it gives me my me time, something I need. Come on, we need to go back a couple of hundred yards, and go deeper into the trees. It wasn't meant to be found, I reckon.'

The three of them trudged back up the main road carefully. Lack of a pavement made life a little difficult, but with Ray in the lead they tried to keep up. Suddenly he veered off, and pointed across the road to the 30 mph sign.

'Remember that sign when you're bringing somebody back to collect the wheelbarrow.'

Chris gave a brief nod, and they followed Ray into the wooded copse, suddenly out of the rain.

Within a minute they could all see the splash of yellow that had attracted Ray earlier.

All three stopped as they reached it, and stood looking at it. The main body of the barrow was a deep green, and blended into the vegetation surrounding it. The handle was like a pram handle, not two handles side by side, and was a bright yellow. Impossible to ignore.

It was upturned and the bottom of the barrow was facing the weather. Chris felt hopeful that if there was DNA evidence to be found, it would have been protected by the way the wheelbarrow had landed once it had been abandoned.

He took out his phone and contacted forensics. The inkling was back and he knew this barrow was important.

\* \* \*

Chris, Tia and Ray were all squashed into Chris's small office, drinking welcome cups of tea and trying to dry themselves off with paper towels purloined from the ladies' toilets. Tia's blonde hair sprang into a myriad of curls as she rubbed at it and she groaned. 'Half an hour of straightening this lot this morning, and now look at me.'

'It suits you when it looks all over the place and messy,' Ray said.

'Thanks, Ray. I think,' Tia said. 'Bit of a back-handed compliment, but I'll take it.'

Chris took a long sip of his tea, then sat back. 'Ray, we felt we needed to talk to you. This investigation is progressing, in that we've now linked the missing woman Hannah Wrightson to Lauren Pascoe. Everything I am about to say to you is for your ears only, because this is very much an ongoing investigation, and we don't want to put Hannah's life into any more danger than it already is. Can I have your word that you won't speak about it to anyone, please?'

'Of course,' Ray said. Yes, he'd found the body, but that was it. He'd told them several times he knew nothing else. He hadn't even known about the day's employment they'd given to Lauren three years earlier. He waited.

'Thank you. We've had a couple of brainstorming sessions, our entire team of seven. We've talked through everything we know and everything that is guesswork, either educated or uneducated. We have no idea where Lauren has been held for three years, and no idea where Hannah is now.' He paused for a moment to gather his thoughts. 'We actually feel that in all of this, you are connected. We don't know why, we don't know how, but Lauren was left there in that particular spot hidden from the sight of everybody except somebody standing by her and looking down on her. You.'

'I know.' Ray frowned. 'Do you seriously think I hadn't reached the conclusion that I was meant to find her? What I can't get my head around is why. I'm nobody. Less than nobody. I live the quietest life imaginable, just me and my music, and still living with my mum taking care of me. I don't think I was meant to see the wheelbarrow, that's accidental because I wouldn't normally go that deep into woodland, but it was a twofold thing today. There was some rubbish from a couple of

McDonald's meals that I put into my bag, and it was a brief respite from the rain that was starting to come down heavy. I simply stood for a couple of minutes, did a quick glance around to make sure I hadn't missed any brown McDonald's bags, then spotted the yellow. I moved deeper into the copse, saw what the yellow was and knew I would be calling in after my day's work had finished to tell you. You coming to find me changed all that, of course.'

'It's now cordoned off, and it's a much bigger area than simply where the wheelbarrow is. It's possible we won't find anything else, but it will be thoroughly tested for any DNA left in it. And fingerprints, of course, but the rain today won't have helped with that. Ray, one thing I need to mention is that you had a severe mental breakdown.'

Ray nodded his agreement with the statement.

'We just wondered, could somebody be attempting to send you back to that dark place?'

'Why?'

'I don't know. In our brainstorming session we threw it out as a possibility. Could there be somebody who feels so angry with you that they would try to destroy you once more? To send you in a downwards spiral once again?'

'You actually believe she was placed there so I would find her?' He looked and sounded utterly bewildered. 'My mental state is nobody else's business, and although I kind of knew of Lauren, it was only because she was a friend of one of our girls at work. And I saw her picture. I didn't actually know her, so why should finding her body tip me over the edge and back to where I thought I would never see daylight and warmth again?'

'You're right, it doesn't make sense, and I have to tell you that I would be wrong if I didn't tell you our thoughts on it. You have to be aware that this is what we are thinking, that for some reason you are being targeted. The next obvious question is who could be doing that.'

Ray lifted his hands up as if in surrender. 'I can honestly say there are only two people I value in my life. My mum and my best mate. Both these people worked together to bring me back from the brink. Mum gave up her independence by putting her own home into cold storage, so to speak, and moved into my home to look after me, and Mark bought me out of our very successful business, because he knew I was done with numbers. They encourage me so much with my music, my gardening, my life as it has become now, and the only other person I occasionally speak to is Mum's friend from across the road, and that's generally to find out if Mum is doing okay, because Mum certainly wouldn't tell me, in case it caused me to regress.'

'That would be the friend she is teaching to crochet?'

'It would. Janet Standall. If Mum isn't with me, then she's over at Janet's. Not sure what number she lives at but it's the bungalow with the dark green door directly across from my house. Large buddleia in the front garden, you can't miss it.'

'She's okay with you?'

'Brilliant. Buys me Mars bars and sometimes plain chocolate Bounty bars.'

Chris licked his lips at the thought of a Bounty bar. 'We can write her off as a suspect then. Anybody who buys Bounty bars can't be as evil as we think they are in this case.'

## 22

Maria had made copious notes on improving and enlarging CCTV images, and had slipped headphones on in the hope that everyone would think she was listening to something important, leaving her alone and in peace to work.

In reality she was listening to Take That, turned down very low so she wasn't tempted to suddenly start singing along about lighting her fire, baby... She simply needed to cut people out, and headphones told them to back off. She stared at the picture on her screen of the white van the whole country was looking out for, and highlighted a square inch of the top corner of the visible section of the back door. She would tackle this one square at a time, because no vehicle was immaculate, especially white vans, which were usually the workhorses of the vehicular world. Somewhere on this damn van there was a mark. A scratch, maybe a small piece of a different-coloured paint where some random car had touched it, there had to be something. She just had to hope that the mark she was looking for was on the left back door or the passenger side of the van, because the right-hand side, the right back door and the whole of the front hadn't been visible on Marjorie's CCTV set-up.

She was aware of a hand sliding over her shoulder, and a large mug of coffee was placed on her desk. She turned her head to smile her thanks and saw Tia. She held up a thumb in thanks, not wanting to get involved in a conversation now she was so focused on her screen.

Her eyes switched back immediately to the van, and she zoomed in as much as she could before it took on a blurriness. She made a note of the optimum setting for the clearest shot, and began to pay much closer attention to the paintwork.

It took two hours for her to find it. At the very bottom of the left-hand back door there was a tiny mark with even tinier rays running outwards from the core of the mark. The whole thing was only about a quarter of an inch in size, and she guessed that the door had been opened at some point, accidentally hitting some sort of street furniture such as a concrete post or a streetlight. To the naked eye it was negligible, and Maria knew she wouldn't have spotted it without her computer. It wouldn't really help to get the information out to the general public as it was difficult to see just by a glance, but if the van ever came into police hands, the mark would confirm it was the van that had been seen outside Sainsbury's when Hannah Wrightson had disappeared.

She did a screenshot and forwarded it to Chris, drawing a red circle around the tiny blemish.

She then moved on to the side, giving it the same degree of scrutiny she had used on the left door. She finished her now cold coffee, switched off Take That and leaned back in her chair, rubbing her eyes. She had a dull headache, caused, she knew, by the intense peering at a computer screen for the entire afternoon. Definitely not caused by Take That. She'd seen Ray Eke come and go, and yet nobody had disturbed her to fill her in on what was going on.

'Maria, go home, take some headache tablets and close your eyes.' Tia gave the young officer instructions, and Maria smiled.

'I'm going. I'll fill everybody in at the morning briefing tomorrow. Seven?'

'I guess so. We have to find her, Maria, she's been missing for days now, and we don't seem to have moved forward at all. I've not had a chance to fill you in, but Ray found a wheelbarrow while he was out working today, and it's now been recovered by forensics. We don't know if it's anything to do with this, but it's in good condition so no need for it to be dumped. Hopefully, we'll hear something from the forensic lads early tomorrow.'

Maria nodded and slipped on her jacket. 'Is it still raining?'

'Not as heavy now, but you could be swimming by the time you get to your car.'

Tia headed back to Chris's office. 'I've told Maria to go home. She's obviously got a headache but she's been staring at that screen nearly all day.'

'She's found a small mark on the van, tiny but enough to confirm we have the right vehicle if we ever come across it. It's on the left back door, virtually at the limit of what we can see because of the angle of the camera. I'll get this email forwarded to everybody on the team, but I actually think we should get it out to everybody who received our original notification about the van we're looking for.'

'I agree. A job for tomorrow – it's time to go home, Chris. We're all tired, we're working long hours so an early night will be welcomed by everybody, I'm sure. We'll all be back again by seven tomorrow, so go home.'

'You're a wise woman, Tia Monroe. Come on, I'll walk you down to the car park.'

\*\*\*

The evening had been good for Ray. He had walked home after leaving the police station, pleased he had followed up on his decision to tell DI Chandler about the wheelbarrow. His job required he reported anything like that to the StreetScene cleaners who would turn up with a little truck and remove it, but it had been in good condition. He also realised StreetScene might actually report it when they added two and two together, so it made sense for him to maybe tell Frank Carter about it, at the very least. It had seemed like fate was telling him it was the right decision when DI Chandler and DS Monroe had caught up with him.

He hoped they would tell him the outcome of the forensic tests on it, but didn't actually think for a minute that they would.

He had been considering heading upstairs for a shower when Mark had turned up, and they had spent an enjoyable hour in the gym, then had a very large latte in the coffee shop afterwards.

'So they actually took the wheelbarrow for testing?'

Ray nodded. 'They did. If it had been really ancient with a flat tyre and suchlike, I'd simply have rung it in to be collected by the truck, but I knew it would seem odd to the StreetScene lads. It seemed in too good a condition to be dumped, and why would you dump something like that? I had to report it to them.'

'You didn't touch it?'

'Not likely. It was actually upside down – DI Chandler said that was good, the rain wouldn't have touched the inside. He also said that if it is connected to Lauren Pascoe, there could be some DNA to prove it. So then I went back to the station with them. I was planning on calling in after I'd finished anyway, to report what I'd seen, but they caught up with me. I forgot to ask why they were looking for me, because the wheelbarrow took over the conversation. If you get what I mean.'

Mark grinned. 'So it's a talking wheelbarrow now?' He was beginning to see his friend come back to life. It had been so long since Ray had spoken more than a three-word sentence, and now he was starting to return to the world he had been in before his breakdown.

'You going to follow it up? Ask if they got any DNA?'

'They'll tell me if they want me to know, I suppose. I'm not going to ask, it's a bit out of my pay scale getting forensic results.'

'They're no nearer finding Hannah?'

'Not as far as I'm aware.'

'It's the first thing the girls ask every morning, and they've all linked finding Lauren's body with Hannah's disappearance. I'm spending my time moving into your old office, and installing Gareth into mine, but I still hear them talking. Nobody goes to the shop on their own now, they go in twos. I make sure nobody goes home on their own, which they appreciate, and I've had to explain the situation to Gareth, tell him the whole story, so now we both take anybody that looks like going home alone. They're scared, and even though they don't think the disappearances have any connection to us, beyond them both having that link to our business, it's rattled everybody.'

'Your business.'

'Okay, my business. Have you given any thoughts to a more suitable job for your brain and your skills?'

'Nope. Love what I do, love the fresh air even when it's like it's been today, and I love the peace. Mum's like you, I can see in her face she doesn't understand it, but I understand it, and that's the most important bit.'

Mark admitted defeat and held up his hands in surrender. 'Okay, I'll shut up. You want another coffee?'

'No, thanks. I've had that much today I'll never sleep tonight. I'm going to call round to Marks and Spencer's if you don't mind taking me before you drop me off. I want to get Mum some flowers. I've hardly seen her lately, she spends more time with Janet and their crochet hooks and doing any other bits and bobs she needs to do, than she does at home, so I thought I'd let her know how much I appreciate everything she does for me. Do you mind?'

'Course not. Come on, let's go. Fingers crossed it's stopped raining now. And your mum does so much for us, so make it a big bunch of flowers.'

* * *

It hadn't stopped raining, and Mark stayed in the car while Ray sprinted across the concourse and into the shop. He chose a beautiful mixed bunch of brightly coloured flowers, threw in a box of mint creams, Ziggy's favourites, and headed back to the car.

'Okay, I'm done. I'll be her number one son now.'

'You're her only son. In fact, you're her only child.'

'She could be thinking about adoption... probably you, you know she thinks the world of you.'

Mark laughed. 'Not likely. She's probably been put off any sort of family because she's had you.'

'Well, I'll be back in favour now, that's for sure. Flowers and mint creams, and she deserves them.'

Mark nodded but wisely said no more. He slipped the car into drive and pulled out of the parking space. He drove Ray home and Ray waited until he saw the flash of the brake lights at the end of the road before heading into the house. It was strangely quiet, and he guessed Ziggy had headed over to Janet's house for the blanket making.

He actually felt relieved she had made a friend. Although her own house was only a ten-minute walk from his, she had left her neighbours, and anybody else she had known well, to move to his area, a much quieter place. It had worried him that she only seemed to have him in her life, but now they were a bit like the proverbial ships passing in the night; it made him feel better.

He checked the fridge, saw she had left him a prawn salad plated up, and he carried it to the kitchen table.

Pulling the music manuscript towards him, he ate the salad with a fork in his left hand and a pencil in his right, hearing the music in his head clearly. He made a couple of marks to indicate he should try a different note, or even a different length of note, and almost before he realised it, the plate was cleared and almost dishwasher ready. He felt a little surprised. The latte had filled his stomach and he hadn't particularly wanted food. Strange world when a pile of prawns can change your mind, he mused.

He rinsed the plate and stashed it in the dishwasher before heading into the lounge. He sat at the piano and rested his hands gently on the keys. This was where he truly belonged.

# 23

With the dawning of Tuesday came the return of the sun. Chris Chandler hoped it was a good omen, but wasn't convinced. Solving crimes didn't seem to depend on whether the sun was shining or not.

The frustration around the lack of any sort of lead, or evidence to help them along the way, was reflected in the fact that all of his team had arrived before him, and he glanced at his watch: 6.45. And he thought he was early...

'Morning, everybody,' he called out and several heads lifted. Everybody except Maria, who was clearly engrossed in her screen. He smiled. Maria and her dedication had made him smile since his first introduction to her.

He pulled up a chair beside hers, and sat down. She ignored him for a few seconds, then turned a startled face towards him. 'Oh, morning, boss. You're here.'

'So are you.' He waved a hand to encompass the room. 'So is everybody. And I'm assuming nothing new has come in?'

'A picture of the wheelbarrow now it is upright and in dry conditions, with a stain in it that is showing as blood. No results as to whose blood it is, it's a little early for that, so as it stands at the moment this could be some gardener who's had a nasty accident with a chainsaw and is blaming his wheelbarrow. I've forwarded the picture to your inbox in case you haven't got it already. I rang forensics and asked if they'd got a picture, so I don't think they've sent it out to all and sundry yet.'

Chris grinned. 'You reckon a gardener? We need to know local suppliers who sell this make of wheelbarrow.'

'Homebase, Argos, B&Q – that's all I've found so far. There's going to be a lot, and I don't think the information will be of any use to us, it could have been bought a couple of years ago. That's what I was searching for when you made me jump.'

'What time does Homebase open?'

'Already looked it up, 8 a.m. to 7 p.m. today. You think Homebase?'

'Only because it's the most local one. I'm not thinking Argos because there's always a paper trail at Argos, but Homebase you can simply pay cash. It just feels as if it's a local crime. The dump site, the place where the wheelbarrow was left, even the abduction point was only half a mile away. And this killer seems to be really good at not drawing attention to themselves. We haven't even worked out if it's a man or a woman yet. I just feel Hannah is being held locally, but heaven only knows where.'

He left Maria to her web searching and headed over towards the larger conference table, where Bryn and Danny had spread out their map.

'Any luck?'

Bryn lifted his head. 'Not yet, but we've ruled out about a million people.'

'That's good. Soon we'll be left with just one.'

'We're covering Owlthorpe today. We do a general drive round first, then make it more targeted. We've had a few stroppy ones who seem to think they don't need to answer police questions, and I just agree with them. Then I tell them they've to be at the station for eight o'clock in the morning, and they might want to engage a solicitor. That shuts them up and they become a bit more amenable to answering us. So far nobody is turning up with a solicitor.'

Chris turned to the younger officer. 'You're learning a lot then, Danny?'

'Not half, boss. And we're not stopping till we find it. Couldn't sleep last night for thinking about it. I reckon it's in a garage. Nobody leaves an unmarked white van out on the road with the wrong number plates, not in these times when we can check everything from inside a police car. If we find a garage with a window we look inside, but most of them don't have windows, they have up and over doors.'

'I don't doubt you're right, Danny,' Chris said with a sigh. 'We just have to keep following the checks, because we'll find it sooner or later. And at least you're tracking down a white van, I'm tracking wheelbarrows.'

He left them to their deliberations and went to stand by Tia, staring up at the whiteboard.

'Where is she?' Tia whispered. 'Where is she?'

'I don't know, and with every day that arrives I feel sicker. It concerns me that whoever took Lauren has realised a dead one can be replaced. There's no need to keep Hannah alive, he or she can do what they like, and hang the consequences. There's plenty of others.'

Tia looked horrified. 'All that pain. That concerns me more than Lauren dying. What she must have suffered for three years before her body gave up. Where do we go next, boss?'

'Homebase? They've apparently found bloodstains in the bottom of the wheelbarrow we collected yesterday, so I thought we'd have a look at a new one, see what comes to mind. They stock them, Maria was about three steps in front of us. Argos do as well, as do B&Q apparently. She's probably got another dozen on her list by now, with Amazon leading the way.'

'Huh, it won't be Amazon and it won't be Argos.'

'Too easy to trace, agreed. Not so much so from Homebase though, or B&Q. But to be honest I just want to look at one the right way up, to put myself into this killer's mind, see if it was bought for this specific purpose. Because if it was, it was bought within the last couple of weeks, which narrows everything down.'

'Okay. Is everybody sorted and doing stuff?'

'Andy and Sally are going back up to Gleadless to catch anybody who wasn't in first time round, because we know some were on holiday. It's just something that's needing tightening up, we don't want to miss something for the sake of not doing it.'

She glanced at her watch. 'By the time we get there they'll be open. I promise not to go looking at wallpapers.'

'You're decorating?'

'Trying to. I'm okay at the painting, but the wallpapering is a bit more difficult. But I'm a woman, I can do anything once I put my mind to it.'

'Course you can. Shall we walk to Homebase?'

'Not worth taking a car, and we can always flash our warrant cards if we need to ask something or someone officially. And it's stopped raining.'

* * *

Apart from staff, they had the shop to themselves. It had only been open one minute. They walked through, with Tia diverting her eyes away from the wallpaper section, and reached the garden centre part. They walked through the back doors and back out into the sunshine. It was a green oasis of beauty. Well-kept plants, gate posts, gates, fencing. And wheelbarrows.

'That's the one.'

Chris took hold of the yellow handlebar and pulled it away from the stand on which it was being displayed. 'It's more like a pram than a wheelbarrow, isn't it? Even the sides are more square-shaped than sloping,' Tia said, walking around it and giving it a close inspection. 'It didn't strike me like this when we got the upturned version of it yesterday. And I reckon it was bought for the reason it was specifically used for – the transport of a body. This is deeper than a conventional wheelbarrow. It also has two wheels rather than one, which makes it more stable, and that pram-like handle. It didn't register with me that it had two wheels when I saw it yesterday.'

'Well, it's definitely the same model.' Chris took out his phone and took several pictures of it from different angles. 'I imagine it was abandoned because of the rough terrain in that wooded copse, it would have been hard work with the body in it, and then not needed any more once the body had been disposed of. Let's hope they don't need to go and buy another one before we find out who it is.'

They both turned as an assistant approached them, and Chris held up his warrant card. 'DI Chandler and DS Monroe. Do you sell many of these?' He pointed to the barrow.

'Yes sir, this is the last of our current stock, but a new delivery is expected tomorrow. It's a very popular model, because of the double wheels, and it's our own-brand – I don't think there are many like it. It's much more manageable than a single-wheeled barrow. A bit more expensive at £80 but worth it.'

'Do you work this department all the time?'

'I do, it was a nightmare yesterday. We didn't have to water the plants last night though.'

'I don't suppose you keep records of who buys them?'

'If they pay by card, you could trace them, but if they pay cash, then no.'

'CCTV?'

She nodded. 'Yes, but you'd have to speak to the manager. I know nothing about that. There are definitely two cameras at opposite sides of the entrance. Would you like me to get him for you?'

'Thank you, that would be helpful.'

She disappeared and Tia groaned. 'A very popular model, she said.'

He grinned at her. 'Nobody ever said policing was easy. And just to add insult to injury, we don't even know for definite it was bought from here. The CCTV is clutching at straws. The killer got rid of the body quickly after Lauren died. So we can come up with a twenty-four-hour slot when he or she would have bought the barrow, provided they did buy it for this particular reason. But if they already had it, then the CCTV can tell us nothing. Two steps forward, one step back, all the time.'

After speaking with the manager, who confirmed there were no cameras in the garden centre section but there were two in the shop entrance foyer, they arranged for Maria to visit later in the day with details of what dates she would need to see videos for. She could also sort out credit card purchases for at least a month earlier, with the manager agreeing that would be no problem to organise.

They thanked him and walked across the retail park, stopping to pick up three lattes at Starbucks before returning to the office.

They filled Maria in on what they needed her to do, and she immediately began to make notes regarding the date brackets she'd want to look at.

'You may find nothing,' Chris warned her. 'There's always the possibility that it's not a new barrow, but one they had prior to Lauren dying.'

'I know, but everything's a hope when you've got nothing else to go on.'

She took a sip of her drink. 'This is nice. Will I be able to afford Starbucks coffees when I'm a DI?'

'Doubt it,' was Chris's dry response. 'I had to sell my body on the Town Hall steps to buy these. In the rain,' he added as an afterthought.

Tia placed a packet of ginger biscuits on the desk. 'Well, I didn't sell my body anywhere, so I can only provide ginger biscuits. Help yourself.'

They sat for a moment enjoying the quietness of the normally noisy office, drinking and nibbling on biscuits, when the peace was shattered by the strident ringing of Chris's phone in his small office. He moved quickly to answer it, and they heard him say, 'We'll be there in ten minutes.'

Both women turned to face him. Some tones of voice generated that feeling that all was not well.

'What's wrong?' Tia asked, putting down her cup as she prepared to go to wherever was ten minutes away.

'We've to go to the Birley Lane tram stop. They're currently closing Birley Lane, both ends, and blocking other entrance roads onto it. There's a body. A female. Unclothed but covered in injuries is the description I've just got. Forensics are on their way. A couple of dog walkers found her. Tia, you're with me, Maria, can you bring the others back. Even if this isn't who we're expecting it to be, it's still our case. Postpone the CCTV at Homebase until tomorrow. Okay?'

Maria nodded. 'Okay, boss. Take care.'

## 24

The tent had been erected a couple of minutes before Chris and Tia arrived. They waited until Andy and Sally joined them, and then Chris walked across to the tent. He could hear Kevin Hanson's voice inside, so inserted his head into the tent flap.

'Okay to come in?' he asked.

Kevin looked up. 'Of course, but you'll probably wish you hadn't. It's a bad one, Chris.'

Chris stepped inside, and made sure the entrance behind him was closed. The body was clearly female, as she had no clothes on her at all. She had simply been dumped towards the top end of the pub car park, where it met the field that accommodated the tram tracks that headed to and from Gleadless. She was lying on grass, and her face was covered in blood.

'Her eyes have been removed,' Kevin said quietly. 'You have to find whoever did this, and find them quickly, Chris. If the killer is the same person who killed Lauren, they're going to want a replacement soon.'

'Do you know the cause of death?'

'I can't say at the moment, but I'm leaning towards a similar scenario as with Lauren Pascoe. I think her heart gave up, but that's only a guess, until I get her on the table for a proper post-mortem.'

'Well, I can confirm it's definitely Hannah Wrightson.' He took out his phone and held the picture out to Kevin. 'That's Hannah. Is this a recent death?'

'Hours, I would say. Maybe ten. I believe she's been in this field since probably late last night. Look at her legs, Chris. They're badly infected, and they've had patterns drawn on them with a knife. She must have been in terrible pain. She's obviously been shackled in some way, because she has severe lacerations around her ankles where her legs have been tied together. And what's bothering me more than anything is that whoever has done this could be on the streets right now trawling for the next victim.'

'Well, I imagine this will be hitting Facebook any moment now, so I have to go see Hannah's mother before she gets some garbled version of events.'

Kevin nodded. 'I'll send my full report as soon as I have it. I'll prioritise this, Chris. Whoever has done this is escalating the actions. Removing eyes? And no clothes on this one, so maybe the clothes could have told us something. We won't know until you catch the bastard, Chris, but I hope to God you find him soon.'

'You think it's a man?'

Kevin sighed. 'Figure of speech really. I just don't want to think that the gentler sex could do something as horrific as this. I won't know if there's been any sexual activity until I get Hannah in my room, so I'll let you know as soon as possible. Do you have a feeling for the sex of the killer?'

Chris shrugged. 'We've talked about it as a team many times, because one member of my team keeps insisting, in her words, *there's no fucking semen.* And she's right, there was none on Lauren, but it could be different with Hannah. I'm off to look round the area now, see if there's tyre tracks or anything that could give us a clue as to how Hannah got here. Then I'm going to break the news to her mum. It will devastate her, they were very close.'

'I'll be in touch as soon as I have anything, Chris. Just between you and me, because I'm supposed to be clinical and impartial at all times, taking her eyes has absolutely knocked me for six...'

Chris turned and left the tent, crossing towards Sally and Tia. 'Anything to tell me?'

'Not really. There's no vehicle tracks, just like there was nothing at the Pascoe site. And Maria has confirmed for us in the last couple of minutes that the blood in the bottom of the wheelbarrow did belong to Lauren, so unless the killer has been out and bought a second barrow, we have no idea how Hannah arrived here.'

Chris did a 360 degree turn slowly. 'Could a vehicle have driven to the top of the car park and the body been transferred over that hedge and onto the field?'

'It could, but the pub has CCTV,' Tia said. 'Andy is inside speaking with the manager, organising for us to have access to any video recordings. There's a camera pointing upwards so that all the car park is covered by it. If the killer did as you've just said, it will show up on it. I just think it's not going to, I think he or she is too smart for that. I believe in Lauren's case they parked a vehicle out of sight of any CCTV cameras and transferred her body into the wheelbarrow to take it to somewhere where it would be found. I suspect the same sort of thing has happened with Hannah's body, which is why we need to go looking for a wheelbarrow. Something else may have been used to transport this one, but I think it's basically been the same.'

'I agree,' Chris said. 'Who found the body?'

'A man and wife. Carl and Tessa Green. They actually only live just across the road, on the other side of Birley Lane. They're sat outside the pub, having a cup of tea. They're badly shaken, especially the man. I don't think he really believed what he saw, but his wife was much calmer, trying to unwind her husband, I think. They have a little white Bichon Frisé with them, that's why they were in the field. I've asked them to hang on until you've spoken with them, and the pub manager supplied them with a pot of tea, so they're okay.'

'I'll go and have a chat, then we can let them go home.'

He walked down the steep incline of the car park, and saw the couple sitting at a picnic bench.

'Mr and Mrs Green? I'm DI Chandler, lead investigator in this case. I'm so very sorry you've had to go through this.'

'You've seen her?' Tessa Green asked.

'I have. A brutal sight. Before you go home, can you leave your address with one of my team please, just in case we need to contact you again. Thank you for calling it in, it must have been a dreadful shock.'

'It was, especially for my husband. He can't stand the sight of blood.' She reached across and grabbed her husband's hand. 'Come on, Carl, finish that tea and let's go home. The walk is cancelled for today.'

Chris watched them walk slowly towards Sally, who made note of their address, and then continued to watch as they crossed the road towards their house. It was virtually on the same level as the site where the body was lying, just a road separating the two areas. They would never be able to leave their house again without seeing that field, and the body.

Danny left the pub and joined his colleagues, a glum expression on his face. 'I couldn't spot anything at all, but I'm no Maria, am I? However, the manager couldn't spot anything out of the ordinary either. But let's not dismiss it, we're the amateurs here. I think Maria needs to come up to check if we've missed anything.'

Chris nodded. 'I agree. I can't do video stuff, I get distracted too easily by my thoughts going off at a tangent. Give Maria a call, Danny, and tell her I'd like her up here first thing tomorrow morning to go through the CCTV again before we write it off.'

'Tia,' he continued, 'let's go up into that field. That body didn't walk there on its own, somebody brought it. In view of the fact we completely missed a discarded wheelbarrow when Lauren was dumped by the roadside, we need to take a much closer look, at least as far as the other side of the field where the tram tracks rejoin the road, and the other traffic.'

'Boss, shall we head back to Moss Way to organise getting people up here to do house to house? Or shall we make a start on that? I'm easy either way.' Sally spoke quietly.

'Thanks, Sally. Go back and get me a team sorted for tomorrow morning, to start at eight-thirty. Strangely enough there's not a lot of houses up here, partly because of an Academy full of school kids taking up most of the land. I'm just thankful it's the school summer break, or else kids would have probably found the body. Give the door-knocking teams their instructions; we're going to walk the field, then Tia and I will go to see Paula Wrightson. I know it seems as if I'm prioritising the field, but I have to just in case there's something else that this...' he hesitated, 'person has used for transporting Hannah. So let's get to it. Briefing meeting at half past four, we'll decide what happens after that when we've all had our say.'

\* \* \*

In any other circumstances, the walk across the field would have been idyllic in the sunshine. They covered as much of the area as they could, having to allow for the fact that tramlines went across the middle of it, and only stopped when they reached the Bay of Bengal Indian Restaurant.

'Any good?' Chris asked, nodding his head in the direction of the restaurant.

'Very good. It's a takeaway place as well. Used to be a pub not so very long ago called The Old Harrow, and locals tend to still call it by that name, so just be aware as we're now working this area. You could end up a very confused DI.'

'I'll bear it in mind. So, tell me your thoughts. We've found nothing that could have got that body to the top of this hill and down the other side. So how did it get there?'

'A car? Driven right to the top of the car park, body already in boot, and just chuck it over the hedge?'

'So we're back to assuming it's a man? I know Hannah is only tiny, her mother said she was only five feet tall, and she's very slim, but even so it would be hard for a woman to get her over that hedge. I think tomorrow we'll go from here up to the top of Birley Lane walking on the roadside, then drop down the other side and walk to the bottom. There have to be other ways of accessing this field, it has school kids walking this route all the time, causing the odd spot of arboreal damage. And is the whole of Sheffield built on hills like this mountainside we're currently on?'

Tia laughed. 'Oh yes, every bit of it. It's tough going if you're a cyclist, I'm telling you. And you should see the summit of this particular mountainside if you drive over it when it's a bit foggy. The top is totally obscured by thick fog.'

'I'll remember that. It occurred to me the other day that wherever we went it was all uphill and down dale, there are no flat bits.'

'Part of the city is built on land as you start to climb up into the Pennines, that's where a lot of sporty cyclists go for their training regimes. It's hard work living here. Thank God somebody invented the motor car.'

They returned to the car park, where Kevin was still waiting around. He moved across to speak with them.

'Find anything?'

Chris shook his head. 'Not today. We're going to search the roadside tomorrow, so this place is going to remain closed off. I don't suppose the landlord of the pub will be very pleased, but that's the way it's going to go.'

'We're about to remove our young lady, and I'm going to start the PM immediately. We need answers. And we need them quickly.'

'Thanks, Kevin. You'll email as soon as you know anything?'

'I will.'

The sound of the coroner's hearse reversing up the car park filled the air, and everyone fell silent. Within a couple of minutes, the stretcher was wheeled out of the field, the closed body bag strapped securely to it.

Nobody spoke, and everyone dipped their heads in solemn silence. Tia brushed away a tear, and said a silent prayer that they could find who had done it before they got the chance to take somebody else off the street in what appeared to be the easiest of fashions.

The vehicle disappeared, and yet still nobody moved. It was simply too much to take in.

# 25

Paula Wrightson knew as soon as she opened her front door and saw DI Chandler and DS Monroe.

'No...' she said, whispering softly.

'Can we come in, Paula?' Chris's tone was gentle. He knew the closeness of this mother and daughter. It was a repetition of the Janey–Lauren relationship. For a second, his mind froze on that thought. He shook his head, parked the thought in the recesses of his brain, and followed Janey through into her lounge.

'You've found her?'

'I'm sorry, Paula, but we have.'

'On Birley Lane? I've seen on Facebook there's police cars up there and it's all cordoned off. But I hoped it wasn't...' The tears rolled down her face. 'She didn't suffer?'

'I can't really tell you very much, but it is Hannah. I recognised her from the photo you gave to us. I'm so very sorry, we've had teams out all over the place searching for her, but this morning we received a call to say a body had been found.'

'Can I see her?'

'In a couple of days. It's of vital importance we get the post-mortem done as quickly as possible, but she is being well cared for, I promise you. As soon as Dr Hanson has completed his work, he'll let us know and we'll arrange to collect you and take you to formally identify her, and to give you some time with her. I'm so sorry it's ended like this, Paula.'

'Do you have any idea who did it?' Paula was shaking, and Tia stood.

'I'll make us all a cup of tea. Can we ring anybody to get them to come and be with you?'

Paula handed her phone to Tia. 'My sister. Fran.'

Tia nodded and took the phone with her to the kitchen. She spoke to Fran, told her what had happened, and there was an immediate promise to be there within ten minutes. Tia made the drinks and carried them through.

'Thank you,' Paula said. 'I don't know what to do. I need Fran. She's been with me almost non-stop since Hannah disappeared, and her belief that we would get her back is what has kept me going. Now we've got her back, but not in the way we wanted.'

'Drink your tea, Paula,' Tia said. 'I promise you it will help soothe you, although it's not going to ease any pain. We can't tell you anything because we know very little ourselves at the moment, but we will keep in touch when we do hear anything, and it will be either me or PC Sally Duroe who will come to collect you to take you to see Hannah. Fran obviously can go with you if that's what you want. Are you close?'

'She's my twin. You'll see how close when she arrives. Even when we try to be different, we end up looking the same, so yes, we're close.'

'And Hannah's father?' Tia was cautious about asking – sometimes it could be a bomb going off when exes were mentioned.

'He died some years ago in a motorcycle accident. We weren't together, he didn't want the responsibility of a baby. He'd only seen Hannah once, and that was an accidental meeting in Morrison's. I have to break the news to Mum, she'll be devastated. She'll be here as soon as she can get a train, she lives in Manchester.'

'If we can help...' Tia said.

Paula shook her head. 'Fran will ring her. In fact she may already have done it. She always knows what I'm thinking and planning before I do.'

She reached across and pulled a fresh tissue out of the box, dabbing her eyes with it. 'I knew really this would be the end result. She's been missing for too long. It's a quiet house without her. She always used to ring me from the bottom of the garden path, and talk to me about every step she was taking to get into the house. I used to howl with laughter at some of the things she came up with, yet it seems she was such a quiet person at work, took her job very seriously.'

Chris and Tia let Paula talk, in the hope that it would help her. They heard the front door open and Tia stood.

She met Fran in the hallway and controlled the gasp that threatened to leave her mouth. So alike. 'I'll make you a cup of tea,' she said. 'Paula is in the lounge with DI Chandler. I'm so sorry for your loss.'

Fran nodded. 'Thank you. I'm going to take Paula back home with me for a few days. She wouldn't go when I suggested it earlier, because she believed Hannah would come home, but now I can look after her properly. I'll leave my address with you before you go.'

She opened the door to the lounge, and Tia continued on into the kitchen.

\* \* \*

It was a sombre journey back to the station and they walked quietly into the reception area. Even Frank couldn't find anything to say apart from how sorry he was to hear the news. 'I can tell you we've put two uniforms up at the site overnight and the whole road will remain closed off until you release it, boss.'

'Thank you, Frank. This whole case is a bloody nightmare. We hardly know any more since finding Lauren's body to now.'

'It will come. It will just take one little thing to lead onto the flash in the brain that shows you the way. Go and find that flash, you two. The rest of your team are upstairs awaiting instructions.' He glanced at the clock. 'It's gone four now, maybe it's time for a quick briefing and then home. The best thoughts happen at home anyway, and I'm sure they'll all be thinking about today for the rest of the evening.'

'You're right,' Chris said. 'And we've just come from Paula Wrightson's house. She's in bits. We'll be back here for seven in the morning, and we'll all be over at Birley Lane talking to people, trudging up and down the mountainside, searching. So far there's nothing to show how the body got to that spot. I'm sending Maria to the pub tomorrow to go through their car park CCTV, but I'm not hopeful.'

They headed upstairs to the briefing room, and everyone stood as they walked through the door. Nobody spoke, and Chris looked around them all. 'Sit down, everybody. It's been a shitty day, so we'll have a quick briefing and then I want you to go home. Maria, your priority tomorrow is to look at the CCTV, the camera trained on that giant sloping car park, and get as many car registrations from it as possible. I would say from ten o'clock last night until eight this morning. Hannah was placed in that field at some point during those hours. Go and check where the forensic tent is so that you know exactly the position you need to be looking at. This time, if a wheelbarrow was used, it wasn't dumped anywhere. It has to be a vehicle of some sort, not necessarily the white van because we've asked for sightings of that too much. They must have another vehicle.'

'I agree,' Danny said. 'I've been thinking about this wheelbarrow a lot. Why was it dumped? I think there is a much smaller vehicle that was used to get Lauren to her site, and possibly used to transport Hannah to Birley Lane. In Lauren's case, I suspect it was a dark-coloured small car that was driven actually into that wooded area as far as it could be, then the second part of the journey towards Donetsk Way had to be taken in the barrow. But if the car was like mine, too small to have anything in it apart from a driver and a passenger really, it would make sense to dump the barrow.'

'Now I'm curious,' Chris said. 'What car do you have, Danny?'

'It's a Sirion,' he said, trying not to blush. 'But there are other little cars like the Fiat 500, you know. And I'd certainly struggle to get a wheelbarrow in my boot if I had a dead body on the back seat. I suspect the white van is well tucked away now, and they're left with a much smaller vehicle.'

'Maria, bear this in mind, will you? And well done, Danny, for pointing this out. I wondered why they dumped the barrow, but couldn't come up with an answer. It's obvious that a smaller car could be driven off road and into the woods and in the late evening it wouldn't be spotted, especially a black or a dark blue one, and it's equally possible they were in a rush to leave the area after leaving Lauren there by the side of the road, so they would be hampered by the barrow. It was large, and heavier than a single-wheeled one. A Sirion?'

'Daihatsu. Mum bought a Range Rover, and gave me her old car because she said it was too good to trade in. Best car I've ever driven, really fast, automatic, and the blurb says it can seat five six-foot men, which I don't doubt for a minute. They just couldn't have any luggage because the boot can only accommodate a couple of loaves of bread.' He creased with laughter. 'So don't point your fingers at me, I definitely couldn't carry a wheelbarrow and a body in it.'

'It's a black one, boss,' Sally called out, trying desperately not to laugh.

'Okay, if we don't come up with any clues or answers tomorrow, we take this Sirion apart. Yes?' Chris tried not to smile. He'd never even heard of a Daihatsu Sirion, but clearly his loan PC enjoyed it.

Chris switched on his serious face. 'I want to mention a thought I had while we were at Paula Wrightson's home. I don't know where the thought will lead, but it occurred to me that the situation with Paula and Hannah is the same as the situation with Janey and Lauren. They were so close, almost a sisterly relationship, doing so much together. A lot of love, a strong family bond. Maybe these girls weren't randomly taken off the street, perhaps we're looking for someone who doesn't have that type of bond with the family members. I may just be grasping for stuff here, but think about it while you're mulling over everything else tonight, because I know you will be.'

'Can I say something, boss?' Sally sounded tentative.

'Go ahead, Sally.'

'It's this thing about is it a man or is it a woman. I'm not closing my mind to it being a man, but what you've just said speaks to me of a woman. Both girls were small, dainty, handled more easily by a woman. There is no semen, as I believe I mentioned before, and I don't know if you've seen it yet but we have an initial report from Dr Hanson. He says Hannah was menstruating, and had a Tampax inserted. Would a man seriously provide sanitary protection for his captive he was torturing? But it would be second nature to a woman to provide it. I know that statistics will show that when abductions of women take place it's usually a man who has taken them, but in this case I'm not convinced the statistics have got it right.'

The others looked at her, all of them thinking the damage inflicted on the two deceased women was even more horrific if it had been perpetrated by a woman. A woman who would have known how excruciating the pain of having a broken glass bottle inserted into the vagina would be, or the intense constant suffering after having thousands of tiny cuts all over her legs and both eyes removed.

## 26

Chris didn't want to believe Sally could be right. Chris liked women, he liked to think about the gentler side of them, the laughter every woman he had ever known had brought into his life, even his ex-wife.

On his way home he had driven as far as the crime scene tape would allow and then walked up Birley Lane to speak to the two officers on duty until midnight, when they would swap out with two different uniforms. He handed them a coffee each, and they thanked him, telling him it had been a quiet evening. One or two people had edged close up to the tape, but hadn't stayed, just wanted to be there. Flowers had been left, and Chris could see quite a few bouquets by the roadside.

'I didn't know where to put them,' one of the officers said. 'So I've put them on the roadside. People can be really nice, not like the bastard that killed Hannah.'

'You knew her?'

'No, but we've been in the teams out asking questions and just talking to people. Done some driving around in spare time looking for white vans, that sort of thing. We were both on duty protecting the spot where Lauren was found as well. It's been a harrowing few weeks, but I guess you know that, sir.'

Chris nodded. 'I do. And thanks for doing this. Enjoy your coffee.'

He walked back to where he'd left his car, turned it around and drove down to the traffic lights. He was deep in thought for the rest of his journey home.

Although he hadn't said much to Sally, everything she had tried to put into words made sense. He dug out a ready meal, not really looking at what it was, as he figured if it was in his freezer he must have fancied eating it at the time, poured a can of beer into a glass and put the can in the recycling, then waited for the microwave ping. A woman. He couldn't get his mind off it. A woman. But even if he accepted the premise, it didn't particularly help as they had no suspects of either sex in mind anyway. Just because he didn't particularly like Mark Griffiths didn't make him a suspect.

Chris put what proved to be Spaghetti Bolognese into a dish and finished it quickly without really tasting it. His mind was anywhere but on food, and after tidying everything away he headed into his lounge. He asked Alexa to play Gold Radio, lowering the volume to level two so it didn't distract him, and he took out all the notes, the reports, everything that had already been read over and over again, then pulled a notebook toward him.

He went back to the beginning and began to list women. He knew he had no reason to think any of the women he had encountered in the case so far could be a genuine suspect, but he also knew he couldn't dismiss any of them out of hand. That was the point he realised just how much credence he was giving to Sally's words.

He was surprised to see just how many names there were

Some didn't have a name, but he added the three ladies Bryn had mentioned worked in the vets simply as three vets. He hoped he had got them all because it was proving to be a hefty list.

He rang Sally.

'Hi, boss. I hope you're not ringing to tell me somebody else is missing.'

'No, I wanted to tell you I listened to you, and as a result I have a very lengthy list of names for us to investigate, all women.'

He heard a swift intake of breath. 'So have I. I've gone through reports from everywhere and if a woman is named, she's now on my list.'

'I've done the same, so we'll check them off tomorrow, make sure we haven't missed anybody. I even added three unnamed woman who work at the vets because Bryn told me there were three assistants there.'

'I'll add them to mine now. So how do we tackle it?'

'No idea. We have to work our way through them, I suppose. We need to know exactly who on this list knows Janey and Paula. These two women have been targeted just as much as their daughters were, because neither of them want to carry on living without their loved ones. My whole thinking on it has turned around since I spoke to Janey this afternoon. She's apparently staying with her sister now for a few days, if we need to talk to her.'

'Okay. So... we re-interview all these women? Is that the plan? Are we splitting the list and all taking some, or are we doing this between us?'

'You don't do anything on your own. Does your mother love you?'

'She does, and actually couldn't manage her illness without me. I get what you mean – I'm a potential target. Okay, I'll take Danny with me. And you and Tia go together?'

'Yes, but it's bloody ridiculous working like this. We've got to stop whoever is doing this to us, and stop them soon, Sally.'

* * *

It was a phone call from Mark that broke the news to Ray of the discovery of a body on Birley Lane fields.

'The grapevine is saying that it's Hannah.' I'm about to ring her mother, and offer the condolences of everybody she worked with, but I thought I'd let you know first, that I'm going to do that. I thought you might not know they'd found her, because it's some way away from your routes. All Birley Lane is closed off.'

'Before you ring her mother, watch the local news. They might be able to confirm it is Hannah, and you will be able to tell her that's where you got the information from. Don't just say you've heard it as gossip.'

'You're right. I thought DI Chandler might have let you know, but maybe he hasn't had time.'

'No reason for him to let me know. I'm nobody really, I just found a body and a wheelbarrow, neither of which is actually connected to me. If you hear anything else, Mark, let me know, will you?'

They disconnected, and Ray sat on the sofa staring into space. He could see Hannah – very pretty, long dark hair that she wore in a ponytail for work, tiny, slim, and nothing was too much trouble for her. He knew he had been awful to her when he couldn't speak to her, and she had seen the results of his complete breakdown when he had smashed everything he could smash in his office. She had held him, tried to comfort him, and he had been aware then of how tiny she was.

She had stepped aside when the paramedics arrived, and hers

had been the first get well soon card he had received. And now she was dead.

He poured himself a rare drink, a brandy, and sipped at it slowly, hoping it would have a reviving effect on him. Hearing the news had been a shock, even though it wasn't unexpected. He headed for the garden looking for his mother, but she was nowhere to be seen.

'Mum!' he shouted from the bottom of the stairs, but received no answer. He headed up and checked each room but decided the silence actually spoke volumes – his mother wasn't in. He'd have a chat with her later, once he had seen it confirmed on *Calendar*.

Just for a few moments, his mind drifted towards Chris Chandler, and he wondered how he would have taken the news. Presumably he was lead officer on the case, and Ray guessed it would weigh heavily on the DI to know they hadn't managed to find Hannah quickly enough to save her.

Returning to the lounge, he switched on the television, and very shortly had the confirmation he knew was going to be revealed – Hannah Wrightson's body had been found. They gave very few details, just a brief shot of many sprays of flowers that had been left on Birley Lane, and images of a couple of police officers and crime scene tape shutting off a large area.

He stood as he heard the front door open, and walked out into the hallway to greet Ziggy. He bent down to place a kiss on her head, and followed it with a hug.

'You've heard the news?' he asked.

'News? What's happened?'

'Hannah Wrightson's body has been found. It was in the field where the tram tracks cross at the top of Birley.'

'Really? Such a lovely girl. Are you okay?'

'I'm fine. Are you?'

'I'm good. That DI seems a smart man, I'm sure we just need to keep the faith. He'll sort it.'

'Where've you been?'

'I went to the garden centre just for a bit of a mooch around because I'm fancying having a water feature in the back garden, so I'm at the research stage, then I called at my house just to check it's all okay. Everything's good, I did some heavy duty cleaning that needed doing, and I saw a water feature with fairies flitting around on it that I'm going to treat myself to.'

'Maybe we can both go at the weekend and get it. Would you like to do that?'

'I would. It'll make a change to crocheting all the hours God sends. The pile of blankets is becoming mountain sized. I'm going to see about delivering them over the next couple of weeks, then they've got them before the winter sets in.'

'You're a good woman, Ziggy Duly,' her son said. 'What you do for me is above and beyond, and I couldn't be more grateful. You know that, don't you?'

'I know,' she responded, 'and if she had a good son, he would make her a drink of tea to soothe her weary soul.'

\* \* \*

Janet Standall was sitting in her front garden, hidden from the rest of the world by the privet hedge that bordered the lawn. She was enjoying a shandy that Philip, her husband, had made for her, while basking in the warmth of the late-evening sun.

'Okay?' he asked, watching her select a different ball of wool.

'Yes, I think I'm going to stick with pink, red and cream for this one, it's a lovely combination. And now I can turn corners properly they look so much better.'

'So Ziggy taught you then?'

'Did she heck. No, I found some instructions on YouTube, apparently that's what everybody does when they can't work out how to do something.'

Philip stood and tucked his chair underneath the table. 'Well, I'm going in to watch some cricket. You need anything?'

She shook her head. 'No, I'll just get this colour started, and then I'll join you inside, watch a bit of cricket with you.'

'Fine by me. Did you know they've found a body up the top end of Birley Lane? Top side of the pub, so I believe.'

'A body? No, I didn't. That's two in the last fortnight or so, scary times. Was she called Hannah something?'

'I think so. Not absolutely certain because I was only half listening, but I seem to remember Hannah. Can't recall her surname.'

'Poor lass. She was the reason we were all asked to look out for white vans. I'm truly sorry if it is her they've found, she was only a young woman, and worked for Ray when he had his accountancy business. Think she still works for his ex-partner at the office. I never knew her, but I think it will upset Ray, he's a warm-hearted soul, nothing like his mother.'

Philip stared at her. 'And I thought you and Ziggy got on well! You never cease to amaze me, Janet. I'll go and put the TV on, come in when you're ready.'

## 27

'Is it Thursday?'

Tia looked at Chris. 'It is, boss. You not sleeping too well?'

'Are you?' he countered.

She shook her head. 'About three hours last night. So if I nod off while we're trudging up and down this hill, just lay me by the roadside and come back and get me when you're ready to go back to the station.'

They stood side by side where Birley Lane levelled out before beginning the steep incline down the other side.

'It didn't used to have any streetlights on, this road. It was nightmare to travel it at night, but then, a few years ago, they installed some. They're not the brightest of lights, but they're better than none at all. They would certainly have helped anybody dumping a body after dark. Whether we're looking for man or a woman, they definitely know this area, don't they?'

'They know how to not be seen, that's a fact. So, let's get going and see how they've managed to dispose of a body with apparent ease.'

The downhill side of the road was much shorter than the pa

that they had driven uphill. They stopped every few yards to check any openings, but both of them were clearly disgruntled by the time they reached the bottom.

'I can't see it,' Chris said. 'How the hell did they get into that field while hiding what they were doing? Caught a tram?'

Tia smiled. 'We have conductors and drivers on trams, not sure they'd be allowed to take a dead body on one. And on this stretch of the tram network it isn't even on a road, it runs through this field, so nobody could have seen if anything a bit sus was going on.'

'A bit sus? You mean like carrying a dead body in your arms? Could this spot have been chosen because of exactly that? That they couldn't have been seen?'

'We checked the field yesterday. We saw nothing out of the ordinary. And now we've walked the side of the road next to the field and still seen nothing.'

'Let's head back. We have other avenues to follow, like re-interviewing every woman we've already seen.'

They walked back in the warm sunshine that was promising another beautiful summer day, and stopped at the pub doors.

'Let's see if Maria is ready to go back.'

\* \* \*

Maria was immersed in the transfer of CCTV videos to her memory stick. She looked up as she sensed someone behind her.

'Hiya, you two. I'm downloading everything. These screens here are a bit ancient, so I'm taking it all back to my desk and I'll go through it there. Can you hang on five minutes and I'll go back with you?'

'No problem. I'll go and have a word with the manager, tell

him he can open up in the morning. We should have covered everything by then.'

Tia sat by the side of Maria. 'He's tired.'

'I can see. I think we all are. It's been that sort of a case, hasn't it? We're not able to leave it at work, it's on our minds every bit of the time. And we don't have a big enough team. I might have to plant a little seed about keeping Danny permanently. He's smart, goes above and beyond, a right asset if you ask me.'

'You fancy him.'

'No, I don't.'

'Yes, you do. I'm not daft. But for all the right reasons, you're right about him. He would be good for the team. I'll plant seeds as well. Our erstwhile leader can't hope to win against two women.' She looked up with a smile as Chris rejoined them, completely unaware of their discussion.

'The manager is making us a coffee while we're waiting for Maria to finish up. I don't think we'd have even been offered a glass of water if I hadn't jumped in first to tell him he could open up tomorrow morning.'

\* \* \*

Sally, Tia and Chris crowded together around Sally's desk, as hers was the tidiest. Tia, a newcomer to the discussion, was impressed by her boss and her colleague producing a list of each of the women they had either seen or heard of during the course of the investigation.

'We're taking it as fact that it's a woman?' Tia looked sceptical.

'Not fact, but bordering on a probability. When we get the full report from Kevin, we'll possibly have to change our minds, but at the moment both Sally and I think there's a strong chance it is a woman. As a result, we're going to link up the two lists until they become one, to make sure we've covered every female already met in this case, and then we're going to visit them all. And we have to do this because we have nothing. Even the wheelbarrow has nothing in the way of fingerprints, just a small amount of blood that proved to have come from Lauren. We learnt nothing new.'

Tia looked thoughtful. 'And we're battling time, aren't we? Whoever it is, they're going to be wanting a replacement soon for their sick satisfaction. Okay, I'm on board. Now I want to make a suggestion that we partner differently, because I think you, boss, should be coordinating the rest of us. So, we need a man and a woman in each two-person team, and my suggestion is Maria and Danny, Bryn and Sally, and I'll head off out with Andy. Throughout the interviews we report back to you here in the office, and you can take in any other reports that may need acting upon. We're still waiting for forensics on Hannah, and maybe you could take Paula and Fran to confirm identification of Hannah?'

'You're a star, Tia. That sounds like a plan. I'll leave you to notify everyone. Sally, can you blend these two lists into one, and make sure everyone has a copy in their inbox? I seem to miss out on doing the admin side, so I'll take this couple of days and do the job I'm paid to do in addition to solving murders.'

\* \* \*

Tia worked on notifying the others of the planned day for Friday, and as she pressed send on the emails she waited. She watched Maria open up her emails, and then she saw her head swivel round.

She walked across to the younger woman and grinned. 'You can thank me later,' she whispered.

\*\*\*

The post-mortem report was even more horrific in black and white than it had been in the brief discussion Chris had had with Kevin at the crime scene. Both eyes removed, possibly with skewers, definitely not with a knife. Cuts all over both legs made with a knife, and with soil rubbed into them, causing massive infection, both nipples removed, both pinky fingers removed, dehydration, completely empty stomach. Tramadol and Gabapentin found in system.

No semen present.

Menstruating, old Tampax removed.

Cause of death: heart attack brought on by physical stress. Aggravated by blood infection.

Chris felt sick. Who the hell could do all this, and stand and watch the results? He forwarded the report to the members of his team, then rang Kevin to thank him for the speedy work. He explained they needed to bring Hannah's mother in for a formal identification, and Kevin said it would be okay for Friday afternoon.

He contacted Paula and arranged to collect her and Fran from Fran's home at Gleadless at two o'clock, and then sat back in his chair, and literally drooped. He was tired. He was frustrated by the lack of leads, and the inklings he had always respected in the past seemed to be non-existent with this case.

He left his office and headed out into the main room. Tia was making drinks for everybody, and she was just placing one on Maria's desk. Maria rubbed her eyes, and turned to thank Tia.

'Maria,' he said. 'No more today. No more computer work. It can wait. You've looked at it once at the pub, and it's too much to be repeating it here. It can be done after everybody has finished their interviewing of all these ladies.'

'But...' Maria started to say.

'No buts. My instructions. There seems to have been a lot of computer work with this one, and it's to be shelved for the moment. We may have to work Saturday to finish these interviews, so schedule this memory stick for Monday, okay?'

'Yes, boss.'

'Good. In fact, remove it from the port, and I'll lock it in my drawer.'

Everybody laughed. 'We've all been telling her she's doing too much screen time,' Sally said. 'But don't take her memory stick, she'll go into a decline.'

Tia did a quick head count. 'Right, everybody got a drink?' She handed one to Chris. 'You can take this back to your office, we're having a meeting to decide who's doing what and the plans for tomorrow. I'll keep you informed, but you're not needed for this.'

He felt a little shellshocked, but did as he had been instructed and headed back to his own office, where he allowed his eyes to close for five minutes. When he opened them, his team were all laughing and clapping, obviously having agreed all campaign plans for the following couple of days. It felt good to see how well they all worked together, and he wondered what would happen if he accidentally put in a request for a permanent transfer of Danny from traffic to Major Crimes.

Might be worth a try, he thought. And then, as instructed, began to type up reports of everything completed over the course of the day. His mind would then be free to concentrate on other things such as the deaths of two young women, and not on administrative stuff that, while he appreciated it was a necessary part of the job, he also detested doing.

He finished his rapidly cooling cup of tea and left his own

office to take it back to the kitchen. Maria was gathering her things together ready to head home, and he smiled at her.

'I don't thank you enough,' he said. 'I really am truly grateful for everything you do on that computer, but it is my job to ensure that you are safe doing it, and today you've done enough.'

She nodded. 'I know. The headache was already there, and I was having to rub my eyes to clear my vision, so you stopping me was a smart move. I'm going home to chill, maybe take the dog for a long walk, do normal stuff. And it will be really good to have a couple of days of normal policing, talking to people, using different skills like instinct – but you understand that, don't you?'

He sighed. 'Normally I do. It's a bit lacking with this case as far as I'm concerned, but we will get this killer, don't ever doubt that. We just need it to be soon, before anyone else is taken. That is our biggest worry at the moment, so everybody's instinct needs to be on full alert over the next couple of days.'

Maria slung her bag strap over her shoulder. 'Don't worry, Tia has us organised, and the ladies on that list are going to be mighty surprised when we come knocking on their doors tomorrow. And I'm taking the memory stick home with me, just in case I need something to do over the weekend.'

## 28

It was a sombre gathering that Friday morning, with all six aware of the importance of what they were about to do. Tia checked everyone had a notebook and at least two pens – nothing worse than a pen suddenly deciding it couldn't produce another drop of ink, she had said.

Frank was a little surprised to see such a mass exodus of the Major Crimes team, minus their boss, but a quick shrug dismissed the thought from his mind. That new DI seemed a canny lad, and he would know what they were doing.

And the canny lad did feel better. He had enjoyed a FaceTime call with the kids the previous night because they had now returned from their impromptu holiday, and they looked so brown and healthy. They had made arrangements for him to drive up and collect them in two weeks' time, for a long weekend with him before their return to school. He missed them so much and FaceTime calls didn't really fill the gap – he needed to hug them, to laugh with them at the stupid television programmes they all enjoyed watching, to just be with them. It was only later that he had realised he didn't actually miss his ex-wife.

\*  \*  \*

The visits had taken some organising, so Tia hadn't had an easy night chatting to anybody, FaceTime or otherwise. She had tried to get every female grouped into three separate areas, then juggle around with them to save any crossovers. Finally it had looked okay, and she had emailed it to herself so that it was simply a matter of printing off six copies when she arrived at work.

Seven copies. She realised that while she had tried to protect Chris a little, to give him time to do other things, he would still need to know what they were doing and where they were.

It was her final thought of the night as she wearily climbed the stairs to go to bed, but it dawned on her that if their theory was correct and it was a woman doing these awful things, tomorrow, two of them could potentially be speaking to the killer.

She didn't sleep much; her dreams were vivid, not very nice, and definitely not worth going back to sleep for. She gave in at six, got up, had a huge mug of coffee and drove to work, booking out three squad cars immediately upon her arrival.

They had decided it would be a smart idea, and slightly intimidating, to advertise just who they were, visiting several homes in the area that was all too aware of the two murdered girls who had lived in their community.

\*  \*  \*

They disappeared on the dot of half past eight, and Chris's last words to all of them were, 'Keep me informed.'

Danny and Maria reached their car and Danny looked at her with an eyebrow raised. 'You or me?' he said, waving the keys at her.

'You done the advanced course?'

'All of them,' he grinned.

'Then you drive, I'll sleep.'

They got in the car and he turned to look at her. 'I really don't mind doing the driving, just to let you know. If you want to take over, tell me. That okay?'

'It's absolutely fine. For me, driving is a necessity, I rarely do it for the hell of it, so I'm quite happy to be the passenger who sits and thinks.'

They didn't talk much until they reached their first address, a lady by the name of Marsha Jackson, who worked at Griffiths Accountancy. She was standing in her doorway as they pulled up, and she frowned.

'Can I help you?'

Both officers held out their warrant cards, and Maria introduced them.

'I'm just about to leave for work. Can it wait?'

'No, I'm sorry, it can't. Can you call work and explain you'll be a little late? I'm sure it won't take long, but we do need to speak with you.'

Reluctantly the front door was held open for them to enter, and she led them through to the kitchen. She took out her phone, rang the office and explained to the answer machine that she would be in later because the police had just arrived to speak with her. She disconnected and sat down at the table opposite Maria and Danny.

'You live here alone?' Maria opened the questioning.

'No, my husband has already left for work. Did you need to speak to him as well?'

'No, that's fine, just you. As you probably realise, this is about the Lauren Pascoe and Hannah Wrightson investigation. With the finding of Hannah's body, linking the two investigations definitively, this has escalated the danger to all women, because it seems that this killer needs to have an abductee. However, Lauren and Hannah were connected. I can't go into details, but we're now re-interviewing everyone who has even the most minimal connection to them. This is partly to put them on their guard because the killer is still walking, probably driving, the streets, but partly to try and draw out further information that we didn't collect at the beginning of the investigation.'

Maria's words seemed to soften Marsha's attitude, and she gave a gentle nod. 'Then thank you, I appreciate this. Hannah and I didn't mix outside of work, but of course I knew her at work. This has quite devastated all of us hearing that her body has now been found, but I'm not sure I have anything to add to my first statement. She was a lot younger than me, and apart from a love of reading and of books in general, we had a working relationship only. I used to know her mum because we went to school together, but once we'd left school, I don't think I saw her again until she popped into the office one day to see Hannah about something. It was really strange how we recognised each other after all these years.'

'And can you remember what she came to see Hannah about?'

'I can, as it happens. Paula had been across the road to the charity shop to drop some stuff off for them, and had picked up a couple of books for Hannah, both J. D. Robb, who Hannah really enjoyed.' She stood. 'One minute.'

She returned holding two books. 'These are the books, Hannah passed them on to me after finishing them. As I say, this was a shared enjoyment between us, but that was really our only connection. I'm sorry I can't really help you.'

Danny flicked through both books, then placed them back on the table with a brief shake of his head to indicate there was nothing in them apart from J. D. Robb's own words.

Maria entered the titles in her notebook, noted that Marsha had known Paula at school, and they both stood. Maria handed the woman her card with a request that she contact her if she remembered anything else, and all three of them walked to the door.

Maria turned. 'You didn't know Lauren Pascoe?'

'Briefly. Very briefly. She only worked at the accountants for a day or so, her heart was set on being a vet, and if she'd only waited a further week we wouldn't actually have known her at all. I seem to remember she said she had been good at maths at school, and so thought she could maybe carry that on into a career, but the animals were a stronger calling, clearly. I don't think I ever saw her again after that day. Slip of a thing, she was, a bit like Hannah to be honest. She never even made it to the payroll, said she didn't want paying because she hadn't actually done anything except a bit of photocopying and running errands.'

They went their separate ways, and Maria completed her notes in her book. Finally she turned to look at Danny. 'Well?'

'Smart woman, once she'd got over the shock of a police car pulling up outside her garden gate. I felt nothing, no worries, no alarm bells, and she was quite forthcoming with whatever she told us. How did you feel?'

'The same. And it will give her something to tell the others at work, won't it? We probably made her day, although she was definitely annoyed when we first arrived.' She gave a brief smile. 'And we're quite nice really.'

'You are,' he said, and switched on the engine. 'You want to put the next address into the sat nav? I've no idea where it is.'

'Huh? Thought you were in traffic!'

He laughed and set off. 'Just find me a route, woman. You're much smarter than me.'

* * *

Bryn and Sally arrived at their destination with Bryn having handed over the keys to his partner with some alacrity. 'Got a thumping headache. I've taken some painkillers, so I'll drive when they start working, but think we'd be better with you behind the wheel at this moment in time.'

'No problem,' she said. 'Too much beer last night?'

'I wish. No, I think it's lack of sleep. This case has really got to me, to the extent that as soon as my head touches the pillow, it starts galloping round my brain. I should have taken some tablets earlier but I'm an idiot and thought it would go away. It hasn't, so tablets now taken. I just think we'll survive the journey if you drive.'

The journey out to Hillsborough took some time, but they were keen to get this one out of the way. The lady's name was Caroline Bent and she hadn't been interviewed before. She was also on the employee list for Griffiths Accountancy, but off work due to illness. Mark Griffiths had explained at the beginning of the investigation that she was a senior member of his staff who was currently in hospital having a hysterectomy.

Sally figured the lady would be expecting them at some point but they had taken the decision to keep it pretty informal and just turn up.

Caroline opened the door wearing a pink fluffy dressing gown and huge pink fluffy slippers.

'Hi,' she said quietly. 'If you'd warned me, I would have made sure I was dressed.'

'It's why we didn't,' Sally said. 'You need to be comfortable, you're recovering, not dressing up for visitors. Can we come in?'

Caroline led them through to the lounge, where she sank o

to the sofa, indicating the two chairs for the officers. Introductions were made, and Sally asked if Caroline needed anything.

'No, I'm fine. Currently living pretty much on water, but I'm a lot better than I was a couple of weeks ago. I'm getting there, and the results from the hospital were encouraging. They were removing cancer with this hysterectomy. Please don't mention that to any of the others at Griffiths, they think it was just a straightforward operation to remove bits I no longer need. It wasn't.'

'Then we both hope things continue to improve and they've managed to get rid of it. We won't keep you long, we're out interviewing every woman who has had a connection, however minor, to the Lauren Pascoe and Hannah Wrightson case.'

'I knew Hannah quite well, really liked her. Nothing was too much trouble, and she was quite a knowledgeable person. I suppose because she was an avid reader. Some people are a loss to this world, and Hannah was one of them.'

'And that's a lovely thing to say. Did you ever go out with her, socialise in any way?'

'No, but that's me really. I don't particularly socialise, I'm definitely a homebody. I make things, and that's my enjoyment, although I'm sure I'd spend less money if I did go out getting drunk every night,' Caroline added, smiling.

'What do you make?'

'I do a lot of paper crafting, "have spare room, have a studio" is my motto. I make junk journals, which I can tell from the blank looks on your faces you don't know what I'm talking about, I always make any birthday, Christmas cards I send, and I knit and crochet when I'm not in the studio. I've crocheted many a blanket while pretending to watch football with my husband. I'm just a creative person, and it's getting me through this awful time,' she said, pointing to the half-finished pink and white blanket at the side of her on the sofa.

Both officers stood. Bryn handed her his card, and they left her still sitting on the sofa, asking that they see themselves out.

'So glad I'm not a woman,' Bryn said as they settled back into the car. 'She was in pain.'

Sally nodded. 'She certainly was.'

# 29

Andy and Tia had opted for the list of women the closest to Moss Way, and headed up to the Griffiths's place as their starting point.

Mark Griffiths came down to greet them. 'You seem to be disrupting my ladies this morning,' he said with a smile. 'Marsha has rung in to say two police officers are grilling her mercilessly, and now you're here disturbing the peace in my domain.'

'They grilled mercilessly?' Tia asked. 'I trained them well. Do you by any chance have a spare room we can borrow for a couple of hours? We need to chat to three more of your ladies, and this will save us having to visit their homes.'

'Of course. My assistant is with a client for a couple of days working on site, so his office is free. If you'd like to follow me?'

He led them to what used to be his own office, and showed them in. 'I'll have our receptionist bring you drinks. Tea? Coffee?'

'Both coffee, white, no sugar, thanks,' Tia said. 'We need to speak with Rose Arnott, Olivia Chase and Lyra Grayson. Singly.'

'No problem. Lyra will bring you your drinks, so I'll prewarn her she will be staying to answer a few questions. Don't scare her, she's a very meek and mild lassie.'

'We don't scare anybody,' Tia said, smiling at him.

'You scare me,' he said as he left the office.

Andy burst out laughing. 'Well, that's told you, DS Monroe. I always said you were scary.'

A few minutes later there was a strange knock on the door and Andy went to open it. Lyra was standing before it, holding a tray of drinks and biscuits. 'I had to knock with my head,' she explained. 'Two coffees, no sugar, and some biscuits so Mr Griffiths said.'

Andy took the tray from her. 'Thank you, Lyra. We just need a quick chat with you, won't take long, I promise.'

She sat down opposite the two officers, and brushed her fringe from her eyes. 'This is about Hannah?'

'It is. You didn't know Lauren?'

'Only of her, didn't actually know her. I was still at school when she was here. Since all this has blown up with Hannah, and you finding Lauren's body anyway, it's kind of been the thing everybody's talking about, but even Hannah, I didn't know that well.'

'You now work on reception?'

'I do. I was set on as an office junior, doing post, photocopying, making drinks, all that sort of stuff, but I've been on reception since the day Hannah disappeared, and now it's an official position with a pay rise. I enjoy it.'

'So, the day Hannah was taken. Do you remember anything at all?'

'Not really. I was going to go for the milk...' Lyra hesitated and then realised the implication of what she had just said. 'I was supposed to go for the milk, that was part of my job, but Hannah asked me to sit on reception for a couple of minutes while she went. She said her period was due and she wanted to pick up some tampons, and maybe get her mum some flowers.' Tears appeared in her eyes. 'Was she taken instead of me? I should have gone to the shop! I should have been taken!'

Tia shot around the desk and pulled the young girl close to her. 'Don't ever think that, Lyra,' she said, into the girl's hair. 'We can't possibly know that. Nothing that happened was a result of you not doing something. We believe Hannah was targeted for some reason, and once we know that reason, we will know the killer. And just to put a smile back on that pretty face, you're too tall anyway. Not to say you shouldn't still be cautious now. But we think one of the reasons Hannah was targeted was because she was small and easily manhandled, as was Lauren. They were both five feet tall, you're what? Around five feet six?'

She sniffled, and reached for a tissue on the desk. 'I am. Both Mum and Dad are tall, I'll say a special thank you to them tonight.'

Tia returned to her chair. 'And that's it? Think carefully. Did you see anything out of the office door or window that made you think?'

Lyra closed her eyes for a moment, trying to take herself back to that awful day. She sighed. 'I'm sorry, it all seemed so everyday and normal. Trams going past, cars always going past, nothing that would make me feel it was wrong. I wish I could help more, I miss Hannah, she was always so nice. She got me reading books, lent me a couple and since then I'm always across the road at the charity shop. Mum bought me a Kindle, and that's magic. I can have it under my reception counter and nobody knows I'm reading. Don't tell Mr Griffiths though.'

Andy handed her his card. 'If you do remember anything, give me a call will you, Lyra? And good luck with the rest of your career, whether it be here or in a library.'

She smiled. 'Plans are in place. Sssh. Who would you like me send in now?'

'Rose Arnott, please.'

* * *

'Lovely girl.' Andy picked up a fig biscuit. 'Love these.'

'She is. It rattled her to think it could have been her, and it actually could. I know I tried to reassure her by saying she was too tall, but she's no weight on her. It could have been her, so was Hannah targeted, or could it have been anyone being bundled into that van? I don't suppose we can guess, but I tried to stop her thinking like that.'

There was a gentle knock on the door and Rose popped her head around it. 'You need me?'

'Is it okay if we call you Rose?' Andy asked.

'Call me whatever you want. I'm a rose by any other name type of person.'

'Oh, smart. I like that.' Tia grinned at her. 'Okay, Rose, you've probably worked out why we're here, and I know we've interviewed and taken a statement already from you, but things have moved on now with the discovery of Hannah's body. We are re-interviewing a significant number of people we've already spoken to, partly because we believe things occur to witnesses who don't realise they have witnessed something. A second chat usually jogs memories, there is something there to jog, so please don't think you're suspect, you definitely aren't, you're simply somebody who could have seen or known something that would lead us to the killer.'

Rose gave a slight nod. 'Neither Olivia nor I can actually see anything out of our office windows. I know we look out onto the main road, but it's frosted glass, unlike the window that looks out of the reception area. We hear the trams rattling past, but w don't see them. It suits us that it's like that, we just get on with our work without distractions.'

'And what do you do?'

'PA duties. All the letters, anything that needs typing I type, organise couriers for returning sets of accounts, I do anything that needs doing that is remotely admin. I also do wages. Mr Griffiths gave me specific instructions to pay Hannah until she returned to us.' Her head dropped and she stared at her clasped hands. 'I'm sorry, I keep crying. I can't believe this has happened. She was so lovely, never said a bad word about anybody…'

Tia nodded. 'You've said exactly the same as everyone else has said. And I'm sorry we couldn't bring her safely back to you. We're all working twenty hours a day at the moment, trying to find this killer. And we will.'

'Lauren was a sweet girl as well. I tried to persuade her to stay when she told me she didn't want paying for that day she was with us, but she was so set on a career with animals. Why would anyone want to hurt them, DS Monroe?'

'It's what we've all asked so many times, and at the moment we don't know, but I firmly believe this re-interviewing of people is going to give us the answer. Nothing has occurred to you since our first conversation?'

Rose shook her head. 'No, and I've never stopped thinking about it.'

Andy handed her his card. 'Just in case something jogs your memory,' he said. 'Thank you, Rose. Will you ask Olivia to step in, please?'

* * *

'And how long have you worked here?' Tia was curious. Olivia was older than Rose by ten years.

'Since Mr Eke first started the business. We both cut the ribbon across the door on the opening day. He was that sort of man, lovely sense of humour, would do anything for anyone. It wasn't so easy-going when Mr Griffiths started, it seemed to all become much more official and less personal, but it's still a good place to work. I have my own clients, usually work in here, but occasionally, with the bigger clients, I go to their premises for a few days at a time. I just do what I have to do, in the best way possible. I shall be retiring in two years, because we now have grandchildren, a cottage in the Yorkshire Dales as a holiday home, and we have plans to travel more, so my husband and I will both retire at the same time. Mr Griffiths isn't aware of this yet, so please don't say anything. I'll tell him this time next year, give him enough time to find my replacement.'

'How well did you know Hannah?'

'Not well, I'm afraid. She called me Mrs Chase instead of Olivia, so that was the relationship we had. Distant, I would say, but I did appreciate the job she did. And she was so scared the day Mr Eke lost everything. I thought she would walk away from her job after that, but she didn't. He'd been funny with her, wouldn't cooperate when she had one of his clients waiting to see him who was turning a bit nasty, and she was the first there when he was smashing everything up. We were all scared, and after the ambulance had sedated him and taken him away, Mr Griffiths sent everybody home, and told them not to return the following day. The day after would be soon enough, he needed to get things repaired and tidied. But Hannah ignored him and came in the following day. She helped him with all the cleaning up, got a skip outside and loaded it up with smashed furniture, generally began to put the business back together for us all to return. Mr Griffiths told me she'd been a star. And now she's an extinguished star. It's so awful.'

'Thank you, Olivia,' Tia said. 'Andy is giving you his card in case you remember anything else.'

Olivia nodded and closed the door behind her.

\* \* \*

The two detectives spoke with Lyra as they left, handing the tray back to her. 'Thank you, Lyra. And if plans are in place, as you said, good luck with them.' Tia smiled at the young girl. 'I worked in a chemist shop when I left school, but I always hankered after being in the police. Just reach for your own stars, I did.'

# 30

By the end of Friday, the bulk of the interviews had been completed, leaving just four names, all within the Owlthorpe area, to cover and sign off.

The full team of seven sat around the briefing table, their notebooks full of notes. Chris stood and clapped his hands, not to draw their attention to him but to congratulate them on a fantastic day's work.

'You're an amazing lot,' he said. 'When I took this job, I had no idea what I would face. I thought I'd have had a bigger team, but it doesn't seem to matter. You do the work of a dozen officers! Today has been huge, whether it throws up any answers or not. The four left to do tomorrow are local to the station, so having had an enforced day of rest, I propose to take on this last four, and the rest of you can type up the reports from the ones that have been seen. Either do it from home, or come in here, it doesn't matter, but it's a routine job that shouldn't take too long, and one that we need for Monday morning. Then we'll convene at seven-thirty Monday and thrash everything out. This is why we need the reports doing tomorrow. Somewhere in the interviews there must be some answers, if everything we believe is correct. Split the reports between each pair, so we're not duplicating stuff, that halves the chore. Say thank you, boss.'

There was a chorus of 'Thank you, boss,' from around the table, not said with much enthusiasm due to tiredness, lack of food and water, and over-heating throughout the long day.

'You're very welcome. I'll type up my own four interviews, so I will feel your pain, I promise you.'

Tia sighed. 'Did we get a choice about which DI we wanted?' she asked the others.

'You asked for the best, so I understand,' said Chris, smirking at everybody. 'And you got it. I buy you coffees on a regular basis, don't I?'

They were tired. From the bits of conversation he had picked up on, it had been a hard day. Hannah had been well loved, mentioned time and time again in all the reports, and emotionally it had been extra difficult. There had been tears, there had been anger that the police still hadn't solved anything, and he looked at all of them.

'Okay, seriously now. Go home. Thank you for not just going out there today, but for all the organisation that went into it. Every one of you is a star, and let's hope we get the right answers from this. Disappear, everybody, I'll see you all Monday, but if you need me, ring me.'

He picked up his papers, and headed back to his office. Everybody stood, and clapped him.

He turned round, grinned, and said, 'Aw, shucks,' before going into his own room. Then he stepped back out. 'Danny, a quick word?'

Danny froze. No. He didn't want to be told his loan period was over. No, he didn't want to go back to dishing out speeding fines and use of phone fines. No, no, no! He walked slowly to Chris's office, and through the door left open for him.

'Come in, Danny. As you know, I'm new here, and when I was offered the job I was told I would have a team of six. It seems somebody can't count because I only have a permanent team of five. I've thrown a bit of a wobbly about it, not a lot of a wobbly, and it seems I can add one to that team, so I've sent a requisition slip in for you, if that's okay. To be permanently transferred from traffic to Major Crimes.'

Danny's mouth opened and closed. Twice.

'Is that okay?'

'Yes, sir. Boss. DI Chandler. Yes, boss. Oh my God. Wait till my mum hears about this!'

Chris laughed. 'Best go home and tell her then. See you Monday, and not in uniform. Okay?'

Danny headed back out to the briefing room where the rest of the team expected to hear he'd got to return to his old post. He told them the news, and Chris heard the cheers and the clap from behind his own closed door. A popular choice then. He had a happy team.

* * *

Tia knocked and opened his door. 'Night, boss. I'm the last one, the others have gone. Don't work too late. What time you here in the morning?'

'I reckon I need to be at the first address by nine, as it's Saturday. They should be up by then.'

She nodded. 'I'll be here.'

'What?'

'Your instructions. We can't go anywhere on our own. So I be here. Don't worry, I had nothing to do tomorrow except wri up the reports, do my laundry and hoover the stairs. I'll be here,' she repeated.

'No, whoever is doing this isn't after a man. Go and hoover your stairs.'

'Sorry, DI Chandler. Instructions are instructions. I'll be here. And don't think you can go early and get away without me, I've got the list, remember? I'll find you.'

He sighed. 'Okay. I'll buy two coffees.'

She smiled. 'Good lad. I knew you'd see sense. Have a good night's sleep. It will be emotional tomorrow. It certainly has been today. Young Lyra, the receptionist at Griffiths, actually cried because she suddenly realised it could have been her that was taken. She was supposed to fetch the milk. And everybody has only had good things to say about Hannah. Not so much Lauren because it's not recent enough, but Hannah is.'

Chris nodded. 'We'll find the bastard, Tia, don't fret. Anybody who can stick skewers into eyes while the person is still alive has to be sent down for life without the possibility of parole, and I think it will just be one small thing that stands out to one of us that does it.'

She nodded and turned to leave. 'Smart move with Danny. We all like him, and he's a bright kid. He'll do well with us. And Maria.'

She closed the door and walked across the briefing room before he managed to get his door open.

'Have I missed something?'

'No, boss,' she said. 'Nothing at all. Yet.'

\* \* \*

'We had a bit of a thing with the police today.' Mark paused to let that sink in.

'A bit of a thing?' Ray spoke quietly.

'Mmm, didn't speak to me but they spoke to our ladies, at some length as well.'

'About Hannah?'

'And Lauren, apparently. They seem a bit fixated on the fact that she was here for a day, but it was more about Hannah and about the day she went missing. It's upset Lyra quite a lot, because she's kind of profited from it by being offered the receptionist job rather than just an office junior, but she was offered that because she's earned it. She does a good job, has a nice way of speaking to clients, and she just gets on with things.'

'Thanks for letting me know. I don't think they'll be here again, I've seen them several times, but as I keep telling them, I only found Lauren's body, didn't see anything, don't know anything, and finding the barrow was a bit of calculated guesswork because it was such a new-looking barrow. Nobody would have just dumped it, unless they felt they had to. They were just fed up with pushing it or something. I don't know. Anyway, I've repeated it so many times now I think they're fed up with hearing it.'

'You fancy the gym tomorrow?'

'Why not? What time?'

'I'll pick you up at ten.'

They said goodbye and disconnected, leaving Ray feeling slightly bewildered and at odds with the world. The police seemed to be doing a bit of straw-clutching by revisiting the accountancy company, and there had been nothing on the news to indicate that they had a suspect they needed help with finding, which was the usual pattern of things these days.

He moved to his piano, and began to play some Beethoven, allowing the notes to wash over him, to soothe him, to bring him into a world he preferred. He thought about Ziggy, about the way she supported him, and knew she would feel quite angry if he told her the women at Griffiths had been questioned yet again. There would be words like 'harassment' bandied around, and he would have to calm her down with a spot or two of Gershwin. That usually worked. But maybe it was better not to say anything. Maybe he should have mentioned it to Mark not to talk to her about it.

He decided he would wait outside for Mark's arrival the following morning, negating any possibility of Ziggy hearing about it, and then he could ask him not to bring it up if he bumped into her anywhere. If only the damn police would get on with it and cold case it for lack of evidence, life would be much easier for this superb litter-picker, he thought to himself.

\* \* \*

Tia made herself a salad, and added some prawns and a hard-boiled egg to her plate. She opened the fridge to see what was in it now she'd emptied her salad bowl, and found there was precious little. She decided she had better go food shopping after her morning with the boss, things were getting to be a bit lacking in sustenance.

She carried the plate out to the back garden, along with a glass of Coke, and decided she actually didn't want to eat it. She felt tired. The emotions of the day had drained her, and she felt so sorry for Lyra Grayson. The second she realised it could have been her and not Hannah who had been snatched had been heartbreaking.

Tears had followed and Tia had felt compelled to make the somewhat stupid comment about Lyra being too tall. Lyra hadn't been aware they were looking at a woman as being the killer, and she couldn't tell her that. She knew she would go back to the girl when the killer was actually locked up, and explain the reasoning behind her comment about Lyra's height.

She popped a prawn in her mouth, but didn't really taste it. Another one followed until she was at the stage where the prawns had disappeared, along with the egg. What was left was basically green, and she had decided long ago that if it was green, it was probably tasteless and/or inedible, so she pushed the plate to one side and picked up her glass of Coke.

The sun was setting, and it was a truly beautiful evening. It was days and evenings like this that woke her up to what Lauren and Hannah had lost, and yet she knew beyond any shadow of a doubt that they would have welcomed death.

Whoever the killer was, she hoped they would get a life sentence, and wished with all her heart that the judge be able to specify without the possibility of parole. This was a dangerous person, and they should never be allowed out into the world again. The danger to the public was evident.

She also wished Janey and Paula didn't have to attend court, but knew they would. They would hear the results of the post-mortems, and even though Tia had no kids, she knew she would never want to hear anything so horrific as Janey and Paula would hear.

She carried her plate back inside the house, finished the Coke and washed the few dishes left in the bowl. She climbed the stairs slowly, feeling so, so weary, jumped under the shower for around thirty seconds, and dried herself before putting on her pyjamas. Within a minute she was in bed, and setting an alarm for 7 a.m. She had no intention of being late – she suspected Chris would go without her, and she was determined that wasn't going to happen. She picked up her Kindle, read one page and it fell out of her hands onto the floor.

# 31

Chris intended arriving early, checking his emails and any reports that had already been filed, then being on his way by eight o'clock. Tia was already there when he arrived.

She laughed at the expression on his face. 'You thought you could leave before I got here, didn't you? Honestly, boss, I've had ten hours' uninterrupted sleep and I'm fine. Raring to go and get this finished. Once we have all the reports and can compare stuff, we'll know the next step.'

'I did intend going without you. You did enough yesterday, but I give up. I'll nip out and get us two huge coffees, and when we've drunk them, we'll set off. Okay?'

She nodded and smiled at him. 'I quite like you when you're being sensible.'

'Oh, good,' he said, and left to walk down to Starbucks.

\* \* \*

By nine o'clock they were outside Janey Pascoe's home. The last four names on their list were the ones closest to Moss Way, and although it was generally agreed that Janey Pascoe and Paula Wrightson were in no way on their suspect list, it was felt that they still had to be interviewed as they were females, and they might just use a throw-away statement that led to another avenue to follow.

Janey Pascoe was puzzled, but she simply opened her door and invited them in.

Chris spent some time explaining the situation, and telling her as much as he dared about why they were there, and in the end it brought a smile to her face.

'DI Chandler, I completely understand that for an exercise to be fully completed, I have to be included. I'm not sure I can help but ask away. Stop behaving as though I'm some fragile teenager who doesn't recognise what is happening, and believe me, understand the need for speed. Now you've found Hannah Wrightson, another girl could disappear at any time. What do you need to know?'

'Probably nothing that you haven't already told us. Did Lauren ever mention she was scared of anyone? Concerned by someone's behaviour, particularly towards her?'

Janey closed her eyes for a moment as she thought back over the years. 'No, I can't remember anything. But don't forget I'm having to think back three years with this. She wasn't a girl who would allow anyone to intimidate her, I can tell you that. Growing up without a father figure, I brought her up to be a bit of a tough cookie, because that's the way I had to live my life. She wasn't scared of anything, my Lauren.'

'She didn't have a father?'

'No, nor a grandfather. My mother was a single parent because my father died before I was born. She never remarried, died quite young of a heart attack. So I've had very little support in the bringing up of Lauren, but I did good, I think. We were so close...'

'So you had contact of some sort with Lauren every day?'

'I did. It's why I panicked so early on, because I knew she had to be in some sort of trouble if she didn't ring or just walk through the door. During this investigation I've told you everything I can remember, but we led a simple, uncomplicated life, did most things together. Please don't tell me that's why she paid such a high price...'

'We don't know why Lauren was picked out to be a victim, but there are similarities with the kidnap of Hannah Wrightson.'

'In what way?'

'Lifestyle. Hannah had the same sort of relationship with her mum, Paula Wrightson. It may be completely irrelevant, but it is a fact that's been included in our investigation.'

Tia had been making notes, and now she looked up at Janey. 'Without us asking any more questions and leading you into answers, can you think of anything else that could possibly have some sort of bearing on this case?'

Janey sat back in her chair, deep in thought. Eventually she shook her head. 'I've got used to being without her, her laughter, her jokes, her lovely nature. For me, she will never die, so whoever did this to my beautiful girl, I hope she rots in hell.'

'She?'

'You think I'm daft? You said you're interviewing females. You've got something that's telling you it's probably a woman who's killed my Lauren. I'm not asking you to tell me anything more, because I think you know that if I find out who it is and can get to them before you do, you won't have anyone to stand in front of a judge.'

Neither officer spoke, each recognising the power inherent in

Janey's statement. Tia put away her notebook, and they both stood. Chris looked at the brave woman standing in front of him, and pulled her towards him for a hug. She folded herself into him, and he whispered, 'We'll get whoever did this. And as soon as we do, I'm coming to tell you.'

\* \* \*

Paula Wrightson wasn't at home, so Tia called her. It appeared she was still at her sister's for the next few days, so Tia said they would call round just for a chat and a bit of a welfare check when she returned to her own home.

\* \* \*

The next on the list of four names was Ziggy Duly, followed by her neighbour across the road, Janet Standall.

'Half an hour and we should be done. We can go back, type up reports and go home. Then the real work starts with reading every report and seeing if anything at all links up, or if anybody has changed their story in any way. I feel strongly that something is going to come of this exercise, although I have to admit we're not there yet.' Chris got into the driver's seat, and Tia slid by his side.

'These are two elderly ladies,' she said. 'Ms Duly is only on our list because she's the mother of Ray Eke, and so far hasn't been anywhere on our radar other than as an address to contact Ray. I'm not expecting a lot from her. And Janet Standall is an even more tenuous link, she's just a friend of Ziggy Duly. We've just got her as a name only. No activity beyond that. But she's a female, so we'll talk to her. She could be the one who says, "Yes, I know of a local kidnapper, her name is Mary Smith."'

Chris laughed. 'Love your optimism, Tia. You do know I'll probably collapse on the floor if that scenario happens?'

'I'll pick you up.'

'Thanks.' He pulled away from Paula's home and drove up the road, hoping he would be able to keep a straight face when they reached their final destination of Janet Standall's home.

\* \* \*

Ray was standing by Mark Griffiths's car as they pulled up. He waited, assuming they were there to see him, but Chris explained they were there to chat to his mother.

'Completely routine, and nothing to concern you. We're just interviewing every female we've come into contact with during this investigation, checking really that they haven't thought of something new since we last spoke to them. You off to the gym?'

'Yes, it's the bullying side of Mark showing clearly. Every so often he turns up and I have to go and do all sorts of unnatural exercises on strange equipment. I enjoy the coffee and buns afterwards though.'

'Have a good day. Your mum is in?'

'She is. Saturday is laundry day. Especially when the sun is shining.'

He climbed into the car, and Chris and Tia waited until they drove off before heading towards the front door.

It opened before they reached it. Ziggy smiled. 'I saw you chatting to Ray. You didn't want him?'

'No,' Tia confirmed. 'Just a quick few minutes with you as part of our investigation, and it's only because you're a name on the periphery of the case.'

'You'd best come in then. Don't want the neighbours thinking you're here to arrest me. Can I make you a tea? Coffee?'

'A glass of water would be good,' Chris said. 'Probably for both of us. It's turning really warm out there. It'll certainly dry your washing today.'

She led them into the coolness of the lounge. 'No sun reaches this room until mid-afternoon, so it stays relatively cool until then. I'll get your drinks. Make yourself at home.'

Tia sat in the armchair nearest the fireplace, and Chris walked around the room, looking at photographs. They were only of Ray and Ziggy. He felt a little sad that it seemed they were so insular.

He sat as Ziggy returned to them carrying three glasses of iced water on a tray.

'That looks so inviting,' Chris said, smiling at their host. 'We had Starbucks lattes earlier, and I've wanted a water ever since.'

He took a long cooling drink of it, and then sat back. 'Just what the doctor ordered,' he said. 'So, you're probably wondering why we're here, and just for reassurance we're not really here for anything. We decided to separate the men from the women in our investigation, and every name that has been in the investigation in some way, no matter how small, has been visited. Sometimes people think about things after we've spoken to them once, and our turning up triggers it again and they speak about it. It's like a safety net for gathering in stray bits of information. We've almost seen everyone now.'

'And I'm on your list because I'm a mother?'

'That's right. The mother of our lovely Ray,' he said with a smile. 'You knew Hannah?'

'I did. Not well, but she was always on reception if ever called in to see Ray for anything. A very pleasant girl. I'm sure she has been missed. I haven't seen her for some time, as I have no reason for calling in now, of course.'

'And did you know Lauren?'

*The Missing Ones*

'No. Not at all.'

Tia continued to take notes. She rather liked this woman, and could see where Ray got his gentleness from.

'Do you have a vehicle, Ms Duly?'

'Please call me Ziggy. Everybody else does, they can't get their heads around Duly as a surname. The men in my life blessed both me and my son with strange surnames. And I sort of have a vehicle. I share a white Astra with my son. It's in the garage if you need to see it. And I say share it in the very loosest possible way. It's registered in Ray's name, but we're both on the insurance. Ray hasn't driven anything, not even a bike, since he had his breakdown. I do all the driving, take him to any appointments he may have, and please don't think I'm complaining because I'm not. It's a lovely automatic car, I enjoy driving anyway, and Ray simply doesn't have the confidence any more to drive. He walks miles, and for work he catches a tram. I've lived here for a long time now, and I suppose I'll stay here until he says he's ready to be on his own again. I look forward to that day, because I did have a separate life completely until he became ill. I closed down my own house, and became a hands-on mother to a grown-up child, who has morphed slowly back into the adult he used to be. It was a massive day when he sat at the piano and played a very simple tune. He's not ready to be left yet, he says, and he's promised he will tell me when he is ready. So I look after him, his home, and help with the garden, I crochet, I knit, I read, and when things start to overwhelm even me, I get in the car and I drive.'

Ray and Tia looked at each other, and nodded. Time to go. 'Thank you so much, Ziggy, and we're both really pleased Ray is turning his life around. I think we've held you up enough, so we'll let you get back to whatever you were doing.'

They all heard three beeps and she laughed. 'Perfect timing, my washer is demanding my attention. Can you see yourselves out?'

'No problem,' Tia said. 'I'll just look through the garage window and confirm the car, and we'll be out of your hair.' They separated at the lounge door, heading in opposite directions as Ziggy went to take full advantage of the sunshine waiting to dry her sheets.

## 32

Chris and Tia didn't discuss anything other than Tia confirming there was indeed a white Astra in the garage and no white van. She laughed as she said it.

They walked across the road to the final visit on their list. All they knew about Janet Standall was that she was a close friend of Ziggy, who visited Janet several times a week to teach her how to crochet. Ray had said he was often alone at night as the two women shared their love of the hobby.

'This should be fast and easy,' Chris said. 'I know you took a lot of notes in Ziggy's place, but I think it'll be a bit slower pace in here. She's not actually connected to anything, just on our radar as the friend who gives Ziggy alibis for nearly every night of the week.' He lifted his hand, saw the knocker was a wise old owl, and banged it.

Janet answered the door, and held it open without them having to say anything. 'I spotted the squad car,' she said by way of explanation. 'Please, come in. It'll have to be in the kitchen, I'm in the middle of baking some biscuits.'

'No problem,' Tia said, and they followed the apron-clad

figure of the elderly woman down a long hallway. The kitchen door was at the end, and the kitchen itself overlooked a magnificent back garden full of colour.

'Wow,' Tia said, drifting towards the large window. 'That is amazing.'

'My husband loves his garden. He's in the greenhouse at the moment. Do you need both of us?'

'No,' Chris said. 'Just you. I'm DI Chandler and this is DS Monroe. We're working on the Hannah Wrightson and Lauren Pascoe cases, and during the course of our preliminary investigations your name cropped up simply for being a close friend of Ziggy, across the road.'

Janet picked up her rolling pin, and began to flatten the mound of pastry rolled into a perfect ball.

'Close friend? Is that what she said?'

'No, she didn't actually. I believe it was her son who spoke about your friendship. He said his mother came across to your home several evenings a week because she was teaching you how to crochet.'

She put down the rolling pin and frowned.

'But that doesn't make sense. Sorry, my manners are all over the place. Would you like a drink?'

Tia said no, but Chris recognised he needed to say yes. This woman needed to talk to them.

'Cancel what my colleague said,' he said, 'we'd actually love a coffee if that's okay.'

'Of course it is. I'd best make one for Philip as well, he's always ready for a drink.' She switched on the kettle and took down four mugs from a mug tree.

\* \* \*

*The Missing Ones*

The questioning resumed with coffees in front of all of them, biscuits in the oven, and Philip also at the table as a bemused bystander. He had absolutely no idea why the police would be wanting to question his wife; she always told him quite clearly she was perfect, and had never put a foot wrong in the whole of her life. He'd always believed her until now...

'So,' Chris continued, as if the biscuit making and the coffee brewing hadn't taken place, 'can we talk about your crochet lessons?'

'We can. Two. The first one she was here for about two hours, she taught me to chain, then a double crochet. I worked at that for a bit, and she asked if I wanted to learn how to do a square. I said yes, because I'd seen a quilt made with small squares all sewn together, and that was what I wanted to make. So from that she showed me how to chain six stitches, link them into a circle, and work twelve trebles into the circle. This was a brand-new stitch to me, and took a bit of mastering. She then said she had something to do at home, but she would be back the following evening to teach me what to do next.'

Tia was writing furiously, hoping she was getting this foreign language down correctly – she had never crocheted in her life, and hadn't come across the terms before.

Chris waited. 'And the second lesson?' he encouraged.

'Oh yes. She came back a couple of evenings later, and I brought out my little piece of work that I hadn't done anything further on because I didn't know how, and she showed me how to form the square with a slip stitch, then begin the second round where the spaces are created. I must say this was a wonderful night. My square took shape before my eyes, and she left me with a promise to return to show me how to reach the end of the square.'

Janet reached behind her, opened a kitchen drawer and

removed a ball of wool and her unfinished square. 'I need help,' she said.

It was a strangely unique shape. Nobody would have been charitable enough to call it a square, and yet it was obviously meant to have equal sides. 'She never returned,' Janet said. 'I think she must be teaching someone else or something, because she goes out for a walk most nights, sometimes she takes the car, but mostly she walks. I've had to resort to YouTube to find out how to do the corners, and believe me, it's been very stressful.'

Neither Tia nor Chris could find anything useful to say about the strangely shaped piece of work, but Chris did have another question.

'Do you know where her own home is? I forgot to ask her.'

'I do. It's on Cavendish Close, and it's actually the same number as our house, number 10. We occasionally look after our daughter's dog, and I took it out for a walk one evening. I bumped into Ziggy coming out of that house, and she said she'd just been to check it was okay as nobody was in it. I thought she would have rented it out until she was ready to move back, but she hasn't, it's just standing empty. Such a shame. It's a lovely old house, extremely big. It must have loads of rooms in it, but I think she wanted to look after Ray in his home rather than her bigger one, because he has his piano here. She doesn't have one.'

Chris's phone pinged. He excused himself, saying he had to answer the message – he knew Maria wouldn't be contacting him unless it was important, as she knew exactly where he was.

It was a message saying could he contact her whenever he was away from whoever he was interviewing, so he messaged back with *fifteen minutes*.

Tia was still chatting with Janet, who was parcelling up a couple of biscuits each for both of them, and they thanked her and left ten minutes later. Chris drove, and almost immediately pulled up. They were out of sight of both homes just visited. He wasn't sure why he felt it was a smart move, but he knew it was. Instinct was finally kicking in.

'Hi, Maria. What's wrong?'

'Are you still out and about?'

'We are, we've just finished our last one on the list. We still have to speak to Paula, but she's at her sister's so we're leaving that one for the time being. She's definitely not our killer anyway.'

'Can you pop round to mine? I'll text you the address. I've something I think you should see.'

'Certainly can.'

\* \* \*

Chris drove quickly. There was a sudden feeling of urgency, and of all people it was Janet Standall who had initiated it, although she absolutely had no idea what reactions her words had created in the two police officers.

There were many things to put in motion, and he needed the whole team there to listen to everything, to read every report, but his inklings were starting to work again.

They pulled up outside Maria's home; she must have been looking out for them because she came out to greet them. 'I have something to show you.' She almost sounded breathless, and Tia and Chris followed her through into her tiny home office. It was a squeeze for the three of them, but she had everything set up so they could view the largest of her screens.

Chris looked around. 'My God, do you actually need three screens?'

She frowned. 'Don't you have three screens?'

'I have the screen that's attached to my laptop, so does that count?'

She shook her head. 'You don't have a home office then?'

'Thinking about getting one now I've seen yours,' he retorted. 'So what do we have that's brought us here at a hundred miles an hour?'

'Well, first of all I confess I brought the memory stick home with me, and I've taken my time going through it. I'm going to take it to a certain point, then I want to see if you notice what jumped out at me. I don't want to tell you what it is, because that would be my thoughts being foisted onto you.'

She pointed to the two chairs in front of her desk, so Tia and Chris sat, quite in awe of this newly bossy colleague.

'Okay, we're ready,' Chris said.

The screen flickered into life, and Maria clicked on her mouse.

It was starting to go dark, and for five minutes there was little movement in the car park. Two adults and two children walked up to their car, got in it and drove down the car park, headlights lighting their way, and out onto Birley Lane. The camera didn't track their entire journey, but there was nowhere else for them to exit.

A lone man walked towards his car and drove away without headlights. A tram, glowing brightly in the late-evening darkness, appeared at the top edge of the screen and slowly came to a stop at the Birley Lane platform, disgorging several passengers who rapidly disappeared from view. The tram vanished from the screen as it continued its journey. Two of the passengers walked down the car park, heading for the pub doors.

Maria leaned between them and clicked on the mouse, halting the picture as the two people reached the bottom of the screen.

'So?' she asked.

'Everybody we've seen was alive,' Chris said. 'Have I missed something?'

Tia shook her head. 'No, I'm guessing Maria watched this in slo-mo, and we've watched it at normal speed. It's something to do with the tram, isn't it?'

Maria nodded. 'It is. Let me take it back. I honestly don't want to tell you just in case my brain is inventing something that's perfectly innocent, but watch it again.'

The screen lit up once again, and they watched the tram approach from the field, running slowly as it prepared to stop at the platform. As the passengers began to disembark, Maria froze the shot.

'Now look,' she said. 'Don't assume anything, look for facts.'

Chris leaned forward and began counting the passengers. 'Seven people got off,' he said.

Tia joined in. 'Two young lads, look to be about fifteen, and punching each other. A woman wheeling a large suitcase returning from a holiday possibly, three women and a man all travelling singly. Well, not talking to each other anyway.'

The tram eased away from the platform and Maria stopped the replay.

'So?'

'We could have missed this,' Chris said softly.

'We definitely could,' agreed Tia. 'Our Maria is a smart cookie.'

Maria smiled with relief. So she wasn't being stupid and seeing stuff that wasn't there.

'That could definitely be Hannah Wrightson and not dirty laundry and souvenirs from a holiday, in that suitcase.'

## 33

Chris stood and turned to hug Maria. 'You're a star, Maria. We definitely didn't connect this when we saw it first time round. She only had to walk to the top end of the platform, and she's straight into that field. Tip out the body, because it's already almost dark, and head off home, taking a wheeled suitcase with her.'

'Now we have to work out where she got on the tram.' Tia frowned. 'I bet she started off in her car, left it parked at a tram stop somewhere back down the system, caught the tram with Hannah in the case, and then after she'd thrown her out of it, she took the much lighter suitcase back to her car and drove home. Odds on she only came one or two stops, she just needed to be near this field without her vehicle being seen.'

'And trams have CCTV!' Chris said. 'We know the time this tram was at Birley Lane, so we can find out which tram it actually was. I have no idea what tram stops are called or anything like that, so I bow to the expertise of you two.'

Tia nodded thoughtfully. 'She'll not have brought her far. I reckon we start to look at stuff from the Manor Top onwards. There is a supermarket next to that tram stop where you could park a car, and it's a flat route to the tram stop. Dead easy there. The next one is at the bottom of Ridgeway Road, at Hollinsend stop. The car again could be easily parked round the corner on Hollinsend Road. Then it travels up the hill to Gleadless Townend, which is the stop used by staff at Griffiths. And there's a car park there that we brought into our considerations before, when we were wondering if the white van had parked in it watching for Hannah going into Sainsbury's. At this point she is only two stops away from Birley Lane. The next one is White Lane, where there is a large car park at the Co-op. Again it's easily accessible for wheeling a suitcase. The stop after that is where she got off with the suitcase.'

Maria was watching her two colleagues closely. 'Do you two know something?'

'Suspect something is closer to it. But I am ever conscious of the possibility of somebody else being grabbed, and so I think we now have to get the rest of the team in for a briefing. Maria, do you have a printer?'

Maria laughed. 'You think I wouldn't have one?'

'Can you get me a map of the tram stops and print it off for this non-Sheffielder, because I'm about to make a phone call to Supertram to ask them for CCTV from that tram. But it would be better if I knew what I was talking about, or else I'll have to say I'm PC Danny Moore, and let them think he's the dumb one.'

'I'll tell him you said that, he'll be here in five minutes.'

'He knows about this?'

Maria shook her head. 'No, only the three of us. Danny coming here is nothing to do with work, we had made plans to go out for a walk, but I guess that will now be a trip into Moss Way.' Her doorbell rang as if on cue. 'That'll be him now.'

She went to let Danny in, who looked quite puzzled as he came through the door and saw half his colleagues there.

'Well, I guess we just need to contact Bryn, Sally and Andy, and we're good to go,' Chris said, trying not to laugh at the expression on Danny's face. 'Sorry, Danny, can you postpone your walk till we've sorted out what young Maria here has dumped in our laps?'

'We're going into work?' Danny asked.

'We are, and we've lots to talk through after this morning anyway, but we've also got Maria's memory stick to watch. It's better if we're all doing this together, and sorting out what happens next.'

Tia was busy on her phone, and she announced the results of the phone calls. 'They're on their way. No grumbles, keen to hear what's been happening, just because they trusted the boss to go out and do four easy interviews this morning.'

'Don't blame me,' Chris said. 'This is all down to Maria and her disobeying orders. I'm sure I said leave this memory stick till Monday. And on top of everything else, it turns out I need to make myself an office in my new home, because every home should have one. Have you got one, Danny?'

'Yes, boss, but that's because I like to be organised. I have a large music collection, all catalogued, superb speakers, so it's kind of morphed into an office facility for me. You should come and see it sometime, you'll be impressed.'

'Tia?'

'Yes, of course I've got an office. Look, when this is all over and we've made our little area of Sheffield safe again, I'll come over to your house – flat? Tent? – and sort something out for you.'

He grinned. 'I live in a house. Full of cardboard boxes because I've only just moved in, but it's quite big. I've got two kids who will occasionally come to stay, but I do have four bedrooms so guess the little one would make into an office. You do realise I'm no Maria, don't you?'

Tia laughed. 'Oh, we do. But you're a DI, you still need an office. Besides, it's somewhere to escape to when you need time out. Right, let's go fill everybody in on what's happened this morning, and I reckon we're going to need a search warrant pretty soon, don't you, boss?'

'The sooner the better,' he said, and led the way out of Maria's home.

* * *

There was a tension in the briefing room that was palpable. Chris walked to the front of the room and looked around at his six colleagues all seated at the table. The large white viewing screen had been pulled down covering the whiteboard and Maria had already loaded up the section of the stick that she needed them all to see, not just the boss and Tia.

'Thank you for getting here so quickly, everybody. I'm sorry we've had to bring you in on a Saturday afternoon, but time is critical, given there's a strong possibility of a kidnap of another woman. Our discoveries today, I believe, show the killer in action, and so I think they will be in custody by this evening. This probably means we'll all be working tomorrow as well. However, I need to hear what conclusions you all draw from what you are about to be told. First of all, watch this small bit of the CCTV from the pub car park on Birley Lane. The steep one. On the mountainside.'

He nodded at Maria, and she used a remote control to start the screening. They watched in silence, with Maria, Chris and Tia deliberately not speaking. They wanted the others to spot it for themselves, although all three were aware it had taken a second viewing for them to see it.

'You could easily carry a body in that suitcase,' Bryn said.

'You carry bodies in suitcases in Wales, do you?' asked Chris, softening his words with a smile.

'If it becomes necessary, we do,' Bryn conceded.

'For the ones who are like Tia and me and didn't spot it first time around, have a second look. Maria?'

She clicked her controller to repeat the showing, and paused it on the woman as she exited the tram.

'For those who don't know,' Chris said, 'and I count myself in that, you walk to the top end of the platform and you're virtually in that field. I know we can't see her face, only the back view of her, but if, as we now believe, that is Hannah's body inside it there will be DNA for retrieval from the case. The killer won't know we have this on CCTV, so will have had no reason to actually dispose of the case, so fingers crossed we can get it during the course of this weekend.'

Chris paused for a moment and looked around at everyone. 'All with me to this point?'

'We need to know where she got on the tram.' Bryn's Welsh accent was getting stronger, as if he could sense impending action in this case.

'I've been on the phone with Supertram, explained what we need, which tram was involved, and the time span we want CCTV for. They've promised it within two hours. That's on the back burner until we get that email. So congratulations to Maria for completely ignoring my instructions and checking out the memory stick anyway. Smart Yorkshire lass we've got here.'

Maria stood, her cheeks rosy red. 'Stop it, you're embarrassing me. Just doing my job, anyway. I'll put away the screen, then make us all a drink. We may need to concentrate on this next bit, you think?' she asked Chris.

'I think. In fact, I'm sure. I'll show the others the tram map while we're waiting, and explain the theory we have about h car having been left near to a tram stop to facilitate moving the weight of that suitcase.'

Maria switched on the coffee machine and the kettle, now completely used to what everybody preferred to drink, and went to raise the screen to tuck it neatly back in its slot in the ceiling. She returned to the tiny kitchen, got out seven mugs and once everything was made carried them through to where they were still talking about the tram route. Bryn was trying to convince Chris to catch the tram and go through to Hillsborough where a short walk would find him at the most important place in Sheffield, Sheffield Wednesday's ground.

'But my kid's suggested I might want to stop supporting Newcastle and change to Sheffield United,' he protested, not admitting his son had already decided there was only one team in Sheffield, and that was Wednesday. Bryn was emitting a huge groan as Maria delivered the drinks. 'No football,' she said. 'It's out of season.'

They collected their drinks, and Chris then sat at the table with them.

'Okay, this morning me and my childminder, Tia, set off with a list of four people to interview. We've not had the chance to type up the reports yet, we'd just finished our last one when Maria messaged us to say we needed to go to hers. As it turned out, I was glad Tia was with me, because things all began to fall into place, and we were singing from the same hymn sheet so to speak, at the same time. Lies were told, and from somebody that had never at any point been on our radar.'

There was silence. The sense of a breakthrough was strong.

'We visited Janey Pascoe first, it was really a courtesy visit checking she was doing okay. Then we tried Paula Wrightson, but she's with her sister for a few days, so we're leaving well alone there. I must stress neither Janey nor Paula have at any point been considered suspects.' Chris hesitated for a moment, trying to put his thoughts in order.

'We only had two names left on our list, neither one of them had been spoken to before, and definitely hadn't been on any suspect list, so we thought we would come back here, type up the reports and head off home. The first person was Ziggy Duly, Ray Eke's mother. Her real name is Sigrid, by the way. The only reason she was on our list was because Ray found the body, and he mentioned he lived with her because of his mental illness. She really was just a name. She's a nice lady, welcomed us in. Ray had just gone out with Mark Griffiths to the gym, and she was doing the laundry, so we figured a two-minute chat and we could go.'

He sipped at his drink, and waited for a moment to collect his thoughts. 'And we were right. Almost.'

## 34

'She basically told us nothing. Confirmed she shared a car with Ray because since he had his breakdown he hasn't driven, so if he needs to go anywhere she drives.'

Chris paused for a moment to put his thoughts into the right order.

'It's a white Astra, and Tia actually saw it in the garage. No other vehicle was in there. We said a fond farewell, so to speak, because she gave us iced water that was delicious, and she didn't actually see where we went after that as far as I'm aware because she was going into her back garden to hang out washing. We went across the road to Janet Standall's home. We didn't actually mention Janet at all when we interviewed Ziggy, so I don't think he realised where we were going next.'

It was as if there was a strange feeling of anticipation around the table. And it seemed Janet Standall, a complete unknown to them, was about to play a part in it.

'So,' Chris continued, 'you lot seriously missed out because she was baking biscuits when we arrived, and she gave us two each to bring away with us. For your information, we've eaten them. They weren't evidence to be logged in downstairs. Anyway, the lady informed us that Ziggy *hadn't* actually been giving her crochet lessons most nights, she had in fact only had two lessons. She did say she thought Ziggy must be teaching somebody else because she goes out a lot in the evening, sometimes walking, sometimes in the car. And let's not forget Ziggy is living with Ray, taking care of him, but does actually have an empty house of her own. I have applied for a search warrant for her house, 10 Cavendish Close, because we need to see what is inside it, and if indeed any vehicles are stored there, such as a small dark-coloured car and a much larger white van. I've stressed the urgency, so I'm hoping to have that within the next hour. I also sent a message to Kevin Hanson as soon as we got back, asking if the skewer mentioned as being the implement for removing Hannah's eyes could possibly have been a crochet hook, and he said it definitely could, without any shadow of a doubt. It definitely wasn't any sort of knife, it was something with a point, maybe a screwdriver?'

'And we'll also possibly find a suitcase when we get into this house.' Bryn's smile was huge. 'You want to bring her in for further questioning, boss?'

'That's why we're all here. A lot of this is supposition, but it's a fact that Ziggy Duly has been lying to her son, because he was the one who told us she was always across the road visiting with Janet, when actually she was probably round at her own home potentially torturing Lauren, and then Hannah. She definitely wasn't where she told Ray she was going to be. So should we bring her in now?'

'Yes. She may have plans in place in the event of being caught out. It would only take a neighbour to ring her to say we were round at her home, and she could vanish.'

'You're right. Okay, two cars to go to the Eke house, Bryn and

Sally in one, Danny and Maria in the other, as we've stopped their afternoon walk. You can have an afternoon drive instead.'

'You're all heart, boss,' Maria said. 'I've never been sent to bring anybody in before, so thank you,' she said with a grin.

'I'm broadening your horizons, Maria. Three screens indeed. Just tell her she's being brought in for further questioning, don't mention the search warrant. As soon as you have her in the car, let me know. We'll have to wait until you get her back here. When you book her in, take all her belongings off her. If possible, we need her keys, but if she doesn't have them with her we'll use an Enforcer to get in a back door that we can board up afterwards. Tia and Andy will be with me as we go into her house. We can break the news of the search warrant when she's being interviewed. Put her in Room A. That's enough to put anybody off. I'll interview her with Tia when we get back. Anybody have any questions?'

'You seriously think it's her?' Andy asked the question on everybody's lips.

'I do. We obviously need further answers, like why leave the body of Lauren where she knew it would probably be her own son who found it, and why these two girls in particular? But despite not having all the answers, I think we'll get them.' He paused for a moment. 'She seems such a nice woman, but...'

'There's something off about her,' Tia finished. 'She didn't look at us. When we spoke, her eyes were anywhere but on us. And at that point we had no reason to think she was involved, but it still seemed a strange chat. Did you notice, boss?'

'I did, but I thought it was just me she didn't like. Seems it was both of us.'

Chris's phone pinged and he looked at his screen. 'It's an email. I'll check it on my computer, as it's going to need printing. Think it's our warrant.'

He headed into his office, and the next sound was the printer in the main office whirring into life.

This caused immediate movement amongst everybody else – time to bring in a suspect.

Chris rejoined them and collected the warrant, then spoke to Sally. 'Text me as soon as you have her in the car. We won't move from here until that happens. If she's gone out, I need to know where she is. It won't make any difference if she's at Cavendish Close, we'll still serve the warrant, but I'd rather she was in Room A here. And please be aware that Ray Eke will probably be at home now, so you will have to deal with him as well, because he's obviously going to be traumatised at you taking away his mother formally.'

The four of them left, and Chris, Tia and Andy paced the briefing room, keen to get on with things. 'Can we do this with just the three of us, boss?' Tia asked. 'Janet said it was a huge house.'

'If we need back-up I'll ring in and get it. At the moment, I'd rather it was just the three of us, but if we find what I expect to find, we'll have forensics there this afternoon anyway. We're really the advance team with this.'

Tia couldn't help the slight feeling of sickness his words brought to her. She had seen the post-mortem reports, knew what the two women had suffered, and seeing where it had happened was going to be... sickening, but more than that it would be sad. So much pain, so much indignity, and she knew it was quite possible they would never know the real reason why a woman could inflict such damage on another woman.

\* \* \*

The two cars pulled up outside the Eke home, and Janet, sitting in her front garden and hidden by the hedge, lifted her head. She stood slightly and looked across the road.

'Two cars! What the hell...' She picked up her phone and messaged Philip, tending to his tomatoes in the greenhouse. Within a minute he was sitting opposite his wife, awaiting developments.

\* \* \*

Sally and Bryn approached the front door, leaving Danny and Maria in the second car, alert and awaiting instructions if they were needed inside the property.

It was Ray who answered, clearly not recognising them but recognising the squad car parked out front, with a second one a few yards behind it. He smiled. 'So, you did want me as well, this morning?'

'No, thank you, Mr Eke. Is Ms Duly around?'

'She is.' He held the door open. 'She's just made us a coffee. We're through in the back garden.'

He led them through the house, and out of the patio doors leading from the dining room.

'Mum,' he said, 'I'm not sure what you've been up to, but the police are here for you again.' They could hear the laughter in his voice; he clearly couldn't imagine his mother ever being in trouble with the police.

She looked up at him, not at the two officers standing either side of him. They might as well not have been there.

'May I have a word with my son, please?' Ziggy asked, quietly.

'No, ma'am, I'm afraid not,' Sally said. 'We have instructions from DI Chandler to take you back to the station immediately.'

Ziggy gave a slight nod of her head and stood. Sally couldn't help but feel this was a very gracious lady, and if she hadn't seen the post-mortem results would have thought that maybe they were making a colossal error. But there was no slip-up.

Ziggy stood and turned towards the table to take a last sip from her glass of water. And Sally knew there was no mistake, colossal or otherwise. She had seen this back view, wearing the same stripy top, on the CCTV recovered from the pub car park, spotted towing a light-coloured tartan suitcase while getting off a tram.

The three of them walked back through the house, deliberately allowing Ziggy to pick up a bag from the hall table, after slipping her keys inside it. 'I might need these if Ray goes out,' she said.

'No problem, Ms Duly,' Bryn said, keeping his face as straight as he could. 'Our duty sergeant will take good care of everything for you, pending the results of your chat with DI Chandler.'

Ray had now joined them at the front door. 'You're taking her to Moss Way? But what can she possibly know that would be helping you? Mum, when you're ready to come home, ring me and I'll get Mark to collect you.'

Ziggy smiled. 'Don't worry about me, Ray. And remember to lock the door tonight if I'm not back by the time you go to bed. I've got my keys in my bag. I have to remind him,' she explained to Sally as they crossed to the car. 'Since he became ill, he forgets things.'

Bryn got behind the wheel as Sally helped Ziggy into the back seat. She then sent a pre-typed text off to Chris saying *suspect in car*.

Janet and Philip had given up all pretence of hiding behind their hedge and were fully standing watching events without speaking. They hadn't a clue what was happening, but it would make for interesting gossip at the Book Club the following week.

\* \* \*

Danny and Maria followed closely behind the car conveying Ziggy towards her second interview of the day. She was escorted as far as Frank by all four of them, where she was relieved of her possessions.

'They'll be returned to you once you're released,' he said solemnly.

'So I will be released?'

'A lovely lady like you, I imagine so.' He tried to be honest at all times, did Frank.

She was escorted to Room A where Sally brought her a glass of water.

Chris, Andy and Tia were on their way to Cavendish Close, bearing a bunch of keys passed to them as Ziggy disappeared down the corridor to the interview rooms.

## 35

'Wow.' Tia couldn't help but say it. The house was enormous, set well back from the road and with a driveway that led to a double garage built on the side. The front door was red and certainly larger than a standard door.

They parked on the road, and simply stood and just looked.

'This is a hell of a house, and yet she still continues to live with Ray. I realise Ray's house isn't small, but crikey – this is magnificent.' Chris shook his head. 'She must love Ray very much is all I can say. Come on then, let's get started.'

He opened the gates at the end of the driveway, and they walked up towards the front door. Andy drifted off to the side to see what there was to observe through the tiny windows set into the garage doors.

'Bingo,' he said softly. He rejoined Tia and Chris in the hallway. 'One white van and one small car, think it's a Fiat 500 or something very similar. I'll find the way into the garage, but need to kit up first, I think.'

Tia handed him shoe covers, a cover-all and gloves. 'Go for it

Make sure your camera records everything, we don't want stuff kicking out of court because we slipped up somewhere.'

'Will do.' He dressed himself in the hallway, took the bunch of keys from Chris and went looking for a door that could possibly lead into the garage.

It was indeed a Fiat 500, and dark brown in colour. Andy shook his head – he had assumed their guesses were just that, mere suppositions about what could have happened, especially with the wheelbarrow having been dumped, and it seemed they had been spot on, guesswork or not.

He pulled out his phone, found the picture of the tiny mark that Maria had discovered on the white van, and dropped to his knees to inspect the left-hand side of the Transit. He took a photograph, sent it to Maria and captioned it with *found it!*

Her response was swift.

> Told you I'm a smart cookie!

Rather than risk any contamination of the scene, he exited the garage and went to find Chris.

'We need forensics here, boss. The Transit and a Fiat 500 are both in the garage, and it is almost certainly the Transit we believe was used to abduct Hannah. I've come straight out, haven't touched anything.'

'Okay, I'll ask for them now. Tia is checking the upstairs, I've just a brief eye over the kitchen, now about to check the other rooms. We need to find where she kept Lauren and Hannah, it's here somewhere. I'm thinking a cellar, but every door in the hallway, and there are quite a few, leads to a room. If there is a cellar here, I don't know where it is.'

'I might. Not sure it's necessarily a cellar, it could also be an added room. And, at the back of the garage, there's a door. It's locked, and there's no key on that bunch of keys that will open it. Before we do anything drastic like kicking it in, I'll go round the outside of the garage, and see what I can see.'

'Thanks, Andy. Forensics will be here shortly, they might have some way of opening that door, but we need a feel for it, if it could be the place she kept them.'

Andy departed through the front door, and walked around the garage. The brick section at the back was clearly an add-on to the original garage, and the tingle he felt told him he'd found what they were looking for.

He continued around the back, but it had no windows and no door. The only entrance was via the garage. He returned to the main part of the house, and waited for the forensics team. Their vehicles arrived as he reached the front door, and he led them in to where Chris was checking drawers in the lounge.

'It's all so straightforward,' he said. 'We need to find where she kept our ladies, it's here somewhere. This feels like a normal household, nothing that would make me say a murderer lives here. Except for the garage.'

'Then tell me about the garage.' Jack Kendall continued to pull on his white suit while he listened to what Chris and Andy had to say.

'There's a small corridor off the hallway that leads directly into it.' Andy held up the bunch of keys. 'These keys belong to our suspect, and one of them opens the garage door. I didn't check if any open the main garage door outside, haven't had a chance yet. However, inside the garage we struck gold, hence your team being called out on a Saturday afternoon. We found the Transit we've been looking for, and we're waiting for CCTV from Supertram to track down what sort of car has also been used for transporting Hannah Wrightson's body to get her on a tram in a suitcase, and possibly Lauren Pascoe's body was also transported partly in that and definitely in a wheelbarrow.'

'So comprehensive fingerprint checks, swabs for bloods and bodily fluids on both vehicles?'

Chris nodded. 'Yes, but there's more. Andy says there's a narrow door on the back wall of the garage, and when you walk around the outside you can see a brick extension that has been added to the original garage construction. There's no key on this key ring for it, so we can't open that door. I'm hoping you brought a magic wand or something to get us through it.'

'We'll open it, don't worry. You're thinking that's where Lauren was held for three very long years?'

'Yes. Doesn't bear thinking about, does it?'

'Follow me, Andy. Let's get you your proof.'

\* \* \*

Andy gagged. The smell was of blood and bodily fluids, all with an overlay of terror. He could sense the fear that must have come out of every pore on the women's bodies and at first he couldn't move. Slowly he stepped into the room and Jack reminded him not to touch anything. This was definitely where they had been kept. The corner of the tiny room had been sectioned off and there was the most miniscule toilet. There was no bed, just a rug on one section of the floor. No bed coverings, no pillow, he couldn't imagine what life had been like for three years, and could easily believe that Lauren had died willingly. It must have been soul-destroying for every day of those years.

Chris stood beside Andy and then Tia joined them. 'Jack says we can't move, basically. We can look but not touch. He says this room is our proof, and we can go charge her.'

Tia spoke slowly. 'In the utility room there is a freezer, a small chest type. I found two plastic boxes, one labelled Lauren and one labelled Hannah. I haven't touched them, and I've told one of the forensic guys about them. I believe they contain body parts that she cut off our ladies.'

Chris shook his head. 'Why? Why would someone do this to another woman? Come on, let's leave the experts to recover what is going to send Ms Duly to prison for the rest of her life, and go and ask her why.'

\* \* \*

Ziggy Duly was staring down at her fingers resting on her lap when Tia and Chris walked into the room.

He listed their names on the recorder then cautioned Ziggy. 'Do I need a solicitor?'

'Probably.'

She thought for a moment, then shrugged. 'Just ask me your questions.'

'First of all, I have to tell you we were granted a search warrant for your home at 10 Cavendish Close. DS Monroe and I attended, and now there is a full forensics team there.'

'I hope you haven't damaged anything.'

'No, we haven't, we used the keys you left with PC Carter to gain access. No damage was done. We have, however, called in forensics because of what we found there. We found body parts in boxes in your freezer, we found a room that is being taken apart forensically speaking, that will prove Lauren Pascoe and Hannah Wrightson were held there, and we found two vehicles in your garage that will be taken to our facility to be minutely and forensically examined.'

They watched as the colour drained from Ziggy Duly's face. 'It's over then,' she said.

'What's over, Ms Duly?' Tia asked.

'Everything,' she said. 'Everything I've lived for, worked for, built my life around. It's gone now. I'd like a solicitor, please.'

Tia glanced at Chris, and he closed up his file. He hadn't needed it. 'Do you have your own solicitor? We can, of course, get our duty solicitor for you.' He tried to hide the look of disgust he knew was on his face.

'Anybody will do,' she said. 'Could I have a coffee, please?'

The whole situation felt wrong. Tia had anticipated a long interview where they would have to coax details out of what was definitely a smart woman, but she seemed to have accepted that she wasn't going to be able to talk her way out of it, and she was in deep trouble.

'Of course, I'll go and get you one. You'll be staying with us certainly overnight, then I'm not sure what will happen to you. Your solicitor will be with you within the hour, and a police officer will get you food for your evening meal later. We'll speak to you again once we hear your solicitor has arrived.'

They left Room A, leaving Ziggy sitting at the table.

\* \* \*

What just happened?' Chris said.

'We didn't even get going. She cut us off at the knees, and she knew exactly what she was doing, asking for a solicitor at that point. It's given her thinking room.'

'Let's go upstairs. We can tell the others what's happening, and see if anything new has come in from anywhere. I'm hoping Maria has taken control of the tram CCTV, that should be here by now.'

Feeling a little disgruntled but knowing they would win in the end, they headed for the briefing room, where Maria was glued to her screen. 'Found where she got on the tram. It was at Gleadless Townend, so that probably means she put her car in that small car park in front of the Methodist church. The good news is that the Sainsbury's exterior cameras cover about three-quarters of that car park. We just have to hope she didn't park in the other quarter. I'm going up tomorrow morning to meet with the manager. They open at ten on Sundays so I said I'd be there for them opening. He was on his way home when I rang him.'

'Brilliant. CPS are definitely going to agree we charge her, when we tell them everything we've got. The solicitor is going to tell her to say nothing, of course, but fortunately she's said the odd wrong phrase or two already, so she might just give us the rest when we go in later.'

Chris thanked her and went to his own office for a couple of minutes' escape. He was feeling overwhelmed. In the end, everything seemed to have happened in a rush, and he just needed five minutes of thinking time.

His phone rang, a strange number, and he said, 'DI Chandler.'

'Jack Kendall, Chris. I thought you might like to know both vehicles in the garage were unlocked, no idea where the keys are. The keys you've left with us are only house keys, plus a fob for a Vauxhall. Anyway, doesn't matter, we got in simply by opening the doors. She really didn't expect to get caught, did she?'

'No, she didn't. She's quite blown away by us keeping her overnight, and getting her a solicitor.'

'What I've really rung to tell you is that there's a suitcase in the boot of the Fiat, squashed in, I might add. These car boots don't hold much. We got it out, opened it up and there's blood smears of it. Not copious amounts, so I think it's indicating the occupant was dead when she was stuffed inside it.'

'What colour is the suitcase?'
He paused. 'It's like a beige colour, but it's definitely tartan.'

## 36

Sunday felt like something of an anticlimax. Ziggy Duly, after speaking with her solicitor, answered every question with, 'No comment,' and rather naively asked when she could go home. She was somewhat brusquely informed that she wouldn't be going home. Nobody added the word *ever*. Everybody thought it.

Ray had been in touch several times by eleven o'clock, trying to find out what was happening, but all Chris would tell him was that his mother was helping them with their enquiries.

Maria went up to Sainsbury's, and downloaded the relevant footage to her memory stick – Ziggy Duly was seen to drive into the car park in front of the church, heave a very heavy suitcase on the back seat of the car, then walk away wheeling the suitcase behind her. Proof that she actually boarded the tram was provided by the footage sent by Supertram, and if further proof was needed she was filmed getting off the tram at the Birley Lane tram stop.

So when Ray rang once again to ask if he could collect his mother, he found out the truth of the situation. Sigrid Duly h been formally charged with the murders of Lauren Pascoe and Hannah Wrightson.

The whole team had come in; nobody wanted to miss any part of the proceedings. It had been a truly traumatic case to be involved with, and they were all keen to be there when Duly was charged.

They celebrated with a McDonald's for lunch, paid for by Chris, and delivered by a taxi driver called Mohammed. Toasting each other with Coca Cola, coffee and banana milkshakes was also a little unusual, but it confirmed a bond in the team that was unbreakable. They had reached that point in their careers where they had seen many different crimes, but nothing had been so horrific as this one, with the dreadful things Ziggy Duly had done to the two women. Nobody would ever forget it, and Tia had felt absurdly traumatised by the two plastic boxes in the freezer at Cavendish Close. Why had Duly saved the body parts? What the hell did she gain by doing that?

DCI Dawson also called in on that strange Sunday, and personally congratulated each and every one of them individually. He also made a point of wishing Danny well, now he was newly transferred officially to the Major Crimes Unit.

They all felt reluctant to go home. Ziggy Duly hadn't denied anything, but neither had she explained anything. They speculated about her reasons for the torture of the two women, with various reasons being suggested for the extreme cruelty used – maybe she was treated with cruelty as a child, maybe she had an abusive husband, maybe an illness was affecting her mentally – but at the end of the discussion they came back to the length of the cruelty, three years. What triggered it in the first place? Or maybe it had been going on for much more than three years, it just hadn't led them to finding Ziggy Duly until now.

Tia thought carefully about the possibility that Lauren Pascoe hadn't been the first. She finished her milkshake, cleaned up all the McDonald's detritus and slipped casually into Chris's office. He was staring at his screen, a frown on his forehead.

'You okay, boss?'

'I don't know. I don't mean that. I'm okay, my brain's not accepting of facts at the moment. Ziggy Duly is almost sixty, has had normal relationships, albeit not long term, has a son who worships the ground she walks on, and she would do anything for him, yet three years ago she started down this route of torture, and ultimately murder. None of it makes sense to my tiny brain.'

'But you're looking something up,' Tia pointed out. 'So that tiny brain isn't so tiny, is it?'

He laughed. 'I'm just casually glancing through cold cases over the last ten years. Trying to see if there's even one little item in any of them that would link to what has happened with this one. Am I being stupid?'

'Only in that you shouldn't be doing it. You're our boss. I actually came in here to put a proposition to you. I'd like to take a sort of sabbatical. Not from the office, I need to be in here, but I'd like to go back through cold cases and see if there is anything at all that would correspond with anything we've found in this case. My sabbatical is just from any other case that might crop up. We've got Danny now, seemingly permanent which is great, so I reckon I could step aside from anything else for two weeks, make full use of our old files that are ferreted away downstairs somewhere, and see if we can't clear up a couple of cases.'

'You're sure? For what it's worth, I think you're right, it does seem odd that a well-educated lady in her late fifties should suddenly take to horrific murder. I mean, pushing somebody off a cliff is one thing, but what she has done is way beyond that. And look at what led us to realising it was her – a bloody crochet hook! Unbelievable. It also seems unbelievable that Ray

Eke had no idea. Maybe since his breakdown his mind has switched off from all things horrible, I don't know. He lives for his music, his gardening, his job where he works completely alone; he's a gentle soul, somebody I really appreciated, yet his mother has done this. I don't know how this will affect him. A relapse?'

'So can I do it, this cold case stuff?'

'Yes, of course. Tell the others, don't tell the others, your choice, but if you tell them they might take the hint and leave you alone to get on with it. I'll clear it with DCI Dawson, he'll not object because if you find something it will have all sorts of knock-on effects but it will also mean more kudos for Major Crimes.'

'Thanks, boss. Duly's in court tomorrow?'

'She is. I shall go, not for any reason other than to see any reactions she makes, listen to what she has to say if anything – she certainly said nothing to us after her solicitor sewed up her lips. If she pleads not guilty they'll give her a Crown Court date then we'll all know where we stand. You think we'll get lucky and she'll plead guilty?'

'Not a cat in hell's chance. I watched her carefully yesterday, and I'm not convinced she thinks she's done anything wrong. Worst-case scenario with this is that she ends up spending the rest of her life in Broadmoor because somebody has decided she's criminally insane. All she needs to do is keep her mouth shut. Imply she doesn't know why she has to shove a broken glass bottle inside a woman, or chop off a nipple, and then come out with the classic, "I need help."'

He shrugged. 'Find me at least another one, Tia. Let's make sure she ends up in prison and not some much comfier mental hospital.'

'Will do, boss. Think she'll admit to any more?'

'Who knows? I've never met anyone like her before, so I couldn't even hazard a guess.'

*　*　*

Janet Standall was saying the same sort of thing to her husband. 'I'm telling you, Philip, if she really did kill those two women, I could have been the next! And who knows how many she'd bumped off before Lauren Pascoe and Hannah Wrightson. I tell you what, it's definitely put me off learning to crochet.'

Philip spluttered into his glass of water. 'What? Are you saying everybody who teaches crochet is a killer? That they get a crochet hook into their hand and start planning ways to murder people with it? And we don't know that she's actually been arrested for anything, she could just be staying at her own house for a bit. The police maybe wanted to ask her a couple of questions, and she went back to that lovely house. I'd rather be there than here, and she must sometimes feel like that. Maybe now that Ray is so much better, she's trying it out for leaving him on his own. We know nothing, Janet, so don't go spreading rumours about this. Leave our lovely neighbours to sort out their own issues, stop trying to control their lives.'

Janet was definitely disgruntled. It would be nice if Philip agreed with her occasionally when it was something as important as this, but he didn't seem to want to agree when it came to the subject of Ziggy Duly. Liked her a bit too much, he did.

'I might just nip over and see if Ray's okay. He's not used to being without her since his brain went funny, is he?'

'For goodness' sake, Janet, leave it, will you? It's nothing to do with us, and when Ziggy comes back, you're going to look proper idiot, aren't you, for saying all this?'

Janet walked across to the window to look at Ray's house. 'I

*The Missing Ones*

unnerving not knowing what's happening. Do you think he knew?'

'Ray? Nah, of course he didn't. Ray's not really part of the world, is he? And he certainly sees no wrong in Ziggy anyway. Loves her to bits. That new music he's writing, he's called it "For Sigrid". Like Beethoven's "Für Elise".'

'He told you that?'

'He did, I could hear him playing it a couple of weeks ago. Thought it was beautiful, so I told him. We got chatting about music in general and that's when he told me what he'd called it.'

He saw her spine stiffen. 'Now what's wrong?'

'Ray's going out. He's gone towards the garage. Why do you think he's going out?'

'Oh my God, Janet, I have absolutely no idea. I am not Ray like's keeper!'

'But he's going in the car. He's not driven since he was taken ill. That's why she drives everywhere. What do we do? Should we try and stop him? She told me he didn't have the confidence to get behind the wheel any more, and now he's getting the car out. Should I go out and say something? What if he has an accident?'

Philip frowned. His wife seemed to be getting really wound up about something that was none of her affair, and totally inaccurate anyway. Why on earth was she saying Ray didn't drive?

'Janet, Ray does drive. Just because Ziggy told you he doesn't drive doesn't mean that he can't drive. Many times when you've moaned at me that Ziggy couldn't come over to help you because he'd just gone out in the car, it was Ray who'd taken it out, so don't tell me he doesn't drive, he very clearly does.'

Suddenly Philip felt uneasy. He didn't know why, and he knew his wife wouldn't understand, but he needed her away from that window, she had to stop watching what was happening over the road, but most of all he wanted her to stop adding two and two together and making up crazy inaccurate numbers.

He hoped they were inaccurate anyway.

He watched as Ray pulled the car out onto the road, and hoped the kind, gentle man would take care. Driving wasn't for everybody, and just lately he'd been doing a lot of it. Sharing a car seemed to have worked for Ray and Ziggy, but Philip really wished Ray would leave it all up to Ziggy, as he had done in the past.

## EPILOGUE
### SIX MONTHS LATER

Ziggy Duly died before the case ever arrived at Crown Court. The lung cancer she had tried bravely to hide from Ray won the fight.

Very few people knew of it until it became the news of the day, and Ray ultimately found himself at a funeral with just Mark by his side, and nobody else there. He was left with an urn of ashes that he took to Cavendish Close while he decided what to do with his life.

* * *

In the end, the decision was easy. He put his own home up for sale at £30,000 less than it was worth, and moved to the home he had now inherited from the late Ziggy. His first job was also a no-brainer.

He hired a digger and knocked down the garage in one mad weekend accompanied by Mark, then brought in a contractor to erect a new double garage. Their conversation over that weekend had been mainly about Ziggy; Ray's first visit while she was on remand was an eye-opener. She had talked of her cancer, of her refusal to have treatment beyond pain relief, and how she knew it would get much worse, but it didn't matter as long as her beloved son was okay.

Until that conversation he hadn't known of her illness. He had gone to discuss getting her out, and telling the truth, but the second he had mentioned that, she had told him her secret.

'You don't need to tell anybody anything,' she had said. 'This is my last gift to you, my darling boy. Let them do what they want to me, but according to my consultant I'll be lucky to still be alive in six months. You live your life how you want now, but please, remember I'm not there to help or tidy up for you from now on. They have arrested me, they're not looking for anyone else, so don't go doing anything dramatic like confessing to the crimes they've got me in here for. Make sure you don't go out looking for another one, because while they think I'm the killer, they're leaving you alone.'

Just six months down the line, and now the snow was here, it was a new year, and he knew he needed help.

Everything had changed. When he had first taken Lauren, he had hidden her away in his workshop in the garden. He had spent weeks soundproofing it, closing off the single window with wood, and installing a cassette toilet that he could empty from the outside. He hadn't anticipated she would live for very long, but what had changed everything was his breakdown.

He wasn't allowed to see Mark. But he was allowed to see Ziggy. And on that first visit after he had been hospitalised, he had to tell her about his prisoner in the shed.

\* \* \*

By the time he came home, the roles had been virtually reversed. Like mother, like son, in every way. To protect Ray, Ziggy had to become Ray. Lauren had been moved from the workshop in his garden to the storage area at the back of the garage at Ziggy's home, the toilet had been transferred to there and plumbed into the garage's water supply, and Lauren had known nothing about it. Transferred in the car boot while unconscious with a large dose of Tramadol, she had woken in a new space and with two of her toes removed.

The mother had to protect the son. This became Ziggy's mantra. The toes had been removed to convince Lauren that nothing had changed, just the person keeping her fed and watered.

\* \* \*

Ray stared out of the window of what was now his lounge, watching Cavendish Close slowly becoming covered in snow. A beautiful sight. He had opened the gates and was watching for Mark's arrival.

Their friendship had been cemented ever more strongly after the arrest of Ziggy; Mark hadn't allowed his friend's mental state to spiral out of control, and they had spent the whole of Christmas at Ray's house, making plans for redecorating, installing a new bathroom, and turning half of the new garage into a tool station. With the scrapping of the Transit and the Fiat used for transporting the women, Ray no longer needed space for two cars. They discussed putting in shelving, having certain tools hanging on the walls, and many diagrams were drawn.

He saw Mark's car pull onto the drive, and Mark get out of the driver's door carefully. He went to open the front door, a smile on his face.

'Glad you made it through this lot. Roads bad?'

'Bloody awful,' Mark grumbled. 'Not much has been gritted, so you can imagine what it's like. I've brought enough clothes for the weekend because I've no chance of driving back in this.'

'Good. I've made up the bed for you, and I've got a stew in the slow cooker for tonight. And dumplings,' he grinned.

'Love dumplings,' Mark responded, shaking his coat outside the door before taking it to hang it in the cloakroom.

'I've also had the blower on in the garage, get it warmed up for us. The shelving has arrived, so I think we need to put that together first, get it screwed to the wall.'

'Will it wait till I've had a coffee?' Mark asked.

'Already made. As if you could do anything without a coffee first.' They headed for the kitchen, and Ray poured them both a drink. 'Here's to a successful weekend of DIY.'

'It'll look like a palace by the time we've finished in there. I'm also giving some thought to a bit of DIY in my cellar.'

They sat down at the kitchen table, and both nursed their mugs, as if keeping their hands warm would help.

'Yes, just a thought at the moment, but I'm going to move the wine bottles. I'm not overfond of wine, and so I thought we could store them over here, in your pantry. It's cool in there, no matter what time of year it is. I'll stick a couple of bottles in the fridge, bring the rest here.'

'Fine by me. Why?'

'I need some space for us.'

There was a moment of silence.

'There's a woman stacks shelves in the evening, cleans the floors and suchlike, works at the Co-op. About the same size as Lauren and Hannah. Still partners?'

Ray smiled, his coffee halfway to his mouth. 'Still partners.'

\* \* \*

## MORE FROM ANITA WALLER

The latest instalment in another crime series from Anita Waller, *Fatal Endings*, is available to order now here:
www.mybook.to/FatalEndingsBackAd

# ACKNOWLEDGEMENTS

My thanks as always go to the amazing team at Boldwood. What more can I say? They did it again, for the eighth time! Isobel Akenhead's structural edit was amazing, followed by Cecily Blench for the copy edit, and last but not least, Candida Bradford for the proof read. I can't thank them enough.

I have three people to thank for lending me their names to use in the book – Ray Eke, Ziggy Duly and Lyra Grayson. I hope you all enjoy seeing your names in print!

I also have to thank Barry Manilow – every book I have written has been written to Alexa playing me Barry Manilow songs. Thanks, Alexa, not only for that but for all the information I get out of you when I'm stuck on anything.

To Valerie Dickenson (Keogh) and Judith Baker (J. A. Baker) I extend my love and gratitude for keeping me sane, keeping me going when the word count feels as though it's going backwards, and generally making me laugh.

My beta reading team of Alyson Read, Nicki Murphy, Tina Jackson and Denise Cutler – thank you for your support. The same goes to my ARC reading team. You make writing books a pleasure.

And to my family, I love you all. Your encouragement supports and fulfils me.

Sheffield

2025

# ABOUT THE AUTHOR

**Anita Waller** is the author of many bestselling psychological thrillers and the Kat and Mouse crime series. She lives in Sheffield, which continues to be the setting of many of her thrillers.

Sign up to Anita Waller's mailing list for news, competitions and updates on future books.

Visit Anita's website: www.anitawaller.co.uk

Follow Anita on social media here:

facebook.com/anita.m.waller

# ALSO BY ANITA WALLER

**The Forrester Detective Agency Mysteries**

Fatal Secrets

Fatal Lies

Fatal Endings

**Standalone Novels**

Flash Point

The Family at No. 12

The Couple Across The Street

The Girls Next Door

Beautiful

Angel

34 Days

Strategy

Captor

Game Players

Malignant

Liars *co-written with Patricia Dixon*

Gamble

Nine Lives

Winterscroft

The Missing Ones

**Kat and Mouse Series**

Murder Undeniable

Murder Unexpected

Murder Unearthed

Murder Untimely

Epitaph

Murder Unjoyful

**The Connection Trilogy**

Blood Red

Code Blue

Mortal Green

# THE *Murder* LIST

**THE MURDER LIST IS A NEWSLETTER DEDICATED TO SPINE-CHILLING FICTION AND GRIPPING PAGE-TURNERS!**

**SIGN UP TO MAKE SURE YOU'RE ON OUR HIT LIST FOR EXCLUSIVE DEALS, AUTHOR CONTENT, AND COMPETITIONS.**

## SIGN UP TO OUR NEWSLETTER

BIT.LY/THEMURDERLISTNEWS

# Boldwood

Boldwood Books is an award-winning fiction publishing company seeking out the best stories from around the world.

**Find out more at www.boldwoodbooks.com**

Join our reader community for brilliant books, competitions and offers!

Follow us
@BoldwoodBooks
@TheBoldBookClub

**Sign up to our weekly deals newsletter**

https://bit.ly/BoldwoodBNewsletter